CALL OF KAYDEN

CALL OF KAYDEN

Book 1 of the Dreamer Series

Steven A. Hellmann

Printed in the United States of America

Published in 2020 by Hellmann Books an imprint of Steven Hellmann

ISBN: 978-1-7344489-0-0:

Cover Design by Steven A. Hellmann with photo attribution to DJI Argas on Pixabay.com, Alex Woods on Unsplash.com, and Johannes Plenio on Pixabay.com

www.HellmannBooks.com

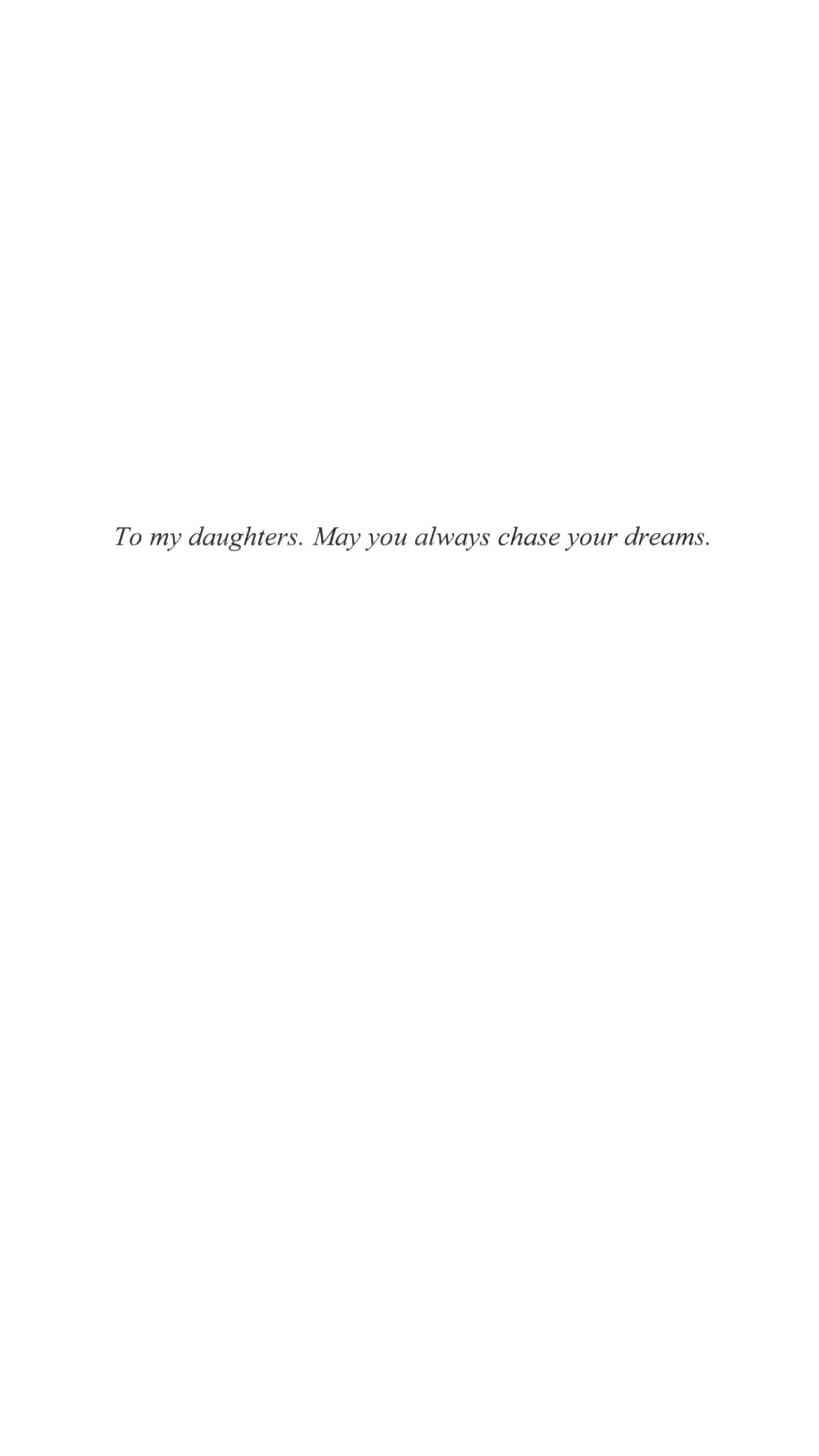

To my daughters. May you always chase your dreams.

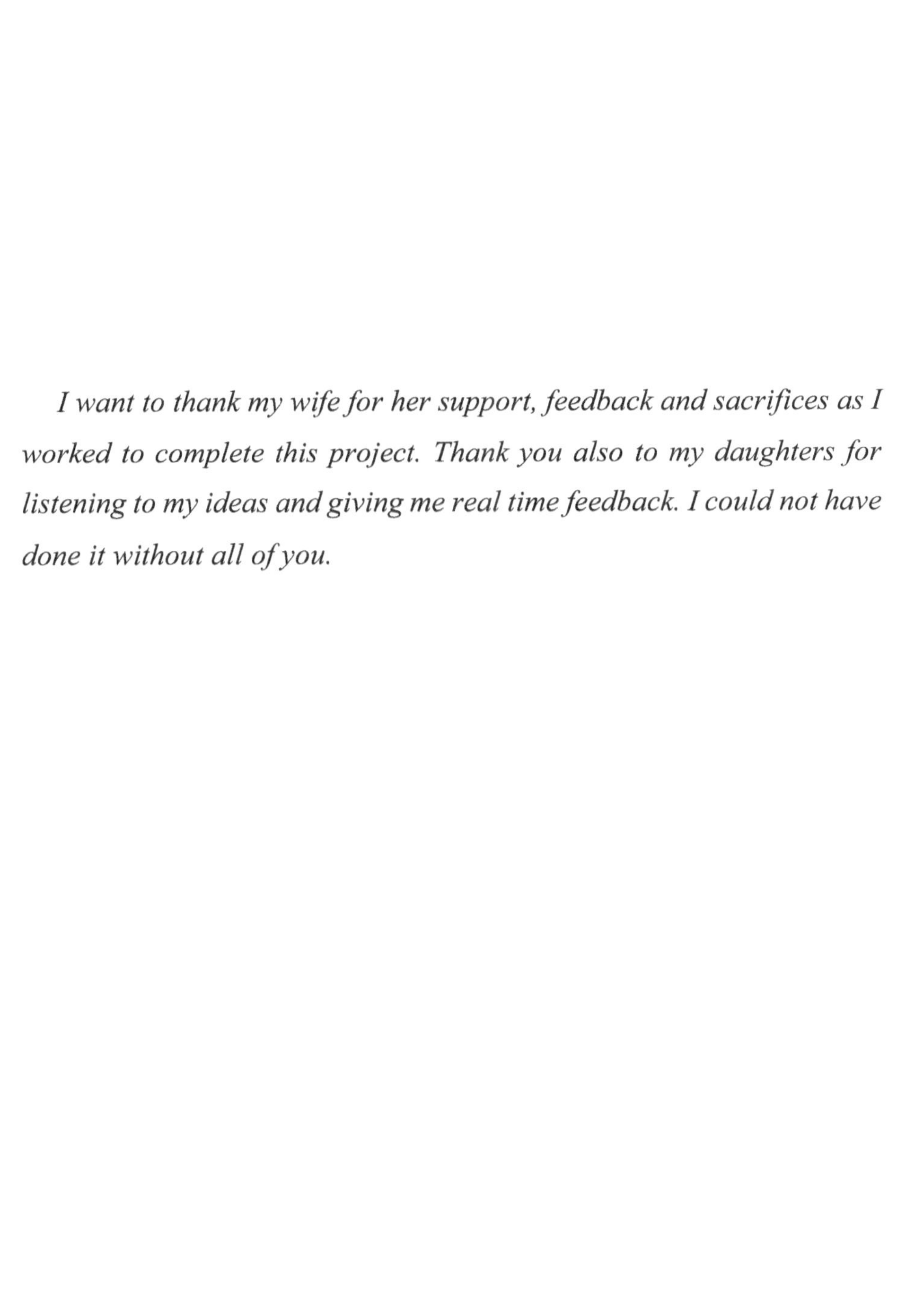

I want to thank my wife for her support, feedback and sacrifices as I worked to complete this project. Thank you also to my daughters for listening to my ideas and giving me real time feedback. I could not have done it without all of you.

Table of Contents

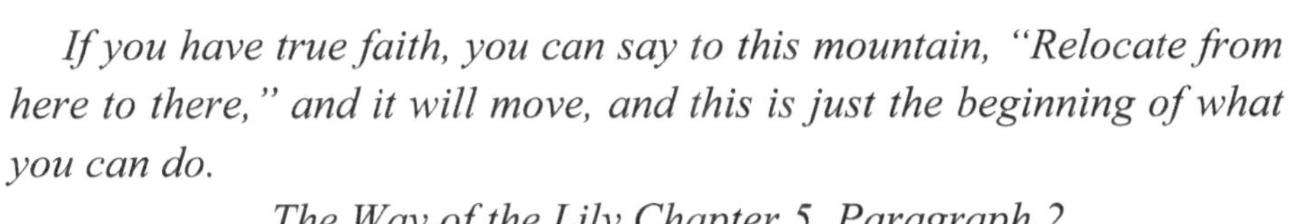

If you have true faith, you can say to this mountain, "Relocate from here to there," and it will move, and this is just the beginning of what you can do.

The Way of the Lily Chapter 5, Paragraph 2.

PROLOGUE

The wind blew strongly across Gabriel's face. There was a sense of disquiet in the air as he heard a howling sound in the distance. Gabriel had knowledge of this place, despite his efforts to forget. The terrain was mostly flat with a foggy mist permeating the air. Gabriel looked around, realizing that something seemed out of place. It was like he was viewing through a lens that stripped all color away. Yes, that was it he realized; all color was absent.

Gabriel felt an unnatural pull to move to the place he wanted to avoid. His legs stirred seemingly against his will, responding to the call that would not let go. Ahead was where it had all happened, where he had lost everything he held dear.

The layout was as he remembered it. There was a building that appeared abandoned within a protected nature area. Oversite had deemed it was occupied by a rebellious faction that was holed up within. These malcontents had started a campaign against the laws governing voiced dissent and were advocating practices that were outlawed after the Scientific Reformation. They wanted to hunt for animals in the nature preserves and advocated the eating of meat. This could not be allowed to continue, and Gabriel had come here with an extraction team from the Ministry of Scientific Compliance to arrest them, ensuring justice was served.

Gabriel's remembrance was interrupted when he saw more than just the building. His team was just beginning its raid. Gabriel usually didn't go into the field to accompany the arresting team, but this time was different. He had tracked and uncovered this group, and when Emily had heard about it, she wanted in on it. Gabriel could deny his fiancé nothing, so he made the request to have Emily and her team assigned and decided to accompany them. And he was reliving it again, devoid of color, anticipating with dismay what he was about to see.

Gabriel predicted they may have access to weapons but did not foresee their level of preparation for being raided. Gabriel watched the assault unfold. The team of six spread out as Emily directed them to their planned locations. There was not believed to be more than four targets, so their team's size, surprise, and superior weaponry should have been more than adequate to subdue them. But Gabriel now knew it would not be enough to escape unscathed.

Gabriel had gone over this so many times in his mind. What could he have done differently to save her? He watched as a booby trap triggered when they entered the structure. It had to be a low technology device, or the scanners would have detected it. But it caused damage as the first team member was injured by something metal capturing and crushing his leg. Emily rushed to extract the injured party to safety while Gabriel stayed back in the rear, as he was supposed to do as an observer. Gabriel watched as he saw one of the law breakers fire at Emily as she was pulling the injured agent to safety. He watched with unbridled dismay as she got hit and fell. He ran to her without thinking and pulled her out of the line of fire as the rest of the team engaged to provide cover for his action. As soon as he and those injured were clear, Emily's second in command deployed a low eco impact explosive device which destroyed the building and all who resisted inside of it. Gabriel should have reacted with the satisfaction of revenge at their annihilation, but instead stayed focused on the non-moving body of Emily. Fear coursed through Gabriel as she lay motionless on the ground.

Gabriel's outlook shifted again, this time later. Emily was badly injured, a husk of herself, without the spark of life that he had known. A stab of sadness went through him at the sight. This was a sight he had seen too clearly near her end. She lay before him in a listless state, not quite awake and not quite sleeping, holding on against her end.

Gabriel moved slowly toward Emily until realizing he was already there in hues of gray. The beeping continued to grow in volume as he walked closer to her bed. The beeping started making a loud, steady sound, broadcasting something was wrong. Her body racked itself in a state of a sudden convulsion, then was still. Despair shot through Gabriel. Past emotions triggered within him. If only he could have saved her. She had the best care medical technology could provide. But it was not enough. She had died anyway, passing into the unknown.

"Do you think you could have saved her?" a voice behind him softly interjected into his grief.

Gabriel turned his head slowly to see a person he did not know standing behind him. It was odd that he had not heard her walk up. She was a tall woman with bright red hair, attired in clothing of a style he was not familiar with. She wore a skirt of bright colors and a white shirt lettered with strange symbols on it of unknown origin. He did not realize it at first, but she represented the only color in his surroundings. It was like her presence did not belong.

"Who are you?" Gabriel asked.

"I am called Raelynn," the woman replied.

Gabriel sadly shook his head.

"I did all I could, and it was not enough," Gabriel answered in a soft voice, barely realizing he had answered.

"The way of man fails, but the Way of the Lily brings hope," Raelynn stated.

He was surprised he had answered her question and was confused by her response. He had kept this burden inside of him and had not shared it. He had struggled. He had summoned many different doctors hoping for a different answer. All had said the same. There was nothing more that could be done. He had stayed with her while she held on to life. Then it just ended. He had failed, and she was gone.

This woman's words did not make sense, and he was not able to process them. His Emily's existence was gone into oblivion. All remaining was a decomposing body and his memories of their time together. It was a memory that was painful trying to let go.

Gabriel looked back up after contemplating her end. He was again alone, the surroundings dissolving into a mist, left with only his grief to keep him company.

CHAPTER 1

*G*abriel woke from a restless night as the first morning rays of sunlight shone through his window. The dreams were a new phenomenon. He did not fully remember when they had started but it seemed like more and more lately, he woke with an increasingly vivid memory of what had transpired in his sleep.

Despite his grogginess, there was a lot on the day's agenda. Gabriel pulled himself out of bed, undressed, then stepped into the shower after carefully depositing his removed clothes in the to be cleaned receptacle. The shower used very little water and was mixed with a sanitizing mist. While he preferred a more soothing, full water-based shower, he only had enough water quota to allow that luxury once per month if he was careful with his usage. Gabriel carefully washed himself in compliance with the Ministry of Hygiene guidelines. It was the duty of every citizen to properly clean themselves to promote good health. He continued his bathing process until the indicator light in the shower turned green, notifying him that the scanner had determined he had cleaned himself to the proper standard. It then sent a notification to the Oversite system which logged his compliance with his assigned daily tasks.

Gabriel stepped out of the shower and got dressed in a clean outfit. He walked to the kitchen where he selected breakfast shake mix number one. He liked this flavor the best of his available choices. It was packed with the perfectly designed mix of nutrients and calories made in collaboration with his medical profile, scientifically proven to provide the optimal response needed to take on the day. Gabriel had been taught that in the past, people had prepared their own meals, often making unhealthy choices. There had been high levels of obesity and other hosts of diseases that burdened society. Gabriel thought of all the life improvements that had been made since the Ministry of Nutrition had implemented changes in eating choices! These medical problems were nearly unheard of today.

After finishing his breakfast, Gabriel placed his finished container in the dish sanitizing machine. The machine confirmed he had consumed his breakfast and logged his compliance in the Oversite system. It was not good to skip a meal, so this helped to ensure people were fully compliant with doing what was best for them. This did not cause any angst in Gabriel's mind. It was just another morning, and he had been following this routine for as long as he could remember.

Gabriel walked to the garage and got into his vehicle. Well, it was not his vehicle exactly, but it was the one that the Ministry of Scientific Compliance had issued him. This vehicle, and having an actual house structure, were some of the perks associated with his rank in the Ministry of Scientific Compliance. Anyone was allowed to have a vehicle or a house, but practically, they could not due to the energy credits that were required to live in and maintain them. Most of the citizenry found they were able to stay under their allotted credits if they lived in apartment style domiciles and took public transportation. There was a standard amount of credits a person was determined to need which balanced the value of their life with the negative impact they had on the ecosystem. This was not initially a popular countermeasure, but it had a great benefit to stabilizing the rate of climate change and protecting the natural resources of the planet. As someone who was a ranking official in the Ministry of Scientific Compliance, Gabriel's contributions and value were deemed at a higher level, thus affording him the extra credit allotments.

"Office," Gabriel spoke to his on-board navigation console.

Gabriel fastened his safety restraint and opened his ministry news feed on the vehicle console.

"Estimated time of arrival is in twenty-seven minutes," the navigation console spoke as his vehicle left the garage and began to transport him to work.

There was very little traffic for the first half of the drive, but it really started picking up as he got closer to the government district. For the most part, he was able to travel about thirty kilometers per hour. This was the speed limit on most of the roadways throughout the sectors that maximized the transport time to energy efficiency ratio. This also was credited with a big improvement in traffic safety before driving by people was abolished. With the fully automated driving algorithms, accidents were extremely rare. However, the environmental benefit of better fuel efficiency was enough to support this speed limit all by itself.

Gabriel became engrossed in a ministry intelligence report detailing something that his office could get involved with. A group had recently begun meeting together with the suspected purpose of challenging government policy on energy quotas. They were apparently using a long-ago debunked conspiracy theory stating that the science used to generate this policy was a government ploy to reduce personal liberties and control the lives of its people. The ministry agent who had prepared the report had been very careful with his approach of this group. Unfortunately, he didn't have any leaders identified but had been able to find some writings hidden on the online public shared network and was still working to trace it back to its source. This would be soon blocked from public view if it had not been already. This was the primary mission of the Ministry of Scientific Compliance, to protect the citizenry from harmful ideas that were contrary to proven and endorsed scientific principles.

The vehicle eased to a stop in Gabriel's marked parking location. "You have arrived. May science and reason guide your day," it announced.

"Without science and reason, all it lost," Gabriel intoned back.

The science mantra was a new Oversite requirement. Studies had shown that each citizen who recited it daily was more likely to be a productive member of society and have improved acceptance of new initiatives and programs that were implemented. Having fulfilled his morning Oversite expectations, the door was released, and Gabriel was able to step out of the vehicle.

Gabriel passed through security quickly and took the elevator up to the fifth floor of the sprawling eight-floor building. This structure housed the national headquarters of the Ministry of Scientific Compliance. Gabriel glanced at the clock on the wall as he stepped out of the elevator. He had about twenty minutes before the morning science reflection. It was his turn to lead today and he wanted to go over his notes before it started. This could be a good opportunity to get noticed by superiors and help his career opportunities. If he was lucky, a visitor from one of the floors above him would be observing today. Senior officials frequently audited reflection and meditation sessions as part of their morning routines, just as Gabriel had the duty to audit the lower floors periodically as part of his routine. Gabriel nodded hello to a few co-workers as he passed them in the hall. Gabriel opened his office door and proceeded to turn on his work station. He took a quick peek out of his window. Having an office with a window was a good indicator he was being considered for promotion to the sixth floor.

"Open reflection notes," Gabriel instructed his workstation.

The workstation responded by displaying his prepared content. Gabriel made a couple of last-minute edits to it then mirrored it to his handheld device. His building was an all-digital worksite. There were still some areas in the sectors where paper was used, but that was becoming rare due to the requirement that all paper contain fully recycled content. *The Tree and Ecosystem Protection Act* was one of many mandatory recycling initiatives that had become law. In fact, there was now very little you could manufacture that contained a newly harvested natural resource. If you desired a newer version of some innovation, you needed to repurpose older components and prioritize their future usage. While inefficient, it protected the planet by not continuing to deforest, mine, drill and complete other destructive actions that had been done in the past.

Gabriel gathered his handheld and walked to the fifth-floor common meeting area. There was a pretty good turnout today. Gabriel glanced around the room and inwardly smiled as he saw Xavier Alexandar walking in. Xavier worked on the seventh floor and had been a key part of Gabriel's advancement in his career. Gabriel had not seen Xavier in a few months and was gladdened by the opportunity to see him today.

"Gabriel Carasa. So good to see you," Xavier said while walking up and proffering his hand.

Xavier was well known in the ministry and was a bit of a legend among the younger workers. He had a lot of field experience that had led to many big wins for the ministry over the years. He rarely got into the field now, but his eyes showed a spark to them of an adventuresome spirit. He walked with a slight limp and was just starting to show gray hair mixed in with his black hair remaining. Xavier had been responsible for several of Gabriel's opportunities in the past and his subsequent advancement in the ministry.

"Good to see you also, Mr. Alexandar," Gabriel replied.

"Sorry to hear about Emily passing," Xavier offered with a concerned expression on his face. "She died in service to the ministry and we will remember her as a hero. How are you holding up?"

"I am doing well, all things considered," Gabriel answered. "Thank you for your help with gaining Ministry support to allow me to pursue medical options and to be with her until her end. With the prognosis she had, I know you could have insisted on conserving medical resources with her."

"No trouble at all," Xavier replied. "Sometimes it advances science to retest that which we already know." Xavier paused for a moment then continued, "I may have an interesting assignment for you. Once you are finished with the reflection this morning, let's talk. Can you be free in an hour?"

"Yes, sir," Gabriel answered. "That will be no problem at all. I'll come up to your office then."

Gabriel glanced at the clock and decided to begin the meditation session. "Good morning, everyone. I would like us to begin by reading an inspiration from the great scientist Hiedel, in his writing of *Cosmos and Beyond* Chapter 3, paragraph 2."

"And into the beyond I gazed. And I saw order, energy and potential. Potential for reaching beyond. Potential to advance. Potential to save our own planet from the wrong thinking of the past. Potential to change our society for the betterment of the greater good. But I also saw great risk. Risk to hold to the flawed ways of the past. Risk to stagnate and revert. Risk of unbelief to the ways of science. But how do we reach this potential and offset these great risks? We must teach the proper ways. We must silence the thinking and actions of impure behaviors that are set against the laws of science. And in doing so, we pursue truth and we can reach to grasp at our potential."

"Let us meditate on this wisdom," Gabriel stated as he glanced at the clock to ensure he did not stop meditation until the full ten minutes past, as was proscribed in the daily requirement.

Gabriel put his body into the meditation pose with his head bowed and hands together. Overall, Gabriel was pleased with how his reading had been received. Hiedel was viewed as a credible meditation source but was rarely used. Other readings which focused more on specific areas of science compliance were often more popular. These included areas such as water conservation, energy use, reducing negative planetary footprints, and other behavior-based items. Gabriel found this reading recently when trying to find something to stand out, and as he surveyed the audience, he could tell it was impactful. After a full ten minutes had passed, Gabriel decided to close the meditation.

"May science and reason guide your day," Gabriel intoned.

"Without science and reason, all is lost," the assembled group answered back.

The gathering broke up. A few people acknowledged Gabriel for the meditation, including Xavier as he exited down the hall. Gabriel still had some time before his appointment with Xavier, so he went back to his office to get caught up on some reports that he had not completed the prior week.

∞ ∞ ∞

Xavier walked to the elevator following the meditation Gabriel had led. He had met Hiedel once many years ago before he had died. Xavier had found him to be very zealous in his mannerisms and someone who had very little patience for those who did not agree with his ways of thinking and the logical policy conclusions to his thinking.

In reality, Hiedel's vision was very close to being achieved today. Sure, there were still some outlying areas of the country that hadn't fully adapted to all the new programs and thinking, but there had been a tremendous amount of progress made in the last generation. If you planted the right seeds when people were young, they were much more pliable to the direction that Hiedel's vision had indicated. And with those who were older, you just needed to move more slowly. As long as you made small incremental changes instead of big, obvious changes, you could generally build compliance over time. It had taken the better part of Xavier's lifetime, but looking back, he could see a monumental change of the land from the time of his childhood to the time he was experiencing now.

Xavier brought his thoughts back to the pressing issues of the day. He really needed to get an operation going to suppress a newly discovered resistance group. There was so little information available, but he was pretty sure they were mainly responsible for the non-compliance in the Xenon, Villron and Brendag sectors that continued to persist.

This was where Xavier thought Gabriel could be of some help. Gabriel's parents had originated from the Xenon sector which was in the center of the believed resistance activity. His parents had died while visiting the capital when he was a small toddler. Well, that they died was technically true, but in reality, they had been conducting some opposition work counter to the ministry's mission and they needed to be silenced. Gabriel was deemed young enough to not be corrupted, so he was placed in government care a bit earlier than the mandated age of four years old that was required in the capital. Gabriel was able to get a top education and was a student who showed high aptitude and potential. Xavier had seen to it that he was placed in the Ministry of Scientific Compliance when he completed his education, foreseeing the potential for such an opportunity as the one he currently had in mind.

Gabriel had thrived in the ministry, becoming a rising star by doing well in his early assignments and proving his reliability many times. Xavier wanted to be sure of his readiness and commitment to the ministry's ideals. Gabriel had never been fully told the story of his parents, and there would be a risk he may uncover parts of it if he were to use the cover story Xavier wanted to give him. But ultimately, Xavier didn't see better options to address this growing threat in the Xenon sector. He would have gladly assigned this earlier, but with the deterioration of Gabriel's fiancé, it would have been likely to backfire if he had asked Gabriel to leave her side near the end.

Xavier had obtained very high-level approval to allow Gabriel to use significant medical resources on her. An unproductive life that cannot be saved is a drain on society and logically should be quickly ended. It is easy to say that, but he could not risk any resentment from Gabriel if he wanted to ensure his loyalty for this upcoming assignment. Gabriel was close to Emily, and by giving him full ability to gain closure, it should pay dividends back. That is how Xavier had secured approval for this policy waiver. Gabriel was led to believe the approval was due to the esteem of his and Emily's service was held, but it was really about enabling this upcoming assignment.

Xavier walked to his office on the seventh floor and peered outside at the view from his office window. If he could get this mission to a successful conclusion, it was all but assured that he would be moving up to the eighth floor when an opening was available. The head of the ministry had all but promised him that when he sought approval for Gabriel's medical waiver. But to do that, he would have to roll up this new resistance cell and he would need Gabriel's help to do it so the assimilation of Xenon, Villron and Brendag could be completed.

∞ ∞ ∞

Gabriel entered Xavier's office reception area and checked in that he had arrived. Xavier's assistant promptly notified Xavier of his arrival and told Gabriel to go right in. Xavier stood up to greet Gabriel.

"Thanks for coming on such short notice," Xavier said.

"Anytime, sir," Gabriel replied.

Gabriel had had some time to think of what prompted his invite up here, and honestly did not know what it could be. Assignments coming from Xavier were almost always interesting and career beneficial. It was good that he had a sponsor of Xavier's stature in the ministry.

"Gabriel, I know you have been through a lot recently, and what I am going to propose to you may be more than you are ready to take on," Xavier said. "I won't order you to do this assignment, but I am hoping you will be willing to volunteer. I have a unique opportunity to do a lot of good for the ministry, not to mention your own career advancement. I will warn you, this may come at a high personal cost and could be very dangerous to you."

This was a very unusual way of offering an assignment. Typically, you were assigned something, and you did it. Gabriel had never been asked to volunteer on something like this before. It must be something risky if he was offered this choice. He was restless lately and the more he thought about it, something to immerse himself in may help him take his mind off the passing of Emily.

"You haven't said anything to disinterest me," Gabriel carefully replied. Not exactly saying yes but wanting to hear more about the assignment before giving final commitment.

"Good, I had hoped that wouldn't dissuade you. I have a field assignment I need covered, and your particular background is uniquely qualified to be useful," Xavier explained. "We have some resistance activity happening in the Xenon sector primarily. The problem I have been having is my attempts to get agents infiltrated there have been woefully unsuccessful. These people are a very close group, not to mention the unique physical characteristics they have. So far, they have politely rebuffed my agents, and as a result, we have not been able to gather any evidence to determine who the leaders of the resistance are. If we are going to make sustainable progress in these sectors, this needs to change. This is where you come in."

Gabriel showed some confusion. He didn't know very much about this sector and their people. And for sure didn't know how he fit into this assignment to be able to do something that top agents had been unable to accomplish.

"Birth parents are not something that is discussed much here in the capital," Xavier continued, about to add clarity to Gabriel's unanswered question. "We have become enlightened in most of the sectors. When children are of a particular age, their care is given to the Ministry of

Education. While there is an acknowledged affiliation with birth parents, it is common that people are not aware of their parentage. It is also common that people do not spend effort seeking out their birth parents later."

Gabriel listened carefully to what Xavier was saying, wondering where he was going with this. Gabriel had never taken a field assignment that sounded anything like what Xavier was describing. It sounded very interesting.

"We had a lot of hope about thirty years back," Xavier continued, "that we could obsolete physical birthing. But as you probably know, while we were able to genetically grow children in a lab setting, we could not develop a way to simulate the human connection which was established in the infant years. We do continue to fund studies to develop a solution for this, but we do not yet have an answer for this. That being the case, we continue to encourage targeted birthing as one's duty to the state when our population target projections demand it."

Gabriel remembered this study. There was a coldness to the personalities of those who had been grown artificially and some were not compliant to ministry edicts and requirements. Much stability would be lost if that continued. Last he had heard, the study had been terminated with organ harvesting as about the only good thing that had come out of it.

"The reason I am discussing this," Xavier continued, "is that Xenon and the adjacent sectors have not been compliant in giving their children to the Ministry of Education. They are still allowing their education but have insisted on being able to house them and oversee them until they reach adult status. We have been slowly working to change this mindset, but it takes time. Things like this resistance harm our efforts and I need your help infiltrating them so we can overcome this negative influence. Sure, we could be more forceful in making the changes in the outlying sectors, but we have learned that slow changes are most sustainable. They still see strong value in familial bonds, and I believe a program of gradual change will resonate with them best if we present it properly."

Gabriel still wasn't sure where this discussion was going, but Xavier definitely had his interest. He didn't know much about his birth parents.

He knew that they had died when he was young, and he had been put in the Ministry of Education like most other children were. It was interesting that this Xenon sector continued to put so much emphasis on familial bonds. It was known that family structures tended to protect dynastic tendencies, where those without the best capabilities rose to the highest positions of power and influence. Science taught that society is best served if the most capable rose to the top positions, survival of the fittest so to speak. Familial structures tended to run counter to this, which is why there had been such an effort to eliminate this connection in society. It was best to give everyone equal opportunity to succeed, rather than one skewed by built-in advantages or disadvantages.

"You may not be fully aware of this," Xavier continued, "but our records indicate that your birth parents were from the Xenon sector. They were visiting the capital when they died. Since our sector policy here in Preath is to assume care for children near the age you were when they died, we took you into the care of the Ministry of Education. You do have the distinct coloration and facial features common of the Xenon region, so I think you will be able to fit in well. Also, we have determined that you have some connections in this sector. Some family members made inquiries about the time when you entered the care of the Ministry of Education requesting to take over your care. We believe there are still living relatives of your birth parents. While we are not sure if they have any role in this resistance, we believe getting their acceptance would give you credibility to identify this resistance activity. It is particularly important to find out about this Kayden that keeps coming up in the intelligence gathering we have been able to complete."

Gabriel hadn't really ever traveled much out of the capital that he had memory of. The government made it difficult to travel outside of your home sector. The fact that there were some sectors that did not fully comply was known to Gabriel as part of his role in the Ministry of Scientific Compliance, but it was not widely known amongst the general populace. This was a great honor to be approved for outside sector travel, let alone to an assignment to the outlying sectors. It indicated great trust in him by the ministry and by Xavier. He did not want to let them down. Gabriel had wondered why his features had a unique aspect to them, but it was not often commented on. Every student's education provided much focus on not noticing such differences in appearance. This answered some curiosities he had mildly entertained when he was younger. The residual familial connection was somewhat interesting, but he did not understand why that had any significance based on what he had been taught.

"For this to be effective we will need a cover story for you," Xavier explained. "And you will need a lot of training. I don't think we will be able to effectively hide the time you have spent in the capital, so I think we should admit it, even to the point of you being in the Ministry of Scientific Compliance. We can arrange for a high profile falling out, where we create a story that will resonate with those in Xenon. You can be seen as leaving your job and traveling back to the place of your birth. This will take some work and a lot of training preparation to get ready. Do well on this, and you will advance quickly in the ministry and have my gratitude."

"I would be honored to take on this assignment, Mr. Alexandar," Gabriel quickly interjected. "Thank you so much for having confidence in me to trust me with an assignment of this importance."

"No, thank you for your service and being willing to do this," Xavier offered. "I will send you an encoded message with next steps. It is critical you discuss this with no one."

"I understand fully," Gabriel replied. "You can count on me."

Gabriel politely dismissed himself and left Xavier's office. This was going to be an exciting assignment and he had a lot of work to do to get ready.

CHAPTER 2

Gabriel looked out of the shuttle as it approached the Northfalcon stop in the Xenon sector. It was hard to believe that his training was finally over. When he agreed to accept this mission, he expected that he would be deployed in a matter of a few weeks. The reality was something completely different. Six grueling months later, he was through his training and embarking on this new assignment.

The ministry had a training facility near the city of Morfort in the Preath sector that taught the many skills he would need to complete this mission. He had learned how to covertly communicate in a way that would not get him caught. He also received extensive training in the cultural norms of the Xenon sector. This had perhaps been the most surprising. Gabriel had grown up thinking that all regions of the country believed and behaved in a very similar manner to the capital, but the reality of that was not true.

Each sector had some policy autonomy, but still had to comply with the same core laws. The government placed sector wide policy priorities on energy conservation policies, wellness policies, scientific compliance programs, and some public educational requirements. They had not, however, gained autonomy over the family structure and while practice of religion was banned, there was still underground practices occurring. Gabriel also learned that enforcement on daily Oversite requirements and other programs common near the capital were laxer.

Gabriel refocused himself to be in the right mindset for this new assignment. While the knowledge of the underlying dynamic of Xenon had been very interesting, it was only a small subset of what would be required of him. His so-called exit from the ministry had been a lot higher profile than he had envisioned. He had been publicly humiliated on a local news report for not complying with his energy allowance. By itself, this would not have been damaging, but when it was illustrated how favorable the allowance he already had was, it was much more devastating with a general public who had to make do with much less than he had been living on.

Following this, it was announced that he was being taken into confinement to allow him a period of reflection for his poor actions. This provided cover for his training period, but also provided a plausible story about his falling out with the ministry. He was curious how he would be later re-integrated back into the good graces of the capital, but he was sure Xavier had that all thought out.

The shuttle came to a stop in Northfalcon. This was the biggest city in the Xenon sector. Gabriel used most of his energy credits to get the shuttle ride and would have to live on very little until his next allotment. It was common for people to walk distances of one hundred or more kilometers in order to travel, and Gabriel had researched that there were primitive sleeping locations available along the route. If he made good time, he should be able to cover this in two to three days. There was available drinking water in route, and he could mix up his food packs with water along the way. Before leaving the transport terminal, he was required to register his presence with the government authorities.

Gabriel cleared the shuttle exit area and promptly presented his travel credentials to the Ministry of Travel officer who had met the shuttle.

"Purpose of visit?" a disinterested looking official asked him while running his identity through Oversite.

"Here to look for work prospects," Gabriel answered, being careful to follow the script his case officer had advised him to use.

"Says here that you have been in the capital for a lot of years," the official stated. "Seems odd that you would come here now for work after all those years."

"I am sure you can see it in the system," Gabriel replied, "but I was born here in Xenon which gives me travel rights to be able to come here.

Since I lost my job at the Ministry of Scientific Compliance, I need to find another option that will provide me with credits."

"Says here you tried to steal energy credits you didn't deserve and that you were confined for it," the official stated. "We don't need any of that behavior here. We already have enough people who don't do as they are told as it is. So why come here now?"

"I think I have some relatives near Deerbarrow," Gabriel answered. "I am hoping they give me better work prospects than the general laborer pool."

"You will be given thirty days to find suitable accommodations and employment," the ministry official stated after determining he didn't have a valid excuse to deny Gabriel entry. "If you are unable to find a useful source of employment, the Ministry of Trade will assign you one."

The Ministry of Trade positions were very rarely coveted and were typically low skill tasks that provided the minimum of energy credits and compensation needed to live on. This provided a great motivation to be accepted into a better source of employment, doing something more useful to society. A sociology study had determined that if you aligned the societies overall goals with how the populace was rewarded, people would act in their self-interest to pursue those goals, especially if the alternative was equally negative. Ultimately a non-contributing member of society should no longer be supported by society. But those who had the ability to show some contributions, even if meager, were able to be supported with enough to live on. Gabriel wanted to avoid that outcome both because it would mean an uncomfortable existence, and due to the fact that it would make his mission here more difficult to achieve.

Gabriel thanked the ministry officer and walked through the checkpoint into the Xenon city of Northfalcon. Gabriel had traveled quite a bit throughout the Preath sector, where the capital was located, and his first reaction was how rustic that this city appeared. One popular recreation activity in Preath was to go on an overnight excursion into a designated nature area and spend a few days without technology assistance. While this wasn't quite to that extreme, it had a very similar feel to Gabriel. If this was the largest city in Xenon, then he wondered what a smaller one would look like.

Close to the shuttle area there was a lot of the technology he was accustomed to, but the further he walked, there was much less evidence of it. He saw several bicycles and what looked like human pulled carts for moving on the roads but didn't see any powered vehicles. He did see a couple vehicles parked near the Ministry of Travel checkpoint, but beyond that, everyone seemed to be moving under their own power. There did not appear to be evidence of any mass public transportation system which likely explained why so many others were walking or using manual forms of transportation.

Gabriel pulled out his handheld device to orient himself to where he needed to be traversing. He inputted his target of Deerbarrow into his handheld and specified that he would need directions at a normal pace. He was given a way to proceed and began to walk along the suggested path. If he was careful at keeping the charging panel exposed throughout the day, his handheld should last several weeks without needing an energy charge. The government wanted to encourage use of these devices, so they discounted the credit costs if it did need a recharge. Handheld devices provided a lot of tracking information on the population, so their use was encouraged. Amid the seemingly lack of technology, he did see handhelds on most of the people he passed on the road.

In his role in the ministry, he had read a study that experimented with imbedding devices in people's bodies to provide the same handheld convenience. This was thought to be more convenient, but the sociological impact created a lot of paranoia and angst in the test subjects. The test group who had the same technological availability but appearing to choose for themselves to carry the devices, had a much higher acceptance rate than those whose equivalent technology was imbedded.

It was always important to ensure the subjects really found value with the devices and kept them with them. There was even a mode where you could turn off location identification and use other privacy indicators. This took away some convenience features, but Gabriel had learned that the same content was still being secretly uploaded to the Oversite system. He supposed that he was being currently tracked via his handheld by the ministry and his case officer. He had been warned he may need to surrender his device at some point in his assignment and, as such, had had been trained on other mechanisms to communicate if the situation demanded it.

Gabriel followed the directions he was given, and soon found himself on the edge of Northfalcon. Looking at his handheld, he found a primitive rest station about three hours walk from his current location and decided that would make a good stopping point for the night. His route was lightly traveled. There was a paved surface that a vehicle could safely traverse, but there was also a smaller walking path off to the side.

His first observation was that there appeared to be a lot of farms. Food stuffs were the best-known exports of the Xenon sector. The food that he ate was already processed for optimal nutrition, but the raw ingredients before processing still needed to be produced from nature. The fully synthetic versions that had been developed performed very poorly in studies, so the farms were still needed to provide foodstuffs to the rest of the population. Gabriel began to wonder if he would end up finding labor in a farm role if he could make a connection with his family relations. His training hadn't covered much of expected work on a farm, but he would try to be a quick learner if it came to it.

Time passed quickly and Gabriel's thoughts were interrupted when his handheld announced that he had arrived at the primitive rest station. The rest station consisted of an open structure with a roof on it. There were some elevated benches big enough to lay down on under the shelter. There was also a bathroom building offset behind the rest station. It looked like there was a heat source and water source available, provided you were willing to spend credits. This station didn't have a nutrition dispensary machine, but probably only being a three hour walk from the city, it wasn't deemed close enough to be needed. Gabriel logged his presence in the console and added enough water to his nutrition mix to make his dinner shake. After consuming it, he used his handheld to verify he had drunk it all, so it could be logged in the Oversite system.

"May science and reason guide your day," Gabriel's handheld spoke out.

"Without science and reason, all is lost," Gabriel faithfully replied.

If he wanted to be able to earn his full credits allotment, he would need to stay current on his daily Oversite requirements. He was surprised that no one else stopped at this station and that he hadn't encountered any other travelers once he had gotten an hour or so outside of Northfalcon. Gabriel adjusted his travel bag into a makeshift pillow and laid down to sleep. It was a bit uncomfortable, but the temperature was still nice out, so he was able to get to drift off quickly.

∞ ∞ ∞

A foggy haze clouded Gabriel's vision as the sun shone brightly, well above the horizon. Gabriel felt an urge to walk, and as time passed, the fog began to diminish. There was a lack of color in his view, as he saw only in shades of gray. He could see the top of a mountain in the distant horizon. As he turned to his right, there was bare nothingness. Sand, heat, rocks and desert filled his senses. The air was now dry, which was odd following the fog, but he spent little thought on it. It seemed normal to have the abnormal here. Gabriel continued to walk. Further ahead showed shades that may be an oasis, or it may just be a mirage. It was hard to tell. But he continued onward and surprisingly felt no thirst, only a desire to move forward toward this apparition ahead.

"Do you think it is real?" a voice beside him asked.

Gabriel turned to see who had spoken. He had heard no approach and was certain he had been alone. But the rules seemed different in this place. The voice belonged to someone who had familiarity to him. He tried to remember the name that she had given him before. He reflected on her bright red hair and strange clothing, willing his memory to give him her name.

"I think we have met before," Gabriel answered, "but I cannot recall your name."

"I have been known by many names, but you know me as Raelynn," she answered.

Gabriel blinked with recognition at this name. It seemed an eternity ago, but the grief during their last meeting was still fresh in his heart. But it was clearly her. She had asked if he had done all he could and now she was asking if it he thought it was real. He thought it was a very loaded question. Was the possible mirage ahead real or did she mean the place he was walking or life itself?

"I cannot tell," he finally answered. "I see an oasis could be ahead, but science also teaches that light waves will curve in hot flat surfaces and make the appearance of water ahead. Because it could be fake does not make it fake, but neither does it assure it is real."

"Spoken like a true adherent of the path of science," Raelynn replied with a slight smile on her lips. "To say so much, yet to believe so little."

This was not the response he had expected to his answer. Granted, he was being evasive, but the fact was he didn't know. He did not understand where he was and what rules governed here.

"What is the truth of the answer then?" Gabriel asked. "You ask like you know the answer and you quiz me for something I have no reason to have knowledge of."

Raelynn gave a mysterious yet patronizing smile. "You have the answer within you. It is not my place to make your journey more certain, only to keep you close to the path. I will ask you this, do you want it to be real? What action will you take to that purpose?"

Gabriel stopped short. He stared ahead trying to see the image ahead. As he turned back to answer her, she was gone. Her absence was no more a surprise than her appearance had been. That still begged the question she had asked him. What did he want it to be? What was the point of wanting? Wanting something did not make it so. Reality was different than that. He could want to have Emily back, but that did not make her come back. Maybe the question was more about taking actions to make your own future. But the more he thought about it, he didn't think this was what Raelynn meant.

Did he want it to be an oasis? He was starting to feel thirst. So, while he was initially indifferent, yes, he did want it to be an oasis. Gabriel continued to walk toward the possible oasis. He reached the location in question. Looking upon the land, he saw a parched and dry area.

He had to admit he was disappointed and had thought he would find water here. As he continued to scan the horizon, he noticed something resembling a small puddle a few paces away and walked toward it. As he got closer, he bent down to check it. Sure enough, while only about half a meter in diameter, it contained water. Not only was it water, but it had an essence of color to it that contrasted the lack of color surrounding it.

"Was it what you wanted it to be?" Raelynn asked appearing beside him. "Was it in proportion to your desire?"

Gabriel wasn't sure how to answer her question as he reached down with his hand to sample the unexpectedly pure taste of the thirst-quenching water. He had wanted a water oasis, and he had found one. Was it as big as he expected? No, but at the same time it was there. He turned his gaze to respond, but he was again alone, drifting back into the foggy haze.

∞ ∞ ∞

Gabriel awoke feeling the heat of the sun coming up in the morning. He felt rested considering his bed and surroundings but could not shake some strange dream memories of looking for water in a desert. Gabriel was glad he wasn't in a desert right now. Gabriel stretched, sat up, and started to stand up, quickly realizing that his feet were half covered in water. He hadn't heard any rain in the night, but a sizable puddle of water was there. Maybe there was a leak from the water machine. Sliding his body to the end of where he had slept, he found a dry spot and fully stood up. Gabriel thought it was very odd about the water.

CHAPTER 3

The High Seat of Kayden raised her arms as she was scanned for the presence of surveillance devices. She had left her handheld at home so her believed physical location would be marked away from the enclave she was attempting entry to. She wasn't sure if the central government suspected her of subversive activity, but the best way to get caught was to be careless. The various ministries had become very creative at imbedding monitoring and tracking devices in the most innocuous of items. These trackers ranged from cameras, recording devices and other locator beacon devices. The general population was not supposed to know they existed, but after some odd coincidences, suspicions began to increase that there was a method being used to monitor and track that was previously unknown.

These had been found recently in some new lines of clothing, embedded into the advanced tech fabric as well as other more portable items like water and food containers. These tracking dots, as they were called by those who knew, were less than a millimeter in diameter and nearly impossible to see with the naked eye. They did not transmit continuously to Oversite but would upload content when they were near a station or handheld equipped with the upload technology. All they needed was a short dose of sunlight to stay active, and they could work for a very long time. There were ways to trick them out, but it was cumbersome to do so and increased risk.

The High Seat had followed all the best practices to avoid risk of contracting tracking dots. She pretty much avoided anything that was newly manufactured. Fortunately, her scanner system confirmed no tracking dots or devices were found. For good measure, she initiated an electromagnetic pulse that had been proven to destroy the electronic components in the tracking dots. It was suspicious to have known devices go completely off the grid, but it was worse to have unknown tracking happening, especially when one was involved in some illegal activities.

The High Seat walked out of the tracker detection area and found the hidden passage to the underground area. It was difficult to move on the surface without detection, but this underground network had provided a very effective way to beat all the surveilling technology that was employed against the population. These tunnels were used in rare circumstances and known only to a critical few. She walked carefully through the winding passages, using a portable light source to illuminate the path.

The leader of Kayden lived just outside of Deerbarrow and had entered this tunnel entry point about an hour's walk from where she lived. From here she had access to a network covering much of Xenon and some points in other sectors. It had a system imbedded in it which could transport you to anywhere in its range within a pretty short period of time. She looked closely for a second hidden entrance to get to the transport area. If the first area was to be discovered, it would appear like an underground cavern, but would have a dead-end and not reveal the transport passage-way. She found what she was looking for and pressed the correct locations on the wall. Hearing a click, she observed the wall shifting slightly to allow her enough space to squeeze through. When she got through the wall opening, she reset it back to its original location.

In front of her was an aerodynamically contoured cylindrical device. There was a circular opening ahead of it that appeared to have some sort of guide system and was only slightly wider than the shuttle itself. The opening did not extend more than ten meters in front of the shuttle device, being blocked by a facing of rock.

The High Seat opened the door and situated herself in one of the seats. She typed in a special code for her target location. Making sure she had everything ready to go, she closed the door and strapped herself into the safety harness. Some time passed where nothing seemed to be happening. During this wait, she was seated quietly with her eyes closed, appearing to be in some sort of focused concentration. Suddenly, the shuttle moved forward with a flash of light into the opening and disappeared.

She came to a stop quickly as her shuttle streaked through an opening and into the staging bay. This was a central hub location, accessible by all primary access points. Most meetings were held here as it was much easier to handle logistics. The central hub had no accessible path to the surface, so there was very little chance of being discovered. She got out of her shuttle and walked to another more advanced tracker detection station. She again underwent another surveillance check until she was confirmed safe then proceeded to walk to the meeting room.

It looked like she was the last to arrive of those who had committed to come. The High Seat looked around the room and moved to take her place at the head of the table on a chair that was slightly elevated relative to the rest. Counting herself, ten had come today. It was a good turnout, proportional to the importance of today's business.

"I call the High Council of Kayden to order," she announced. "Will the Reader please provide us focus with a guiding text?"

An elderly man opened an aged book in front of him and began to speak.

"We shall read from the book of *The Path*, Chapter 2, stanza 3. And in the days of strain, one came amongst the faithful, a stranger who was not. In him was great power to mend the divide, but also great power to destroy. He was a dreamer in all ways but did not believe. Two paths were open. The path of belief leads to the survival of the people. The path to unbelief leads to the devastation of both the Lily and hopes of mankind."

"Thank you, Reader," the High Seat stated.

The Reader nodded in acknowledgement as the High Seat turned her head to the right to call on the Seeker. The Seeker was tall, with long red hair and was, as usual, colorful in her dress. Her report was the reason the High Seat had called this meeting.

"Seeker, please update the council with your report," the High Seat requested.

"The Seeker's role is to search the signs to find those who are gifted in the power of dreams," she stated. "The even more important charge is to look for he who will come as foretold by the prophesy that the Reader just offered to us for reflection. I have been watching in the place of dreams for these things."

The High Seat looked around the assembled council and noted that the Seeker had everyone's full attention. This could be a decision of great consequence and wanted the full council on board with whatever was decided.

"One person I have been tracking is Gabriel Carasa" the Seeker continued. "He is the son of Kayla and Erik who died on a mission to the capital many years back. If you recall, they reported great danger near the end before they were found dead. Their son was taken by the Ministry of Education, even over the protests of his extended family from Xenon. Gabriel's parents were strong in the gift of dreams, and I have been watching for signs he may have similar talents. I have appeared in his dreams a few times, and the most recent event I pushed him to see if he had the ability to create. His skill was very raw, but with some prompting, he managed to create a small quantity of water. I do not think he believes anything unique from it, and when he finds water upon awakening, I think he will likely surmise a different reason for water being physically near him."

"Isn't that risky to start someone to the dream state if we don't have a way to get him a teacher? Especially since he is in the capital area," one of the newer council members asked.

"Yes, it can be very risky," the Seeker went on, "but in this case he is on his way to Deerbarrow and should arrive within a day or two. I found by looking into capital news, that he has recently been disgraced and discharged from a Ministry of Scientific Compliance position and may have entered a period of confinement. His coming has some potential to fit the signs of the prophesy, but some things appear too coincidental about this. He is the closest I have ever observed to meeting the signs of the many prophesies foretelling of the great dreamer, but I am not yet ready to say it is him with full certainty."

The Seeker had a resolute demeanor about her as she looked around to each of the assembled council members. She had never made such a definitive statement regarding a possible identification of the great dreamer. This was not lost on the council who had come to trust the Seeker's judgement, even if she was at a relatively young age for her position.

The Guardian of the Lily had the most skeptical expression on his face. He was responsible for protecting the security of Kayden to prevent infiltration by the government or other dangerous entities.

"I agree he shows potential for being the great dreamer, but he also shows great potential to be a spy by one of the ministries to try to infiltrate us," the Guardian responded. "They have been sending a lot of agents recently who have been trying to find out more about Kayden. They think Kayden is a person instead of the name of our organization, but they have heard enough to be worried, and are actively trying to infiltrate us. What better way than to turn one of our own, and send him back to us knowing we could not easily reject him?"

"Even if he is an agent to try to expose us, that doesn't mean he still isn't the great dreamer," the Seeker answered. "We may need to bring him to our side, while still not exposing ourselves. This carries great risk, and as Seeker I agree. But can we afford not to take some chances? The people here in the northern sectors have shown great strength against the continued propaganda of the various ministries. But despite this fortitude, we are slowly losing with our young ones. If we wait too long to act, it will be too late."

The High Seat listened as the debate continued and other council members weighed in. There had been some minor insights presented, but no other new points presented. This Gabriel could very well be the great dreamer prophesized in the sacred texts, and it was equally as likely that he would betray them all if brought into their circle of trust. This was a personally sensitive item that would require some direct investigation on the High Seat's part.

Recognizing that points were now being repeated without new ones being raised, the High Seat interjected to steer the council to a decision. She proposed her plan for taking on this challenge. The council made some minor suggestions, but agreement was reached with her plan largely still intact. When the meeting finally ended, the High Seat left with a feeling of hopeful anticipation combined with one of concern for the risks ahead.

∞ ∞ ∞

Gabriel arrived on the outskirts of Deerbarrow after two full days of walking since his first night's stop. It was early evening, and he hoped to find a proper bed tonight. The rustic overnight stations and walking everywhere on his feet was very tiring, and he was not sure how so many people operated this way on a regular basis. He had clearly been spoiled in his role in the ministry with automated transportation. Looking back, he now had a greater appreciation of the cover story that Xavier had orchestrated, and why it would have been meaningful to someone who cannot afford to spend energy credits for transportation.

Gabriel encountered a person walking on the road pushing a cart of some sort of produce.

"Good day to you sir," Gabriel stated. "I was wondering if you could recommend a place where I could get a room to stay at for the night?"

The person stopped briefly, putting his cart down to answer. "If you don't know someone here, your best bet is the Deerbarrow Inn. Most visitors usually stay there. I am pretty sure he keeps a few rooms open. Just stay on this road and you can't miss it."

"Much appreciative, mister," Gabriel replied then proceeded to look up the name on his handheld, intending to make reservations. He didn't find any way to contact this place, so he decided he would need to ask in person.

Gabriel followed the directions and found the inn that had been recommended to him. It was constructed like other buildings in Deerbarrow. It appeared to be about three stories tall and was made with the standard composition building material that the government had approved for construction. You could still find some buildings with wood-based construction, but in new building construction, that way was now unlawful due to impact to the environment that deforestation would cause. Instead, builders had adapted to using a new synthetic structural component that was eco-system friendly. It wasn't as visually appealing as some of the pictures of older buildings he had seen, but it was functional for its purpose. The sign in front simply said Deerbarrow Inn and there was a picture of a musical note and a bed on it.

Walking inside, Gabriel found a large common room with several tables setup and a stage area, likely used for the entertainment. It was empty of guests, but most entertainment in inns didn't usually occur until normal work hours were completed if it was anything like the capital. Gabriel walked up to the check-in counter and found someone sitting there engrossed on their handheld device.

"Good evening," Gabriel offered. "Do you have any rooms available? Sorry for not reserving ahead but I couldn't find any contact information on my handheld."

The person behind the desk looked up. "Yeah, I have never gotten around to registering this place in Oversite. We get so few travelers here in Deerbarrow, and I am never booked out. It seems like overkill to put up with all the red-tape of being registered. To answer your question, yes, we do have rooms available. Do you plan on staying very long?"

"I may stay a while, but my duration is pretty open ended right now," Gabriel replied. "I am looking for some family relations, and I am not sure what I will find, and how welcome I will be. If all goes well, I will find some work here, but I am leaving my options open right now."

"We offer a couple of room types," the proprietor offered while directing Gabriel to the rate sheet.

The rates were extremely reasonable compared to the capital, but Gabriel decided he should start with the cheapest option for now to better maintain his cover. He hoped the quality of the accommodations wouldn't reflect the cheaper cost.

"I'll take the cheaper one," Gabriel answered. "After staying in those primitive overnight stations, the past couple of nights, I am really looking forward to a normal bed to sleep in tonight!"

"You are not the first person to say that!" the proprietor said with a chuckle. "Let's get some information from you and we can get you checked in."

Gabriel provided his registration information and then scanned himself to approve the payment for the room.

Glancing at the registration information, the clerk zeroed in on his name. "The Carasa name is one I have known over the years. I think I know most who share this name. You wouldn't happen to be related to Kayla and Erik who used to live here many years back? I know they had a small child before they died that did not come back to Deerbarrow."

Gabriel internally jumped with excitement, carefully masking his outward expression. This would maybe to easier than he expected to make contact.

"Wow, that is interesting," Gabriel remarked. "They were my parents. I don't really remember them, but I recently learned they were from here and was hoping to learn more of my history. I grew up in the capital, so my concept of family has a lot to be learned."

"Well, you are very welcome here. My name is Wallis Ringsdale, by the way," he said while extending his hand in greeting. "Your parents came to my establishment about once a week, many years ago, and I knew them pretty well. Some of your relations still come here after work to listen to the music and to socialize. If you are willing to join me tonight in the common room, I would be happy to make some introductions for you."

"I would be extremely grateful," Gabriel answered. "I wasn't sure where to start on this, and this will make things much easier for me!"

"Well, let's get you settled in your room." Wallis answered. "Things should pick up in the common room in an hour or two if you are able to be back down by then."

Gabriel walked up the stairs to his room on the second floor. It had a window overlooking the street, which would allow plenty of natural light to come through. The room was a good size, had a comfortable looking bed and had its own bathroom. Otherwise, it was basic in accommodations. After the fully rustic existence for the past couple of nights, it looked absolutely wonderful! Gabriel walked around the room, looking for the energy meter used for logging his usage. Not finding one, he checked the water supply and found it came right on without restriction. This was odd, as it should be limiting him somehow to make sure he stayed within his allocated supply. He looked around the room and found the internal messaging device to contact the front desk.

"Hi, this is Gabriel in room 205. I am not seeing any energy metering equipment. Just trying to make sure I don't exceed my energy allotment."

Wallis answered, "That is all factored into your room rate. Feel free to use whatever you need. We don't have all that technology that you are probably used to in the capital."

Gabriel was confused but decided not to press further at this time. He was pretty certain that all energy and water was metered to each location, and there was an accounting that needed to happen to tie usage back to every person. He also wondered about the rate. The number of credits he was quoted per night wouldn't come close to covering unmetered water usage. But he was warned when he took this assignment, that he would experience a lot of things different than when he was in the capital. He could try to figure this discrepancy out later, as he spent more time here. Feeling the dirt of the road, Gabriel got undressed and stepped into the shower. There did not appear to be a mist setting and he experienced an enjoyable, full water shower until he felt refreshed and suitably cleaned.

After getting dressed into a clean outfit, Gabriel logged into Oversite and sent a very brief encoded report on his handheld that he had arrived safely and what his immediate plans were. He didn't see any new instructions left for him. Gabriel then mixed up a dinner shake, did the recommended period of meditation, then skimmed on his handheld until it was time to go downstairs.

In the common room Gabriel noticed a growing number of people present. There was music being performed on the stage. He didn't recognize the song playing, but it was upbeat and had a certain life to it. Gabriel looked around and found an open table and sat down. He glanced around looking for Wallis but didn't immediately see him.

People were mingling around to one another in active, friendly looking conversation. The people were not attired in the styles he was used to seeing in Preath, but they looked comfortable with what they were wearing.

Many were drinking a colored clear looking substance which didn't look like the standard shakes he was accustomed to. Gabriel watched as a patron went to the counter and someone poured him a drink from one of containers on the shelf behind it. He suspected this was a form of alcohol consumption he had learned about in his training. This practice was no longer permitted in the capital. If you needed some stress relief or relaxation, there were meditation methods proscribed for this. If this wasn't effective, you could be prescribed some medication that would simulate the effect, in a proper safety-controlled environment. He was surprised alcohol was still allowed, but this was probably one of the critical issues that risked destabilizing this sector.

"There you are Gabriel," a voice behind him called out. "I trust your room was to your satisfaction?"

Gabriel turned to see Wallis standing with a couple of people he didn't recognize.

"Yes, the room is very nice thank you," Gabriel replied. "It was very refreshing to get cleaned up after being on the road for the last few days."

"Yes, you look much more refreshed," Wallis observed. "I have a couple of people I would like for you to meet. Gabriel Carasa, I would like for you to meet Kelby and Isadora Carasa. Kelby was your father's brother and Isadora is his wife. We would call them your Uncle and Aunt here in Xenon."

Gabriel stood up to greet these new acquaintances. Looking at them, he would place them in their early fifties. Kelby had some similar physical traits to himself including being about the same height. Isadora was shorter and had a reddish hair cut to a medium length. She also had a kind and welcoming expression on her face.

Gabriel reached out his hand and was surprised when Isadora enveloped him in an embrace. Gabriel awkwardly returned the hug and then turned to shake Kelby's hand.

"Very pleased to meet you," Gabriel replied.

"You can't know how happy we are to see you!" Isadora said. "I remember when you were a very small baby. I used to hold you in my arms and watched you when your parents needed a night out to themselves."

Isadora appeared to be holding back joyful tears. Gabriel tried to mimic her happy expression, but honestly didn't share it in return. He was feeling overall indifferent about it other than it helping him on his assignment.

"After so many years, it is so good to see you." Kelby shared with genuine warmth. "Gabriel, what brings you back to Deerbarrow?"

"Well, it is a long story, but the short of it is I no longer have a position in the ministry I worked at and need to find out if a can get a fresh start somewhere else," Gabriel explained. "Things didn't end on the best terms there and the more I thought about it, since I found out I was born in Xenon and therefore allowed to travel here, I thought I would try my luck here so to speak."

"I don't care what happened to get you here," Isadora stated, "I am just glad you made it!"

"That is a pretty big jump to just come up here," Kelby stated. "Last I checked, that is a lot of energy credits to take the shuttle that far."

"Yeah, I used most of what I had saved up," Gabriel answered. "I know it is a gamble, but I really needed a change in my life, and this seemed to be the best one available."

"Do you have any work prospects yet?" Isadora asked. "I assume if you are considering relocating here, that is part of your process? The general work assignments from the government do not provide many credits, and typically are not the best type of jobs."

"None yet, but I just arrived today. I have mostly had desk work as an analyst when I was with the ministry," Gabriel answered. "But I am a hard worker and would welcome a better option than a general laborer. They gave me thirty days to find new work before I need to report to the Ministry of Trade for an assignment. Job prospects are definitely something I am interested in."

"We have an agricultural farm we maintain not too far from town," Kelby replied. "If you wanted to stop by tomorrow morning, we could see what you are capable of, and see if you are interested in the work we have to offer. It probably isn't the same type of employment as you are used to, but it should be better than the general laborer positions. Wallis could give you directions tomorrow if you wanted to come by."

"That would be great!" Gabriel said excitedly. "Thank you so much for this opportunity."

"That is what family is for," Isadora replied warmly.

They talked some more with Gabriel and proceeded to introduce him as their nephew to many of the patrons in the common room. Everyone he was introduced to seemed friendly but had a cautious wall up when they learned he had recently come from the capital. As the night wound down and people began to disperse, Gabriel politely excused himself from the common room and went up to his room to get some sleep. He had a very promising day to look forward to.

CHAPTER 4

*A*nnabel Farwell stretched as she opened her eyes. After staring at the ceiling for a few moments, she stood up as she looked into the mirror to straighten her vibrant red hair. She possessed a slender appearance and a depth to her gaze that hinted at intelligence and great drive. At twenty-three years old, she was considered young for someone with her responsibilities in the Order.

Her sleep time had been productive as she recalled the prior night's experience. She identified two new people who showed some potential gifts in dreams. Both were from northern areas, one in Highgate, at the edge of the Kaybeen Mountains. The other seemed to be near Rockland, on the edge of the Brendag Desert. Annabel took a mental note to send notice to her contacts in these areas, so the people could be evaluated, and if safe to do so, have their talents nurtured.

Those who were identified in the northern areas had a successful rate of conversion, as the populations were still pretty receptive to the Way of the Lily. It was getting harder to convince those on the southern edge of these sectors, as the capital influence continued to push northward. And it was extremely difficult to recruit someone in any of the sectors near the capital due to skepticism and fear of government persecution. The Way of the Lily was relegated as a myth of old when it was even discussed. In sectors where some belief of it was present, the government curriculum belittled it, and made it seem like only those who were not enlightened to the ways of science could follow it. It was against the law to discuss any of the myths with purpose of proselytizing and was also unlawful to meet to study or practice them across all the sectors, unless of course, the study was government sponsored.

That didn't mean that religion was not taught, or that there were not assemblies of those who practiced these ways still. It just meant that a lot more caution was required relative to how these interactions would occur. Science meditation groups were often used as a cover for these assemblies. During the meditation times, dream state actions would be practiced, and the outside viewer would never be the wiser, provided the science text forms were followed. The challenge became how to teach those who were children, or those who were recruited into the Order. With so much surveillance, it was difficult to do this in groups, so creativity was utilized to teach basic precepts in non-surveilled areas, of which there were very few options available. And this continued to increase in risk, especially as the state required education continued to advocate precepts that undermined the teachings of the Order. Those who were stronger in specific aspects of the dream gifts could do some correspondence in the dream state, but not everyone was able to interact effectively with this method, so it was limited in application.

Annabel decided to get ready to journey to Deerbarrow. It had been a couple of months since she had visited her Aunt Isadora and had some items that her Mom asked her to deliver. Isadora was her mom's sister and that close relationship continued with Annabel. It would be so much quicker to use the underground tunnel system, but that would set off Oversite flags questioning how she got from one place to another without being logged in any watch systems. Fortunately, the walk could be done in less than a day, so she could avoid any of those horrid overnight stations that the government had placed along the traveling roads. There was a shuttle service that came through periodically, but the cost was so high, almost no one used it. Mainly it shuttled government ministry inspectors doing their rounds in the outlying areas. And who wanted to be stuck on a shuttle with a government inspector? She sure didn't!

Annabel was looking forward to meeting Gabriel. She was pretty sure he had already arrived in Deerbarrow, and if things had gone right, would have made some sort of connection with her Aunt and Uncle. She didn't usually make first contact after meeting someone in the dream state, but the plan that had been developed deviated in several ways from normal methods. There had to be so many more safeguards than were typically encountered with this contact. It was thought best to let Gabriel make the connection that she was the one from the dream in real life. If he could suspend his preconceptions to do that, he may be more receptive to take more steps without exposing the Order to risk from one of the ministries. This could take a lot longer to play out but was a much safer approach to protect Kayden and all it stood for.

Annabel would have to be very careful to not have any slip-ups in her interactions with him. Others in the Order were given some general instructions regarding interactions. He was not to be treated fully like a visitor from the capital, but they also wanted to limit their exposure to what he was to see. That way, punishments and risk to the Order could be minimized.

She hadn't visited his dreams since the water in the desert interaction a few days back. This had been a very big step for him to make. It normally took someone a lot of training to be able to create in the dream state, and the fact that he was able to do it with some minimal prompting spoke very highly of his potential. This was dangerous what she had initiated. If he continued to push on his own without proper training, he could create some situations that could harm both himself and those around him. This had been observed during the now-called Scientific Reformation.

Prior to the Scientific Reformation, now fifty-three years ago, you could openly practice religions and beliefs. While it wasn't a huge portion of the population, there were many who did so. When the now called Founding Scientists gained full power, they mandated an eradication of these beliefs. They said they were harmful to societies' scientific progress and rallied the population to purge this thinking and practices from their communities. Open adherents were demonized, attributed to deplorable practices they didn't do, and mocked for the ignorance of their ways. Known leaders were taken into confinement of which most were executed, and those who were lower level adherents were given the opportunity to take some reeducation classes and cease all practice of their prior ways.

The intensity of the Scientific Reformation movement was strongest near the capital regions, but the outlying regions still felt the reach of this. Rather than fight a riled-up mob, practices went underground, and most of those who were not arrested went through the motions of complying with the new edicts relative to religious practices, while looking for ways to continue practicing their ways in secret. Those who continued to openly practice their beliefs were quickly arrested and dealt with harshly.

Some tried to initiate an armed insurrection, but that was quickly put down and resulted in the seizure of all projectile weapons. Those within the Order did not recognize any of the people who mounted this insurrection, but the outcome was the same. The prevailing religious practices were largely non-violent, so they were never a large threat to challenge a central government. But there was a large fear that belief sets that went contrary to the central government's scientific program would undermine the compliance of the population. The newly formed Great Scientist Council knew where they wanted to take the population, and anything that was in the way of that was clearly a threat.

During this period of change, there were those living near the capital whose gift had been awakened. The purge of so-called myths, coupled with the strong public sentiment against non-science-based practices, had completely isolated some of those who had been identified to have dream gifts. They hadn't all been publicly connected with the Order, so some had escaped. Having experienced some level of dream gifts, their curiosity and interest was kindled. When it became practically impossible to continue their training, some still tried to advance on their own without a qualified teacher. One caused an earthquake trying to visualize some ground formation changes, which ended up causing his own death as a building collapsed on him. A few others in the area were killed and many more injured. Another dreamer who had some gifts in translocation, redirected himself into a solid rock facing which ended up being fatal. The government thought he had just gone missing, but a dreamer knew otherwise by observing this action and hadn't been able to save him.

It was critical that Gabriel be handled carefully. He needed to have an appreciation that his gifts were real if he was going to be convinced to change his loyalty. However, if she let him get too far along in this process, he could do great harm to himself and those around him.

Annabel gathered her items for her journey and walked on the path toward Deerbarrow.

∞ ∞ ∞

Quintin Conlon briefly looked out the window of his office after logging into Oversite. He had arrived early in the morning to work, wanting to get a jump start on his work queue. Quinton was one of the rising stars in the Ministry of Scientific Compliance and had been assigned by Xavier to be Gabriel Carasa's case officer. This matched well with his assignments overseeing activities in Xenon sector. Quintin had previously been stationed in Xenon early in his career. He knew the geography well and was familiar with many of the people that Gabriel was likely to meet.

While in Xenon, Quintin had uncovered some educational malfeasance where schools were not fully teaching to the capital mandated curriculum. It had been difficult to come by this information, but with a careful investigation he had assembled the needed evidence which had resulted in big changes in how education was managed. Many from outside Xenon were now sent into the area to be teachers and school administrators. Also, increased surveillance was implemented to ensure ongoing compliance with the required teaching content. He also uncovered discrepancies in attendance records where more students were being reported present than were actually in school. It wasn't the same students each time and he couldn't prove what the purpose of the discrepancy was, but after escalating it, attendance practices improved and the record keeping was corrected. The Ministry of Education had been very grateful for his work.

Based on his exposure in Xenon, he could never be an undercover agent like Gabriel was assigned to be. He would have relished this opportunity if it were available to him, but he already had high notoriety in Xenon, having left at the end fearing somewhat for his safety. He was never outright threatened, but other ministry officials who were zealous in the enforcement of their duties had been known to disappear. He had started to see expressions migrate from reluctant tolerance of his presence to masked hostility toward the end. When he had been given the opportunity to transfer back to the capital, he didn't hesitate in accepting it. Moving was the logical next step in his career, and he was more likely to advance quickly in the capital versus being in a remote assignment without a lot of visibility. Now he was still working in the same region but was doing it from a distance.

Gabriel was not the first operative Quintin had managed in Xenon. He managed several agents before and had also planted a few sleeper agents whose initial job was to try to establish themselves in the community. They would likely have a cloud of suspicion over them for a long time, but hopefully the inhabitants of the sector would grow complacent and slowly let them into their confidence.

Once his Oversite portal had loaded up, Quintin checked his message queue and saw the first update from Gabriel. It didn't say much other than he had arrived and made some initial contacts he was hopeful about. Quintin didn't like how brief the update was. He would much rather have it detail out who he met and any relevant details of his contacts. It was possible Gabriel didn't have much opportunity to provide that detail, but Quintin thought it was just a mistake common to being new to this type of role. Often the smallest details were the most important, and he was worried that Gabriel trusted himself too much to decide what was and was not relevant.

Gabriel's handheld had enhanced audio capabilities, so Quintin did have the ability to go back and replay his conversations, but that was very time consuming. Before committing his time to doing that, he would see if he could get Gabriel to improve his report summaries and provide approximate time stamps of relevant interactions. Xavier seemed to care about this agent more than most, and some help by Gabriel would aid at keeping Xavier happy.

After composing a message asking for more detail, Quintin reviewed other activity in his area of control. His contacts were hearing more incidental chatter about this Kayden. He had garnered approval for surveillance drones to be deployed to follow persons of interest should he amass any of note. These drones were a relatively new technology that the ministry had a very limited supply of. They were about the size of a small insect, and they could be programmed to track specific personnel, or move to areas for general intelligence gathering. He was really hoping that Gabriel would be able to recommend some targets to maximize the drone's effectiveness. So far, he didn't risk putting one on Gabriel in case a means for detecting these was known. That would be a good way to shine a spotlight on his agent, and say he wasn't all he was representing himself to be. That may need to change later but was the current approach being used.

Looking at the rest of the new intelligence, Quintin reviewed some footage of a Northfalcon resident in the act of invoking a mythical deity's name during meditation time. He suspected this was more wide-spread than was commonly known. This person had been to re-education once before so the second offense would require more stringent measures. Quintin filled out orders for confinement and had them issued to the local Ministry of Scientific Compliance official in Northfalcon. If the confinement did not correct this behavior, the person clearly was a detriment to society, and no longer had standing to justify their existence. Crimes of thought and speech could be just as harmful as crimes of action.

Quintin looked up as he heard a light knocking on his office door and saw Xavier standing outside. Quintin thought he detected a slight bit of anxiety showing in Xavier's demeanor, but otherwise was projecting his authority and confidence he usually displayed.

"Good morning, sir," Quintin offered.

"Thought I would drop in on you," Xavier stated. "I was wondering how far Gabriel has gotten."

"I was just catching up on that, Mr. Alexandar," Quintin replied. "It appears that he is now officially in Deerbarrow and has contacted some of his relatives. He seems very positive about his prospects but didn't offer much more information than that in his most recent report. I haven't had time to review the audio feed from his handheld yet but can prioritize that if you need more detailed information developed."

"No, that is fine for now." Xavier replied. "I need to give an update on this operation to the head of the ministry this morning and wanted to make sure I had the most recent information. I can't emphasize enough how important this operation is. Please continue to give it your full attention. May science and reason guide your day, Quintin."

"Without science and reason, all is lost," Quintin answered dutifully back.

If Xavier was having to give updates this soon to the Minister, it must be way more important than he understood it to be. Quintin sighed as he decided he would immediately review the handheld audio log after all.

∞ ∞ ∞

Gabriel was glad he allowed plenty of time to walk to Kelby's farm. If he ended up working here, the commute was going to get old very fast. The route to get here had been very straight-forward, it just took a lot of time. There were many fields spread out and there appeared to be a cluster of buildings where some people were gathering around. Gabriel walked up to join them.

"Good morning!" a tall man called out. He was dressed in clothes meant for working hard in and had a slightly mischievous smile on his face. "You must be Gabriel?"

"Hello," Gabriel answered. "Yes, I am Gabriel. Kelby said that I could come by this morning and you may have some work you can consider me for?"

"Yeah, my Dad is out doing something this morning in the fields but asked me to get you started when you got here," the person stated. "You ever worked on a farm before?"

"Not once," Gabriel answered truthfully. "But I am a quick learner and am not afraid of work."

Gabriel looked around and noticed that the several other workers were listening to the conversation with curiosity. He wasn't sure what type of attitude he was reading, but overall everyone seemed mostly friendly in their countenances.

"Famous last words!" he replied with a small laugh. "Farming isn't for everyone, but we'll give you a try. Come with me and I'll get you started."

∞ ∞ ∞

Gabriel looked across the large expanse of farmland. His body hurt all over in ways he had never experienced before. He had always thought himself to be athletically fit until he began this assignment. Any remnant of that belief had evaporated today. The multiday journey of walking from Northfalcon was bad enough, but this completely put that prior complaint in a brand-new perspective. His new-found family had put him to work removing weeds from amongst the crops.

They had technology that would provide a virtual barrier from pests that could damage the crops, but they did not have an available non-toxic method that was effective for keeping weeds out of the fields. There were chemical methods that could effectively remove the weeds, but those had been banned many years before. That left workers to complete the weed removal by hand or greatly jeopardize the yield of the crops. Looking at the task involved, Gabriel was pretty sure that engineers could devise a way to automate the weed removal with a machine-based solution. However, that would require additional energy consumption, not to mention create a lot of idle people in an otherwise rebellious sector.

Gabriel was dying to know the time of day so he could pace himself to his next break. He left his handheld device in his equipment locker, which made looking for the time difficult. They had rules here that required full attention on the work, and they didn't want anything to be a distraction in the fields. But asking about breaks would not make a good impression with those he was working with. He wanted to show he could keep up with his co-workers and that meant no matter how much his body was aching, he was going to keep up his pace. Finally, Gabriel heard the bell ringing indicating it was time for lunch.

That morning, Gabriel was given some training on what the crop that was supposed to be there looked like and was shown how to properly remove weeds by the roots that did not belong. After repeating this for several repetitions, the field was his to weed alone. Although he had been laboring extremely hard, he had hardly dented the quota he had been asked to complete.

Grateful for break time, Gabriel left his equipment where he had stopped working and walked to the edge of the field. Here he found a tree that would give him some shade to rest under. He had been told that lunch was an hour break, and you got twenty minutes mid-morning and mid-afternoon. The first half of the morning break was to complete your required meditation, but they did not require that to be in the presence of anyone else. He internally wondered how much people actually did it when nothing was officially monitoring it being done. Either way, he was grateful it was lunchtime and quickly mixed up a shake and consumed his meal. Feeling dead-tired, Gabriel decided to rest his body in the cool shade, hoping to rejuvenate himself for the afternoon's expected efforts. Gabriel's eyes slowly drifted closed as sleep captured him.

∞ ∞ ∞

Gabriel looked around. The field he had been working on all day appeared to be displayed before him but was dampened by a thick fog and the lack of color. He was already sick of the field. Sick of the weeds. How did people do this all day long? This could so easily be automated, and yet it wasn't.

"I am surprised to see you here at this time of day," a voice behind him interrupted his thoughts.

Gabriel turned to see someone who he had come to know as Raelynn walking up beside him. He had been seeing her in his dreams lately. He wondered why he had envisioned this person.

"This is very tiring work. Figured I would take a quick rest with what is left of my lunch break," Gabriel answered. "I guess I nodded off," he finished sheepishly.

"You don't appear to have made very much progress," Raelynn answered. "Were you supposed to weed this entire field today?"

"I think so. I have been working as hard as I can, but it is a lot slower work than I would have ever expected it to be. I am not sure how people do this all the time," Gabriel answered.

"You are assuming they all do it the hard way you are doing it," Raelynn said. "Why don't you just remove the weeds here by visualizing the field already weeded?"

"What good will that do?" Gabriel asked with skepticism. "I am looking at the field enough as it is and am already sick of it. Why would I want to keep thinking of it when I am getting a much-needed break?"

"Try it," Raelynn challenged. "You might be surprised at your attitude improvement when you wake up, if you see what the hope of completion feels like. You may even dream of more happy things than removing weeds from a field."

Gabriel breathed out slowly. It would feel good to think about the task being completed. He doubted he would get rotated to more appealing tasks until he showed some level of proficiency and understanding of what it took to do this one. Maybe if he could renew his motivation and energy, it would help him when he woke up.

"Ok, I'll give it a try." Gabriel agreed reluctantly. "How should I do this?"

Raelynn smiled with an expression of subdued amusement at his acquiescence. "Take it a row at a time. See where the weeds are, and then visualize what that space looks like with the weeds removed. Consider where you want the weeds to be placed, and as you remove them, mentally add them to your weed pile."

Gabriel looked at the small area in front of him. It had a lot of weeds in it. He looked at each weed carefully and then visualized what the plant would look like if the weed was removed to a pile at the end of the field. This seemed to take a long time to clear it one weed at a time. Honestly, if didn't seem much faster than the work by hand he was already doing. But piece by piece, the small area was slowly completed.

"How is this better?" Gabriel asked. "This takes just as long as doing by hand, and it definitely isn't making me feel any better about it."

"You are not doing it the best way. Don't look at each weed individually," she answered. "Look at the row as a whole, notice the weeds then blur out your eyes and refocus with the weeds not there. Then imagine them added to the pile."

Gabriel was losing patience with this exercise but figured he would try one more time what this strange dream sequence was suggesting. He looked at the row carefully. He saw weeds scattered throughout the row. Blurring his vision, he visualized the weeds removed to the pile. Refocusing himself, they were gone.

"That was much better!" Raelynn encouraged. "Now do the same for the remaining rows. You will probably be able to go quicker now that you have learned how to properly do it."

Gabriel went ahead and repeated the exercise on each of the remaining rows and was quickly completed. He turned around to get Raelynn's approval, but she was nowhere to be seen. Gabriel's searching was interrupted with a faint ringing sound as his environment began to fade.

∞ ∞ ∞

Gabriel couldn't believe he had nodded off. He looked at the sky and saw that the sun had moved a lot further across the horizon than it should have for his lunch break. He groaned internally as he realized that he had lost valuable time, and he would look even worse for his lack of progress. This was not a good way to make a good first impression. Gabriel stood up and grabbed his equipment to see if he could get some additional progress completed before someone came by. He wasn't sure if the bell that woke him was for the afternoon break or for the end of the day. Either way, he wanted to be seen working when he got checked on. Hopefully no one had come by while he was sleeping.

Just as he had got to the section of the field he had stopped at, Kelby called out to him in greeting.

"There you are. How was your first day of work in the fields?" Kelby asked.

"I am sort of embarrassed," Gabriel answered. "I didn't make near as much progress as I wanted to."

"Well, let's take a look to see how you did," Kelby stated as he surveyed the field. "It looks like you did really good to me. Normally someone new at this task doesn't complete a full field on their first day. Not only did you weed it all, you also piled it at the end of the field, so it doesn't again have a chance to take root. Excellent work!" Kelby said enthusiastically as he firmly patted Gabriel on the back.

Gabriel had a look of confusion on this face. He walked a few rows beyond where he had worked, and sure enough, it was clear of weeds. Somehow the work had gotten done while he had been napping. He found the mound of weeds, and it was a very large pile. Had someone completed the work for him while he had been sleeping? Gabriel reflected on his dream and tried to dismiss the connection to the outcome in the field to his dream. No, there had to be a logical explanation. Maybe they were using some technology to clear the field and were playing tricks on him as a way to initiate him. Sometimes a new person would get some jokes played on them. That could be it. But how could he explain the dream, and how were the weeds placed in the exact place he had envisioned them? That couldn't have been predicted if someone was having some fun at his expense, could it?

Gabriel looked up, realizing he needed to respond to his uncle. "Thank you, I think. I hadn't realized I had made that much progress. For some reason it seemed like a lot less. I am glad that you are pleased with what was completed."

"Well, you have worked hard enough for today," Kelby said. "Come on back to the house. You can get cleaned up and spend some time with people we would love for you to meet."

CHAPTER 5

"*I* still can't get over how much of the field you got done today," Kelby said excitedly. "You must really have a knack for this! I'll be honest with you, there are a lot of hands here on the farm that didn't give you a lot of hope of being able to cut it here. There is a big difference from a big-city job, and one out here on the farm. I can't wait to tell everyone what a natural you are at this."

"I really don't understand it either," Gabriel said with a slight embarrassment. "I could have sworn I got a lot less done today."

"Most of my experienced hands couldn't get a field close to that big done in one day, even if they wanted to," Kelby went on. "Between you and me, I think they were playing a joke on you when they told you that you needed to get the whole thing done. They like to mess with a new person sometimes as a way of saying hello if you know what I mean."

"I saw that when I was in school growing up," Gabriel replied. "A new student would often get challenged to see how they would fit in, so I think I know what you mean."

"Yeah, I reckon you saw some of that," Kelby answered. "We really tried hard to get you allowed to come back here to grow up when your parents died, but we didn't get any support at all from the capital. It got to the point where it didn't feel safe to keep asking about it anymore."

"Well, I am glad you are happy with my progress today," Gabriel said with relief. "I know this type of work isn't something I have a lot of experience with. I know I used muscles I didn't even know I had! This can be some really taxing work out here. I am not sure how you manage it. I am most surprised that more technology isn't available to help complete these tasks."

"Yeah, that has been a bit of a sore spot out here, but we have adapted the best we can," Kelby explained. "We are permitted to use more automated equipment for plowing and harvesting the fields. All the work to maintain them has to be done by hand though."

"Seems like a lot of extra work," Gabriel stated.

"Yes, it is," Kelby explained. "It took quite a bit of time to adjust to the chemical ban, but we have learned how to manage. The most difficult area is working around water induced diseases. If we get too much rainfall, it really hurts our crop health and yield, and there isn't much we can do about it since sprays to fight the diseases are no longer allowed. We have improved drainage setups, which helps, but we sometimes still lose a lot of our crops to spoilage."

"What if you don't get enough rainfall?" Gabriel asked.

"We have irrigation available for when it is too dry," Kelby answered, "but it takes about ten different ministry people to sign off on using it, with water being such a controlled resource. Fortunately, we live in a stable area for rainfall, so we don't have to deal with that very often."

"Wow!" Gabriel replied. "I never realized all that went into providing food for the population. And I know I have only seen a small part of what is involved."

"We each have our own part to play," Kelby replied. "We just need to do the best we can with what we have. Give me a few minutes to make sure there is nothing I have to deal with, and then we can go to the house, let you clean-up, and then can introduce you to some people."

Gabriel looked ahead of where they were walking. It appeared there were several people congregating around the main house. He watched as Kelby chatted with each of them, getting a status update on what they had completed and what potential problems they had run into. Kelby impressed him with the rapport with his workers, and how he treated them all with respect and friendliness. The capital was always so serious all the time, but here on his uncle's farm, there seemed to be a lighthearted friendliness that he was not accustomed to experiencing. It was refreshing, genuine, and made him feel welcome.

"Well, I think I got everything squared away," Kelby offered as he rejoined Gabriel. "Come this way and we'll get you a place to clean-up before you come into the house. We wouldn't want Isadora to be cross with you for tracking dirt though the house. I forgot to tell you to bring a change of clothes, so I had Isadora pull an outfit for you that I think will fit ok. I hope you don't mind."

"That is very kind of you," Gabriel answered. "I was wondering how I was going to avoid messing up your house."

Gabriel followed Kelby to a building situated off the main house. It was an older looking building and had some traces of wood in its construction. It looked like it had been repaired a few times. Looking inside, Gabriel saw there were several shower stalls and what appeared to be a changing area.

"There is a shower off that way. If you want to grab these clothes and go clean up and get changed, it would be a good thing," Kelby suggested.

"Sure thing. Just come inside when I am ready?" Gabriel asked.

"Yeah, that would be great," Kelby replied. "Take all the time you need. I think it will be a bit until everyone arrives anyway."

Gabriel quickly got undressed and stepped into the shower. He didn't see a mist setting but tried to hurry in case he took away from someone's water allotment. Once he had scrubbed off the dirt of working in the fields, Gabriel quickly dried off and got dressed in the clothing that was provided. It didn't look like any of the styles he had seen in the capital, but it was comfortable enough and was a similar style that matched what others were wearing around him. Looking and feeling much refreshed, Gabriel carefully placed his dirty clothing in a pile to get when he left, then headed for the main house.

Isadora saw him before he could even get his hand to the door to knock. "Come on in!" she said in an excited and welcoming tone. "Kelby told me you did a great job in the fields today."

"Thank you," Gabriel answered. "It is really hard work out there. Really makes me appreciate my food shakes way more than I ever have before!"

"Come on inside and be welcome," Isadora repeated her offer. "There are a lot of people who are interested in meeting you."

Gabriel followed her inside the house. It had a warm homey feel to it. It was hard to explain what made it feel this way. He was not used to a living space causing that kind of emotion in him. There were pictures on the wall as well as other crafty looking items decorating the living space.

"Yeah, I really like photos," Isadora offered, noticing Gabriel's gaze. "Here come look at this one. You are in it."

Gabriel followed her. The photo showed a very small boy, surrounded by a man and a woman. They had happy smiles on their faces. Looking closer, he realized there was resemblance to some of his features.

Isadora replied, answering his unspoken question, "these were your parents, Gabriel. This photo was taken shortly before you all took the tragic trip to the capital."

Gabriel wasn't sure what he felt about it. He was pretty sure Isadora expected some type of response from him. "Wow, I can see some resemblance to my features," Gabriel said with some feigned enthusiasm.

"Yeah," she said, "you remind me a lot of your father, but I can see some of your mother in there also. Come on in to the main room. I think there are a few people we can introduce you to."

Gabriel walked into a large common room, and saw Kelby conversing with the person who had given him his initial instruction in field that morning.

"You should have seen it!" Kelby exclaimed. "He weeded that entire field, and not only did he weed it, he piled the weeds all at the end of the field so none would have a chance to regrow. And he didn't just do a partial job of it. I walked though that field, and I couldn't find one weed present!"

Kelby saw Gabriel as he was walking in. "There you are, I was just telling my son what a good job you did today. I think you have met?"

"Briefly," Gabriel answered. "Tom gave me my training and assignment this morning."

Tom smiled sheepishly, "I wasn't actually expecting you to get it all done, cousin. I was just trying to have a bit of fun at your expense. But I guess the joke is on me. No hard feelings?"

"I am glad I could get something useful done. But I sure do hurt all over!" Gabriel answered as he shook the proffered hand to signal that all was ok between them.

"Tom, why don't you circulate with Gabriel and introduce him to some others while I make sure your mother has all the help she needs," Kelby asked.

Tom signaled for Gabriel to follow. There were not a lot of people present, but Gabriel's eyes were immediately drawn to a familiar looking person on the other side of the room. Tom, seeing his look decided to lead him in that direction.

"Gabriel, this is my cousin Annabel Farwell," Tom said. "My cousin, not yours. She is related to me through my mom's side of the family. She is staying here for a few days, visiting from about a day's journey away."

Gabriel was momentarily paralyzed with confusion. This person was a spitting image of the Raelynn from his dreams. The hair was the same, the bemused expression was the same, the pronounced sense of style was the same. It seemed the only thing that wasn't the same was her name.

"Nice to meet you, Gabriel. There is a lot of excitement in the house that you have returned. Uncle Kelby hasn't been able to stop talking about what a great job you did today in the fields," Annabel answered with a hint of knowing mirth in her expression.

There had to be a logical reason that a person with her description was in his dreams. He had no knowledge of meeting her in real life before. He didn't recall her on any ministry report. There had to be a reason, other than her reaching out to him in a dream.

"Nice to meet you as well," Gabriel finally got the words together to answer after an unnatural pause. "I am sorry for asking this, but have we met before? You have so much familiarity to me, and for the life of me I can't shake the fact that we have met before?"

Annabel smiled, "Well, I have lived in the Xenon sector my whole life and have never done more than dream of the capital, which is where everyone says you have been living. Maybe I remind you of someone?"

Gabriel was stuck. He didn't really want to explain that she reminded him of someone in his dreams, not to mention the strange deal with the weeds in the field today. Things were quickly becoming confusing. Who could he even discuss this with? Certainly not his ministry case officer. They would worry he had already had a psychotic breakdown and may want to pull him from this assignment before he even had a chance to get started. There had to be a logical explanation for all this somewhere. Maybe he had seen a file on this person somewhere before. Then it came to him, he should pull up her file in Oversite. Maybe that would answer the question and give him a logical basis for this. He quickly committed her name to his memory so he could do this later tonight.

After greeting the remainder of the guests, Gabriel checked the time. It was getting late and would be dark before he knew it. Gabriel looked for Kelby to make excuses to head out.

"It will be dark soon," Gabriel stated. "I figure I should be headed back. It is a long walk to the Deerbarrow Inn. Thank you so much for inviting me here and giving me a chance on the farm work today."

"It was a real pleasure to have you here," Kelby replied. "I think you worked out really well today and would welcome you back for work at the start of next week if you were interested. I think we can definitely make a place for you here if you are willing."

"That is more than I could hope for," Gabriel said gratefully. "I will definitely be here."

"And I really would enjoy it if you stopped by for the weekly meditation session tomorrow," Kelby continued. "If you want, you can return the clothes you are wearing then instead of changing back for the walk home."

"I will plan on coming," Gabriel confirmed before he exited the door. The walk back was lengthy and after laboring in the field all day, it was all he could do to make it back, longing to collapse on his bed when he arrived.

Gabriel arrived at the hotel with just enough light to see. Gabriel made himself up a meal shake and logged into Oversite on his handheld while he was drinking it. He had not been able to check his handheld all day and found some messages waiting for him from Quintin, his case officer. It looked like Quintin had replayed his day from his handheld recording and had several questions about who he had met in the common room the night before. Then there was a message asking why there was no audio for most of the day. Gabriel sighed. He was already exhausted, and they expected him to spend hours on reports? Such was the nature of this assignment.

About three hours later, he finished answering Quintin's questions. Once he finally got this caught up, he realized he hadn't looked up Annabel up in Oversite yet. Ministry guidelines on sleep came to mind and wanting to not miss the opportunity to participate in the meditation group, he realized he would need to get some rest now while he could. Hopefully, there would be time to check her file in the morning.

∞ ∞ ∞

Gabriel looked around to discover a hazy and fog filled area. It looked like a meeting room of some sort, or maybe the room of a house. Silhouettes of two adults were sitting at a table with a small child playing quietly in the corner of the room. Gabriel could only hear voices, unable to clearly make out any of the features of the people present.

"The Way of the Lily is clear. We must journey to the capital, otherwise our Order, if not the world will perish." A man implored with resignation.

"But what of our son? Can't we leave him here?" a woman asked. "Isn't it enough that we risk ourselves, why do we also have to risk him? You know if something happens to us while there, he probably won't be allowed to be returned to our family to be raised in the Way of the Lily?"

"So far, the government hasn't taken children from visiting sectors," the man said. "We can hope that will be a small reassurance. But the seer who dreamed the vision was clear. She saw that if we leave him here, then the prophesy fails, and all is lost. For some reason, he is the key, and all will be for nothing if he does not come with us. There is some part his presence brings. There is no other way. We stay here, it fails. If we only go, it fails. We all must go, and even then, that only buys a hope, a small chance for the Order and the world."

Gabriel watched as the two people held each other in their arms in a period of quiet solace.

"Mommy," a small voice interrupted, "is something wrong?"

"No Gab," the woman answered. Mommy and Daddy were just talking about something important and wanted to say we love each other. Do you know that we love you too? No matter whatever happens, we will always love you sooooo much!"

"I love you too Mommy," the little boy answered and joined the hug.

Gabriel watched this scene with a growing sense of familiarity. It created a sensation of déjà vu, like he had seen it once before. Gabriel decided to move closer to the people. He hoped he did not disturb them, but he had an unexplained urge to be near them, to ascertain their features. And he even had an unexplained urge to join the embrace. Gabriel moved through the fog and began to make out features of the people he was watching. He abruptly stopped, as he could make out the clarity of their features. He had seen them before. Their descriptions matched the picture he had been shown by Isadora. These were his parents and him as a boy. Gabriel abruptly turned and walked quickly back toward the fog.

"Why are you running away?" a familiar voice asked.

Gabriel stopped his accelerated exit to see Raelynn beside him. Gabriel was filled with confusion, looking to understand what he was seeing.

"Is your past so bad that you need to run from it?" she asked. "Do you so fear being who you were destined to be? Will you embrace your path and acknowledge the sacrifice others have made to bring you to this place?"

"What is happening to me?" Gabriel asked. "There is so much going on there that I cannot explain. So much that runs counter to the teaching of science. These dreams where you appear, things occur in them that I cannot explain. How is it that I can go back and see something from my early childhood? I do not remember it, but inside of me, I know it happened. How do I dream weeds out of a field, only to wake up, and the state of the field reflects what I dreamed? And somehow you are tied to this. None of this can be explained by what I know of science. I feel like I am losing my mind!"

"The logic of science is not equipped to explain faith." Raelynn answered. "Faith is hope personified into reality. You cannot explain it with logic, yet it exists. It manifests itself in those who reach for it. And yet, it also offers itself to those who are chosen and respond to its call. Gabriel, you were chosen in the cosmos of the universe, yet you are uncertain of your loyalties, your past, your future, and the path you need take in your life. The path to faith requires you but to take one step. Step toward the path that does not seem to be there, but still trust that it will accept your weight and lead you to where you need to go."

"How do I make this step?" Gabriel implored. "I don't see any paths before me. I only see fog and blurry images. I need a guide to direct me."

Raelynn smiled, "You know how to find a guide. You have seen her, but you refused to acknowledge her for who and what she is. Will you show enough faith to step out on the path toward her and risk the judgement of others?"

"You mean Annabel?" Gabriel answered. "Are you the same? One in my dreams and one in the world?"

Raelynn smiled as she faded away as Gabriel awoke with a start.

∞ ∞ ∞

Gabriel woke up with his mind racing. In most dreams, the detail would fade the more awake you became. But these dreams where the Raelynn person was present, were just as vivid now as when he was having them.

Gabriel decided to get up and grabbed his handheld and logged into to the restricted research portion of the Oversite system. He had a high access level in this system, so he hoped anything that was there he would be allowed to see. After authenticating himself properly, he typed in his search query. After paging through many results discussing the aspects of the lily flower, he found an article detailing a mythical religion. Apparently, adherents believed they could impact the course of the world through some sort of mysticism. The author was very dismissive of this belief set, explaining the likelihood that some of the so-called miracles attested in the stories were explainable with technology application, practiced ahead of its widespread use. There was some belief that it had influenced some of the more recently outlawed religions that the Scientific Reformation had aggressively opposed. Either way, the article presented it as a historical footnote on obscure beliefs but did not seem to have anything that indicated it was viewed as a current threat to the Ministry of Scientific Compliance.

While he was in Oversite, he decided to do some research on dreams. That was not nearly as enlightening. He read several articles by prominent psychologists discussing how dreams were a manifestation of your hopes and fears and provided a platform to live out your fantasies, devoid of reality. After much reading and searching, he did not find anything that explained how he had met someone he had never met. He also didn't find anything to suggest any correlation between a dream state and awake state impacting physical things in real life.

Gabriel logged out of the restricted portion of Oversite and then decided to do some research from the public portion. His training in Morfort advised him not to gain knowledge of people through non-public means. Gabriel started putting in names of people he had met, including Annabel, into the public search tool and found a few articles about the farm he had worked on and some community events they had been involved with. There really wasn't anything of value in the public area. He was curious to pull the non-public records but did not feel like that was a safe thing to do at this point.

Gabriel's mind kept coming back to his dream he just woke up from. There didn't appear to be a good explanation for what had happened. What if his current path was wrong? What if he was somehow being enticed using a technology he didn't understand yet? There were so many questions, and he did not feel like it would be a safe thing to ask advice from his case officer. He needed a way to explore this phenomenon without the ministry misunderstanding. He needed time where he wasn't closely watched, where he could have some freedom to explore this dream oddity. But there was surveillance everywhere. The only place that was truly safe was his thoughts and dreams. He didn't think technology existed to penetrate that, yet.

The ministry would not expect a huge breakthrough immediately. If he continued to work on the farm and cultivate relationships, that would be a good start to keep them happy. The ministry would likely get impatient for results at some point, but Gabriel figured he had a few weeks before that pressure would begin to be applied. In the meantime, he could see what he could learn on this whole dream thing by starting with Annabel.

CHAPTER 6

*X*avier grew increasingly upset while looking at the latest report from the Xenon sector. Another prisoner had disappeared while in transit to a confinement facility. Prisoners who were arrested for crimes of violence or other actions against society had never escaped. But in the last two months, the Ministry of Scientific Compliance had lost many detainees who were apprehended for violating the *Adherence to Myths Act*. This law's purpose was to prevent the propagation of fallacies such as religion from corrupting the minds of the people.

The re-education process was simple. Ministry officials would load prisoners to take them to be confined and re-educated. Those who showed proper reeducation progress were given a final chance to interact with society. Those who didn't, wouldn't keep the privilege of their existence. Typically, over half of those sent to confinement would get one final chance to change their ways. But the escapes were a problem and needed stopped. Hopefully his next meeting would shed light on correcting this.

"A Commander Wilcox is here," Xavier's assistant announced.

"Send him in," Xavier replied.

Xavier watched as a short man of middle age walked into his office offering him the courtesy of a salute. There was an intensity in his eyes that was hard to define. He exuded confidence but did not have the look of being cocky.

"Thank you for coming Commander," Xavier offered while acknowledging the salute. "You are welcome to take a seat."

"If it is all the same to you, sir, I would prefer to stand," the Commander replied formally.

"Suit yourself," Xavier answered. Field agents typically had a higher degree of formality than regular officials in the ministry did. "I asked you here to provide me an update on the recent increase in escapes in Xenon. I believe this falls under your authority currently?"

"Yes, it does, and it is completely unacceptable what is currently happening," Commander Wilcox answered.

"The report I saw is showing an increase in escapes," Xavier stated. "How are they getting away?"

"I wish I knew, sir," Wilcox replied. "They just keep disappearing when in transit to the containment site."

"I saw that mentioned in the report I read," Xavier challenged. "People don't just disappear. They obviously go somewhere! Are your people transporting them reliable?"

"Normally that question would give me offense," Wilcox answered. "We have very dedicated people who serve the Ministry. But honestly, I had to ask the same questions after repeated escapes. I rotated the guard duty teams, I have kept guards in with the prisoners to watch and it hasn't made a difference, they keep escaping."

"Have you been able to gain any clues on how they are escaping? And have you recovered any prisoners?" Xavier asked with a perplexed expression on his face.

"We have recovered no one," Wilcox answered. "Video footage shows them there one frame and gone the next. All we have as a clue is one guard claimed he heard one prisoner saying the word Kayden over and over before they disappeared."

"This is classified for your ears only, but we have been hearing a lot more chatter across Xenon on this Kayden word recently," Xavier replied carefully. "We suspect it is a leader of an anti-government faction but have next to no information that is actionable yet. We are working to change that, but that is a hard sector to get informants in."

"I understand sir, I won't repeat anything you tell me on this," Wilcox answered. "Forgive me if I am out of line, but the number of arrests for the *Adherence to Myths Act* seems to have gone up significantly recently, and they seem to be less severe infractions, even a stray word. In the past we have only arrested for actively trying to convince others to follow a religion or practicing it openly."

"Yes," Xavier replied. "We recently adjusted arrest criteria standards in an effort to make the progression to the way of science move faster. There is still too much superstition imbedded into the culture in Xenon and surrounding areas."

"I understand," Wilcox answered. "We will continue to do our jobs but if you want the escapes to stop, we need much more significant tools made available during transport."

"What do you have in mind?" Xavier asked resignedly.

"I would like to alter the mode of transport," Wilcox added. "Most escapes have occurred in the same general ten-kilometer area of transport. Granted we have searched these areas thoroughly to no avail, but I need a way to mix up the route to be less predictable."

"It will cause some controversy, but would air-transport being made available address that need?" Xavier asked.

"Yes, it would work nicely," Wilcox replied. "but I don't have enough authority to get approval for that."

"I will authorize it out of my energy budget," Xavier answered. "I don't want to use this method forever, but we are losing a huge amount of credibility by not being able to follow-through on the arrests. I can justify it. I will issue the orders to you this afternoon."

"Thank you, sir," Wilcox answered. "I think that will help. I also want to add tracking devices to prisoners going forward. I know we don't typically implant until conviction, but I think we need to do it."

"I will authorize this as well," Xavier replied. "I'll send you approval in Oversite before the day is done."

Commander Wilcox saluted and formally turned around as he exited his office. Xavier watched him exit and contemplated his next steps. Xavier really needed Gabriel to quickly get some actionable information on this Kayden. Gabriel had been instructed right before he left to report all instances of this word being used but each report had indicated nothing had been discovered.

Xavier was needing a soft suppression of Xenon, not one that had to be put down with force. Xavier had worked enough in the field to know that this type of information did not manifest itself quickly, and if you rushed it, you could burn your whole operation. Slowly, he talked himself down from issuing instructions to Gabriel to be more aggressive in asking about Kayden. He would need to let Gabriel build some trust, which he appeared to be on track to do. Once he did though, Xavier couldn't wait to get his payback on those who were thwarting the ministry's efforts to win the minds and overall compliance of Xenon and the surrounding sectors.

∞ ∞ ∞

The High Seat reviewed handwritten reports at her secure reading location. She was pleased with the success Kayden had so far in freeing those who were arrested against this tyrannical *Adherence to Myths Act*. It was one thing to have the government go after those who were actively and publicly stirring up dissent. Those who were willing to do this, knew what they were risking and were willing to be martyrs for their beliefs. Those who were largely quiet and reserved who made an accidental slip up that revealed their inner beliefs were no threat to society. They were compliant and didn't cause active trouble. Why arrest them, and on top of that, execute many of them? Did the human condition only have value if it espoused acceptable traits and beliefs?

Was the practice of science so narrow minded that it prosecuted all ideas that ran contrary to the prevailing belief set? It was no wonder that the pace of innovation and discovery had slowed so much in the past fifty years. Sure, there was advancement in some areas, mainly in the areas that the government had shown clear support of. But anything that may need more energy expended, more natural resources, or risk negative ecological impacts, those things were highly discouraged. If you were not careful, one could meet the same outcome as those who had been arrested for this *Adherence to Myths Act*. So here society was in an age of high technological capability largely living like a pre-industrial culture. Well, at least most of the population was who didn't work in government. It made no sense, yet that was the reality.

The High Seat had initially resisted the factions within Kayden who had called for a more open response to the escalating crackdown that was tied to the *Adherence to Myths Act*. But the arrest pattern proved to be enough of an overstep that she approved working to free those who were unjustly arrested. She let it be quietly circulated that those who faced illegitimate arrest just needed to call out to Kayden and an attempt would be made to free them. Escaping confinement was forfeiting your life if you were caught, so not everyone was willing to make that choice. Some chose to take their chances to make it through confinement and be able to rejoin their families. Others didn't like their chances, and figured that escaping was a better option than a high likelihood of losing their life.

Kayden had those at its disposal with the dream ability of translocation. This allowed them to physically move an object, including a person from one location to another. This could be challenging on a moving transport, but a method had been developed that had shown good success. This was not something easily done over long distances, so by waiting for the shuttle to come near to where those with this gift were stationed, this allowed a way to rescue prisoners.

The escaped prisoners would be translocated to an interim location nearby that had a wire mesh cage, which provided a temporary means to block wireless communication of any tracking beacons. Once the prisoner was cleared of all surveillance mechanisms, they would then be moved to an underground cavern and transported to a safe location that was fully off the grid.

Kayden was building up quite a sizable society this way in the past several months. Once you were rescued, you couldn't leave, but you could do work beneficial to the resistance. When several months elapsed after a prisoner escaped, family members were typically carefully approached to ascertain interest in rejoining with their family member who was in hiding.

At some point, the High Seat knew she would have to do something more meaningful with this growing group of escaped prisoners. But being alive was a good first step for them. At least this way, they could practice any beliefs they may want to follow without fear of persecution.

And they could do it without the pretense of following something else they had been failing at maintaining when they got arrested in the first place.

The High Seat moved through her stack of reports and found one giving an update on Gabriel. There was still debate if Gabriel was a spy or a true returning son. The High Seat had her own opinions on this after doing some personal investigating. Either way, a lot depended on him for the future. At the same time, she still needed to protect her people in case Gabriel decided to betray those who opened up to him.

She wrote up a few instructions in a cypher based on a one-time pad process and put them in the submission tube for transport. With the state of electronic oversight, you just didn't put anything in an electronic form. There was no telling what system would gain access to it. The information she had just reviewed was burned in a filtered device to make sure sensors didn't pick up an unauthorized fire.

∞ ∞ ∞

After a restless night, Gabriel got up. He decided he needed to get around if he was going to get to Kelby's house in time for the Sunday meditation session. This was an exciting opportunity to meet with people in a less formal setting. Hopefully he could learn something useful plus he could maybe resolve some of his confusion with Annabel.

Gabriel was still conflicted about what action to take on the dreams he had been having. He was pretty sure he needed to ask Annabel in real life to provide help with this dream phenomenon. Whether he was prepared to act on this suggestion was something that he was avoiding thinking about. Annabel would likely return to her home in a few days, so if he was going to do something, it needed to be today.

Gabriel gathered his thoughts and made the walk over to his uncle's house. The walk took about an hour. It wasn't that far away, but not having automated transportation really made simple journeys take a lot longer. If he was going to keep working at the farm, it would be more convenient if he had a place to stay that was closer.

"I am very glad you made it," Isadora said, greeting him at the door before he could even knock. "We were worried you wouldn't come."

"Sorry that I didn't arrive a bit earlier," Gabriel answered. "I didn't sleep well last night which made it harder to get up. Plus, it took a while to walk over. Hopefully I didn't get here too late?"

"Oh, not at all," Isadora answered. "We don't usually start the formal meditation for at least another hour. Mostly we just relax and socialize during this time. I think now that you are here, everyone we are expecting has arrived. Here, let me take your handheld. Kelby has a rule of staying off those devices until our actual meditation time starts. If it wasn't for the logging requirement, I think he wouldn't even have one. He feels like if everyone spends all their time looking at their screens, then we won't build our family relationships. I hope you don't mind?"

"No, that is fine," Gabriel answered. "It is good advice to follow. When Emily was still with me, we would set apart time we stayed off our handhelds also."

Gabriel watched her leave his handheld in the entry room and then followed her into the large gathering room. As he started thinking about it, Kelby did a lot of work to keep people separated from their handhelds. Gabriel couldn't use his on the farm during work hours, and Kelby didn't want them in the house. He wondered how much of this was due to suspicions of being monitored and risking any stray comments that an algorithm would flag. The best way to avoid being arrested for what you say, is to keep tracking methods from detecting what you say. At a minimum, not having his handheld would make discussing his dream problem easier with Annabel – if he followed through on it.

It looked like he had met nearly everyone here before, either from the farm or from the inn he was staying at. There was one older lady he didn't recognize who Isadora seemed to be steering him towards.

"Gabriel, I would like to introduce you to your mother's mother, your grandmother," Isadora said. "Isabella, this is your grandson Gabriel."

Isabella was likely in at least her mid-seventies. She moved slowly to stand while looking Gabriel over. Beneath the deceiving slow movements, he sensed a strong sense of vibrancy in her spirit.

"I can see some of Kayla in you," Isabella remarked moving forward to give him a hug. "I haven't been able to hug you since you were a very little boy."

"I do not know my mother's likeness very well, but from the pictures I have seen, she looked a lot like you. It is very nice to meet you," Gabriel replied a bit awkwardly. He still wasn't sure how he was expected to behave in this kind of interaction.

Isabella had a small tear forming in the corner of her eye. It was clear that she was very happy to see Gabriel, while trying to hold her emotions in check.

"Do I have any other cousins or relations of my mother on your side of the family?" Gabriel asked, seeming to feel like that would be an appropriate thing to ask. "I really know so little of my family background."

"No," Isabella said, "your mother was an only child. And as you probably know by now, you were her only child when she died. My husband was, what is the official way it is said now, oh yes, was taken into confinement many years back and was not successful in his reeducation. Anyone who was a known religion adherent was suspected back during the time now called the Scientific Reformation. He wasn't a leader in an Order or anything, but was a stubborn man who wouldn't give up what he believed in. All he had to do was to say the right words, but he wouldn't do it, and he lost his life over it. I never remarried and had thought I had lost all connection to my daughter, but here you are! This gives me great joy to see you."

That was a different answer than what he expected to hear. She hadn't said anything rebellious, but he could sense she still harbored some resentment. If someone had taken Emily away and executed her, he probably would not have felt happy about it either, even if they were in the right for doing it.

"Well, I am glad to be able to come back into your life then," Gabriel answered.

"I am just rambling," Isabella interjected. "Enough about stuff from long ago. So where are you staying? Isadora was telling me you have been helping them some here on their farm. Is this something you plan to stick with?"

"I have been staying at the Deerbarrow Inn so far," Gabriel answered. "I am not sure if my aunt and uncle will want me here full time. I think they are still trying me out, but I am not sure."

"Well, that is a long way to walk every morning if you ask me." Isabella offered. "Deerbarrow Inn is a nice enough place to stay from what I have heard, but more suited for someone who has business in the city. If you decide you want to keep working on Kelby's farm, I have a space available in my home I could let you stay in. It is about a twenty-minute walk from here. You will probably inherit the farm in a few years anyway if that isn't outlawed, so you probably want to get familiar with it at some point. I have hired people to take care of most of the physical work, but I still stay involved with the management of it."

"Well, I wouldn't mind not having that long walk every day, that is for sure," Gabriel answered. "I think I would be interested in seeing this space when you have some time. But I don't want to commit to it until I am sure my aunt and uncle will have a place for me to work here. Otherwise, I will need to be close to the city for the government general laborer work that will likely be assigned."

"Well, if they don't want you, I will find something for you to do at my place," she answered. "But if you want to take a bit of time to decide, there is sense in that also. It is good to get the lay of the land before you make any big decisions I think."

Gabriel looked around the room. He made his courtesies with his grandmother and walked toward Annabel. She was keeping to herself mostly in the corner, making something resembling a piece of clothing.

"That looks interesting," Gabriel remarked. "What are you making?"

"Just a sweater," she answered. "A lot of people around these parts prefer handmade clothing. When I get some idle time, I work on making things to wear. We grow the fiber that is used to make this yarn on our farm, and I am putting some of it to good use in making some clothing."

"It looks like a lot of work," Gabriel remarked. "Don't you get tired of working on it?"

"Not at all," Annabel answered. "I actually find this pretty relaxing and do it for fun."

"I have an odd question for you," Gabriel offered, figuring the best way to get an answer was to ask a question. "Does the name Raelynn mean anything to you?"

"Other than it being my middle name?" Annabel smiled in response. "No one ever calls me by that name, but I have always liked it a lot. Why do you ask?"

Gabriel was unsure where to go with this next. Was she confirming she was the same person from his dream? Technically she had just said she had a middle name. That really wasn't a confirmation of anything. He would have to be more direct if he wanted to get the confirmation he was looking for.

"Well, this is going to seem strange," Gabriel replied. "But I have been having dreams where someone who looks nearly identical to you and calls herself Raelynn is in them. This started before I ever met you. I don't know what to make of it. If you know anything about this and can help me with it, I would be appreciative."

Annabel gave him a quizzical look. He hadn't asked her directly to be a coach but had sort of. He was being a bit cryptic and wasn't sure if she was deciding to trust him or just thinking he wasn't all there.

"Try to fall to sleep when we get to meditation time in a few minutes. I will see if I can help you get answers then," Annabel answered.

Gabriel nodded his assent and walked away to greet the other guests. He had made an indirect request and had received in return a very indirect answer. Had he really received what he was looking for? All he could do is try to sleep during meditation time and see what happened.

Meditation time felt very similar to others he had attended in the capital during the rest day. There were the standard readings and the standard phrases. Those attending didn't appear to be zealous in their passion for the standard program, but they completed it with proper intonations and respect. It almost had a robotic feel to it where they all knew the words and motions. Gabriel was pretty certain they were not just doing it for his benefit. Ministry officials were known to make unannounced visits to check on meditation time. Handhelds also documented the meditation session for compliance. After about twenty minutes of readings and reflections, it was time for the meditation portion. Typically, this would take the remaining time in the hour to be completed. The attendees were supposed to sit in a silent meditative state to reflect on the readings, to determine how to best apply it toward their contribution to society.

Gabriel looked around the room briefly and saw everyone with their head bowed and eyes closed. He was tired from lack of sleep the prior night but wasn't sure if he could succeed in trying to induce sleep. He closed his eyes and worked to slowly empty his mind of other thoughts so he could maybe drift off into sleep. After an undeterminable time of doing this, he began to nod off.

Gabriel opened his eyes quickly, realizing he had gone to sleep. He was worried that he was embarrassing himself if he slept during meditation time beyond the time that everyone else was meditating. Looking around quickly, he quickly realized that there was a fog present in the room, and it was a black and white view like his other dreams where Raelynn appeared in them. Focusing closely, the scene was as it was when he began the meditation. The same people were in a state of meditation. He looked over to where Annabel had been sitting and watched with amazement as right beside her black and white form, a duplicate form appeared in full color. Her head lifted and her eyes opened.

"You are her, aren't you?" Gabriel blurted out.

The woman who was either Annabel, Raelynn or both smiled back at him.

"I was afraid you would not join us," she answered. "It took you a long time to enter the dream state. The meditation time was nearly up when you finally came."

"Does that mean I need to wake right back up?" Gabriel asked.

"Not at all. Time passes differently in the dream state. Much can be accomplished in a very short period of real time. The reverse can be true as well. It is all a matter of controlling it to meet the needs you have," she answered.

"So, are you Raelynn or Annabel?" Gabriel asked. "I don't know what to call you now."

"Names are not important here," she replied. "You may call me what you like. I will answer to either. The question is what is it that you ask of me?"

"I think what I most desire is answers and knowledge. There is much that is happening to me that I don't understand. It flies in the face of everything I have learned, and I still do not know if I am hallucinating or experiencing a reality that I never knew existed," Gabriel replied with raw honesty.

"So, you seek a teacher then? You are asking me to guide you on your journey of discovery?" she asked.

"Yes, Raelynn," Gabriel answered. "Please help me understand what is happening to me."

Raelynn smiled, "I am willing to guide you on this path. Are you willing to trust me and follow my instructions? Not all I will ask of you will make sense to you at first. I will need you to limit yourself as I ask, until you better understand what you are doing. There are many things you can do in this dream world that can have grave danger to yourself and to the real outside world around you. In this, you must trust me explicitly."

Gabriel gave her comments careful thought. He was willing to go along with them for a while at least. No harm in trying to understand what was happening to him. "Yes, I am willing to follow your instructions in this," he replied.

"There are two types of dream states," Raelynn explained. "The first is regular dreams. You can do no harm there. But the second state like we are in now is where the danger lies. My first rule to you as your guide is that if you find yourself with awareness in this state without color and with fog, don't try to exert your will to desire anything different. You remember the water and the weeds in the field? I was here with you then to make sure you didn't do something to cause harm. As you learn more, you may be able to enter this dream state without my help, and it is very important you limit yourself within what I have already instructed you on. Those who have experimented on their own, often find themselves dead or cause a great harm outside of themselves in the world."

"I am not sure I fully understand, but I will follow that rule," Gabriel replied. "So how did I end up in this dream state versus a normal one? And what makes the dream world we are in right now, so much different?"

"I am responsible for drawing you into this dream state," Raelynn answered. "I can sense those who have the potential to do more than observe in the dream state. When they are asleep, I can open a door like a portal that they can pass through into this place. In this dream place, you can alter the reality of the normal world around you, depending on the nature of your talents and gifts. So far, you have shown you are able to do some simple resource creation when you made water in the desert, and you have shown the ability for basic translocation when you removed all the weeds in the fields and put them in a pile. You also were able to pull up key memories with strong clarity. You may have ability to do more than this, but this is what we will need to discover as we complete some lessons."

"Does everyone have the ability to do this? I have never heard of this being done before," Gabriel asked.

"Some are much stronger in the ability than others," Raelynn answered. "But in reality, very few people are able to do any of things you have already been able to demonstrate. Given the current political climate, those who have some gifts in this area don't go out of their way to make themselves visible."

"I would think that prominent scientists would love to study this phenomenon. This would have so many real-world applications. It could change the landscape of the world!" Gabriel said with excitement.

Raelynn gave Gabriel a humoring smile. "Do you really think they would react that way? There is no scientific formula for this gift. It is an action that requires faith in order to succeed. If you don't believe what you are doing will happen, it won't. Would you like trying to explain that to the ministry charged with enforcing scientific compliance? Someone told me you worked there before. How do you think they would react to that?"

Gabriel paused to consider her comments. In best terms, a person demonstrating gifts would be imprisoned in a lab to be studied. Worst case, they would face judgement for violating religion prohibitions.

"Yeah, it probably wouldn't go over very good for the person bringing it forward," Gabriel answered. "But at the same time, this isn't really a religion is it? I am not a believer of any order or religious organization, and you say I have developed this gift."

"You are demonstrating a certain level of faith or belief to be able to change things in the dream state," Raelynn answered. "Faith is the basis for everything the government would label as religion."

"That seems like a leap to me," Gabriel lightly challenged.

"So where do you think the power you have demonstrated comes from?" Raelynn asked. "You may be an effective conduit to have it flow through, but you are assuming the power will always be available to you to use. There are those who have learned that when the power is directed for nefarious purposes, then it is much limited, or the person directing it may lose access to it. Assuming you accept my word on this, how can you explain this? Doesn't it logically follow that there is an entity establishing order and rules on this power? Belief in this sounds awfully close to a religion doesn't it?"

"Then you are saying that those who want to maintain and ultimately grow in their gift in this dream state must seek to understand these rules better?" Gabriel asked.

"That is a very good way of saying it Gabriel," Raelynn answered. "You must be open to taking a much broader view of the world than you have been exposed to in your previous life experiences. Reality does not exist in the way you were taught it to be. I can help teach you these rules if you are willing to learn. But you will need to change your mindset, or you will never reach your true potential."

Gabriel listened carefully as he let Raelynn's words absorb. Was he ready to suspend his beliefs to learn about this new gift? This was a lot of take in all at once, and he didn't think he had even gotten the whole of it yet. He was still struggling whether this conversation was a figment of his imagination.

"I think I would like to try," Gabriel finally replied. "What is the first step I need to take?"

"You need to learn to experience the full range of life," Raelynn answered. "I know you have experienced grief and loss. But have you experienced joy, wonder, taste, smell, true hearing, life itself? That is the first step. This week, when you are working on the farm, I want you to look for lilies. They are prevalent around the farm so I don't think you will need to work very hard to find some. I want you to experience the Lily, meditate on the Lily, smell the Lily and learn all you can about it. Let it consume your thoughts. When you have completed this task successfully, I will reach out to you in your dreams for your next lesson. Now wake. Meditation time is just ending."

CHAPTER 7

Gabriel was clearly getting worn down, Quintin thought. It seemed like he was spinning his wheels on a fast track to nowhere. The process of nightly detailing all his interactions was costing Gabriel much needed rest, which in turn made him more likely to slipup and blow his cover. Quintin could solve much of this by having a surveillance drone shadow him, but the ministry suspected the resistance had a way to detect for this.

So far, there had been no idle comments on the topic of Kayden, and while observed behaviors may not have been up to the capital standards, there hadn't been any violations of law that would have been actionable. The Isabella person seemed interesting, but likely harmless, and not a lead to something bigger. Gabriel had asked for a recommendation on moving his place of living to her house. There was some debate between Xavier and himself, but ultimately, they decided to let Gabriel explore moving there. If nothing else, it would give Gabriel some much needed rest to improve his ability to document observations.

Quintin wrote up the recommendation to pursue moving to the closer house. He also suggested visiting town at a regular interval to interact in the common room of the Deerbarrow Inn. Pursing local customs was recommended to better fit in. He did not want Gabriel to become so isolated that he didn't see what was going on around the community. In time, he could start making some leading statements that could draw those in the resistance into the open.

Quintin moved on to the rest of his to do list. He found another violator of the *Adherence to Myths Act* and ordered her arrest. This was another repeat offender. Xavier had provided a new protocol for arrest, so he added that to the detention orders.

∞ ∞ ∞

Gabriel finished another long day working in the fields. He wasn't being asked to weed at an insane rate anymore. Today and most days recently were spent partnering with his cousin Tom learning a lot about what went into managing and running a farm. He was educated on the different types of crops that grew on this farm and many of the challenges in growing them. This really increased Gabriel's appreciation of what went into providing food to the overall population. Reflecting on this past week, he had to say he had gained a much better appreciation of nature and the ecosystem than he ever had in the capital.

The various ministries had programs and policies that encouraged the right environmental practices and they enforced them to ensure that no one did anything harmful to negatively impact the planet. But Gabriel now realized that those who were working the crops on these farms didn't want to do anything that would jeopardize their livelihood. Their farms would pass down to their progeny and doing anything short sighted would not be entertained if it risked their future. Counter to everything he had learned in the capital, those up here on the farms cared more about the environment than anyone he had met before. They showed it differently, but they truly cared, even as their work had grown progressively harder due to the regulatory changes that had been implemented over the last several years.

Gabriel looked down at the plant he had in a pot. Tom noticed him staring at a batch of lilies and suggested if he liked them, to dig them up and put them in a pot so he could enjoy them in the evening. Gabriel had taken him up on his offer and now had it by the window in his room at the Deerbarrow Inn.

Having completed his nightly report to Quintin, Gabriel fully shifted his attention to the lily plant. This was now his new routine in the evenings before bed. The plant was mostly white, with a small bit of yellow in the flower. It had a fragrant aroma that he was becoming much more able to recognize. There was a beauty and simplicity in this flower, but it also held great complexity. Gabriel had spent some time on his handheld learning about this plant. It really didn't have any practical value that he was able to find. Some small animals were known to be negatively impacted by it, but overall, it was mainly a plant enjoyed for its aesthetic value. Gabriel refocused himself on the plant. He increased his concentration with his eyes closed, reciting in his mind what he had learned about it and what he had observed. He almost began to feel like he was part of the flower, like he was almost one with it.

As he continued with this focus, he began to see an appearance of a foggy and non-colored canvas. It looked like he was in a field of lilies as he looked directly in front of him. They did not have the vibrancy of color he had become accustomed to, but the detail in them was unmistakable. There was a stone lined path in the center of the field that he was standing on. He felt the urge to walk forward, so he followed that calling. At the end of the path, there was a cabana with two chairs in it, one of them occupied. He continued to walk closer and was able to make out who was sitting there. It was Raelynn seated, once again exuding vibrant colors on a backdrop of grays. He had entered the dream space, but he didn't think he had fallen asleep. This was clearly something new that was happening. Gabriel continued to walk closer, and with unspoken consent, sat in the empty seat which faced the field full of lilies.

"I was not sure how long it would take you to reach this place on your own," Raelynn offered. "I have seen it happen by accident and have seen it take months."

"I didn't sleep this time," Gabriel explained. "I was just concentrating on the lily and then I was here. I am not sure how it was a lot different than what I did earlier in the week, but today I got a different result."

"You did well getting here so soon," she offered. "The key is becoming one with what you are concentrating on. It doesn't have to be a lily, but we have found the lily works better than most things. It is simple, yet has subtle complexity. Once you master its essence, it is a lot easier to blend your mind with it to reach this dream place."

"If you didn't know how long it would take for me to figure out how to get here, how did you know when to come meet me?" Gabriel wondered aloud.

"My strength in dreams is being able to hear those who enter it, or have the ability to enter it," Raelynn explained. "I am not perfect at it, but I have learned how to coexist in the waking world and the dream world simultaneously. Well, at least enough where I can sort of hear a sharp indicator if someone I am watching takes an action. If I am in a safe place to join them, I can adjust myself fully into the dream state. Each dreamer has a unique tone, so I just needed to learn yours and when I heard it, I knew to come seek you out."

"That explains how you found me just now," Gabriel answered. "But it doesn't explain how you found me the times I didn't enter the dream state on my own."

"That takes a slightly different approach," Raelynn continued. "For that, I open the potential for a portal in a way only someone who has some ability can enter through. I can scan through the normal dream world offering the path via a nudging to normal dreams. Those with the ability to hear it, sometimes respond. When they do, I can interact with them, and get a sense of their gifts and abilities. Once they have passed through my portal once, it is much easier to pull them though later on. I can then learn their unique tone and can recognize them later if they figure out how to come through on their own, as you just did."

Gabriel was a bit confused by all of this, but it did make sense in its own sort of way. That is, if he could get over the fact that he was in this dream state to begin with. But he had decided he was going to try to give this a serious try, so he would give all his effort to keep his skepticism at bay.

"Our last discussion you said you would give me my next lesson after I had done enough to meditate on the Lily. By coming here, does that mean I have achieved your goals on this?" Gabriel asked.

"Getting here without my help was your next lesson, but yes, you have achieved this," Raelynn explained. "The key for you will be to practice duplicating what you did, developing unity or one-ness with the Lily so you can get back. If you are not at peace or do not have inner calm, it is nearly impossible to enter on your own. Someone can open the portal for you to come through, but to enter unaided, you must be fully focused and at peace to get here. You may find that is often the most difficult thing to achieve. Try to do something in anger or with lack of mental clarity and you will fail in the attempt."

"I think I understand." Gabriel stated, "but how do I leave it? I don't recall doing anything to go back when I have been here before. I am guessing you did something to push me out?"

"We can practice that in a bit, but it is pretty simple," Raelynn answered. "Just visualize yourself awake back where you started from and you will be back. It is all in the mind."

"Ok, that makes sense, I guess," Gabriel said. "I will try that when you are ready for me to. What I don't understand is why am I looking at a field of lilies right now instead of something else? I have been in this dream place several times now, and each time it has been a different location. How is it that they are different, and how do I be in once place versus someplace else?"

"This is your intermediate place right now, a sort of limbo between the dream state and the awake state," she answered. "From here you can go anywhere you want to go. You do need a frame of reference to get there though. You need to envision a real fixed point that exists in the waking world. From there you focus on it, envisioning yourself there. Then you will be there in the dream state. Once you have a reached a point of reference, you can explore and move around from there. Also, the further away from your physical location you are, the harder it is to exact changes. For example, you could probably envision yourself in a place you knew in the capital right now, but to do anything there more than look, it would require a lot of effort. But if you focused on your room at the inn where your body is currently at, then you would be able to do things with the least possible effort needed."

Gabriel was thoughtful for a few moments. "The dreams I have had, don't all seem to fit with what you are saying. I haven't been to the desert. Plus, two of the events seemed to take place in my past. They were not current time events. How does that fit with what you are saying?"

"When I make a portal for someone, I can use a combination of their memories and mine to get them to a location," Raelynn answered. "I have been to that desert before in the Brendag sector. Since you were not actually using your own reference point there, you actually created the water in the same space you were at which is why you probably found water when you woke up."

"I thought that water puddle was strange!" Gabriel exclaimed.

"Relative to memories of past experiences," Raelynn continued, "you seem to be constraining your thinking quite a bit. Time can be traversed in the same way distance can be. You just need a reference point and you can move to it. Most who can do this, can only stay on their own timeline, meaning they can only follow the path of their own memories and life experiences. Some have been known to have the gift to envision possible future timelines and thus have a unique gift of prediction or prophesy as we call it. This is usually less certain, and the predictions of those with this gift are often more cryptic and have less details."

"If I visit my past, do I have the ability to change anything in it?" Gabriel asked seeing possibilities go off in his head.

"Very few have the gift of being able to make changes in the timeline space," Raelynn answered. "Those who do, say that it is a lot like distance in the current time space. Meaning that the further you go back in time; it is much harder to manipulate events. You may be able to change something that happened ten seconds ago fine, but going back several hours or days, is unthinkable for even the strongest we have found in this gift. But if you had the gift and lost at gambling, could you go back and change your bet? Sure, you could. But that wouldn't mean you would be guaranteed to see the same result. Sometimes our actions impact future events and if we change our actions in the past, there may be a different future. Many people have a rudimentary ability to go back and view the past in their timeline. Gifts beyond that are rare."

Raelynn had given Gabriel a lot to think about. "That is a lot to consider for sure," Gabriel replied after a long pause in the conversation. "I will have to think about what you have told me."

"I have explained a lot to you but want you to remember to follow your promise to not act beyond what I have taught you to do," Raelynn instructed. You can do a lot of harm to yourself and others, if you don't know what you are doing. Looking around is pretty safe. Envisioning things different in any way, I don't want you to try unless you have me here helping you. This is very important."

"I will," Gabriel responded. "I can see how this could come with great danger."

"Ok, good," she answered. "So, let's practice moving around for a bit before we call this lesson to an end. I don't want you to exert yourself beyond your strength. Focus your mind on a location you know here around Deerbarrow and envision yourself to being there. You will need to visualize the detail of the surroundings the best you can in order to get there. I should be able to follow."

Gabriel closed his eyes and tried to think about places he knew well in Deerbarrow. As he thought about it, he lamented that he should start being more observant of his surroundings. He had been in many places but didn't have vivid memories of many of them at all. He knew his room at the Deerbarrow Inn well by now, so he figured that would be the easiest place to start. He pictured the room in his mind and slowly imagined himself being there.

Opening his eyes, he saw that it was so. The room existed in black and white, and a fog was present, but it was clearly his room. He had made his first jump in the dream state. Looking around the room he saw an immaterial haze around the place he had been sitting when he was meditating on the Lily and recognized the form of his body there. Gabriel continued to look around and then saw Raelynn materialize beside him.

"A good choice," Raelynn commented.

"I realized when you asked me to do this, how little I observe and retain of the world around me." Gabriel explained. "It was either here, or the place on the farm where I clean up after working in the fields. I had difficulty fully picturing other places with enough confidence to get there. I could have probably visualized places in the capital pretty well, but you asked me to stay around here."

"No, that is fine," she said. "You can start paying more attention to your surroundings in the future. This will naturally flow with my challenge last time to you to grow in your experience of life. Now go ahead and walk around a bit in the room. Things like doors are basically illusions here that you can walk through. Let's start with something simple like moving a piece of clothing."

Gabriel saw his shoes sitting on the floor by the bed. Concentrating on them, he envisioned them to be instead by the door using a similar approach he had used removing weeds from the field. There was a brief glimmer of color and then they moved and were now beside the door. He would need to remember to check for this when he returned to the wakened state.

"Good," Raelynn remarked. "I think that is enough for this lesson. You have my blessing to practice getting to the dream state and out of it and coming here to your room to move items around. Stay within that construct, and you shouldn't cause any harm to yourself or others. Now, if you want to envision yourself sitting back into that chair meditating in an awake state, you should return to the normal waking world."

"Thank you, Raelynn," Gabriel said with sincerity. "I really appreciate what you have taught me. I will practice what you have asked me to do."

Gabriel closed his eyes and concentrated on being in the chair meditating, then awaking. He kept doing it but didn't feel anything differently. Sighing, he opened his eyes only to find that the world around him was now in color. He was fully awake, sitting in his chair in front of the lily plant. Gabriel stood up and walked around the room. He couldn't help noticing with amazement that his shoes were now beside the door.

CHAPTER 8

Tybalt sat with anticipation in his prepared bunker, awaiting the expected shuttle crossing. Based on the intelligence he had been provided, a female prisoner named Zandra was due to be on the prisoner transport headed for containment and likely execution. Tybalt had not been given much more information than this, other than she was detained under the Adherence to Myths Act, for a benign act of saying "God" in the presence of her own home, likely by accident. For some reason the government had significantly increased enforcement of this law recently. With this escalation, Kayden had been put on alert and had responded, working to rescue those from arrest who did not view their prospects favorable for surviving containment.

Tybalt had some ability in the dream state and his area of the gift was in translocating people from one location to another. This skill had been used quite a bit lately with the uptick in arrest overreaches. Noting the time, Tybalt centered himself, bringing himself into the dream state. Having achieved this within a few seconds of focus, he brought his dream self to the shuttle tracks to await its crossing. By now he usually heard the pinging of the word Kayden from the prisoner's lips, but this time he did not hear it calling out. This did not make rescue impossible, but it would instead take longer to find his intended target.

Seeing the train's outline coming from afar, Tybalt envisioned himself on board and proceeded to pass through the various compartments until he could recognize Zandra from those who were in transit. There were prisoners present, but none matched her description. Tybalt frantically searched a second time in case he had missed her, but alas, she was not there. Having reached the limits of his translocation range, he brought his dream state body back to his present location and ultimately came back to the woken state. Why wasn't she there, he wondered with frustration. His contact had told him she had left the holding area in Northfalcon. Something had changed, likely due to the all the successful escapes. It would probably never be as easy as it had been again.

∞ ∞ ∞

"You have all read the report of our agent who tried to perform the rescue of the person named Zandra," the High Seat stated. "Has anyone determined what went wrong?"

"Air transport was used instead of the shuttle," the Guardian answered. "It was a matter of time until they changed the transport protocol. It surprised us all that they jumped all the way to air though."

"And the status of the children?" the Seeker asked.

"Currently in Ministry custody and by the looks of it, armed custody," the Guardian grimly answered.

The High Seat let this new development sink in. Zandra was considered a repeat offender and would likely be executed for her actions. And the worst of it was that she had two small children. This was a new escalation. The children had some relatives who would probably take them in. It still may be possible to get them transferred to their care, but she did not think it likely. The father had previously been executed for other acts against the government, so this was going to impact the care of the children also.

"Options to rescue her?" the High Seat asked the assembled council.

"We have not tried to rescue anyone in the containment facility before," the Guardian answered. "But if we want to save her, that is what we need to be able to do."

"This is the question in front of us," The High Seat addressed the council. "Do we attempt a rescue, and if we do, how do we ensure we have the kids secured as well as the mother without jeopardizing the safety of the other?"

"We can deploy two teams to hit at once in order to protect that," the Guardian offered before becoming more animated. "This has gone way too far! Before the government has honored an uneasy truce. We pretended to obey and follow the rules and in turn, they pretended to believe that we are mostly following them. Those that publicly flaunt the laws know that they risk themselves. But those who have a minor infraction, only to be incarcerated and ultimately executed, is not something I am prepared to sit by and watch any longer."

"But what can we do?" asked another on the council. "Do we really want to have a military conflict? That is what is next if we go further than the rescues we have been doing. We don't have the tools to fight an armed resistance. That really isn't what our beliefs are centered around. Can we really sacrifice our people in a bloodbath, by giving a pretext to invite an occupation army?"

"And if we don't meet them with weapons, is anyone really advocating we meet them with the dream gifts?" the Seeker offered. "To come out into the open? Plus, can those who have these gifts really use them in violence? Can we truly center ourselves at peace with a policy of annihilation?"

"You are speaking of terror as opposed to righteous defense of our people," the Guardian responded. "I would be able to be very at peace responding to this tyranny in a just and measured way. I am not advocating open rebellion with weaponry but am suggesting a combined effort of civil disobedience by shutting off the exports from this and any other willing sectors. What will the other sectors do without our food exports? What will they do without the resource exports that fuel their technology?"

"If we do that, will those near the capital accept the lies that they are being given as to why their food allocations are being reduced?" the Reader asked. "We need to open the eyes of the people all across this land that there is another path. There is a path to life, freedom and hope. And that path does not come from this false and corrupted path of science that they are currently held in the power of."

"How well known is this woman's arrest?" The High Seat asked interrupting the discussion that was quickly escalating. "We have seen the intelligence reports and are outraged. But this is not well known across the sector. Don't get me wrong, there is angst and the people are upset when people randomly disappear, but there is very little information released with arrests. Sometimes hints are dropped to the offense which helps others understand what not to do. But beyond that, is the story of this woman's kids being taken and her arrest for such a trivial charge well understood? I think the people of Xenon have heard whispers, but have they heard it shouted from the mountain tops? Does their outrage match ours? If you want people to rise up in civil defiance, they need to believe in the cause. I think there is an appetite to rise up, but they need to be fed some information to believe in the why. We need a way to get the stories out."

"I would suggest getting the stories posted so they display on handhelds would be most effective," the Keeper offered. "But that technology is so controlled, anything that could be done will trace back quickly to whoever did it and the government would know who actually read it."

"What about paper fliers or pamphlets that tell the stories?" the Seeker suggested. "We could post them around the sector in public places where someone could not be charged for possession of them. Can we print them and then have those with the gift of translocation get them posted? This would be a large effort, but that would get them put up without anyone seeing how they got there. We could also rotate locations of posting so surveillance systems couldn't always see the how they appeared."

Seeing agreement on the council, The High Seat blessed this approach. "Agreed. But what should we do about rescuing this woman and her kids?"

"We need to find out when the execution is planned for, and make a timely rescue," the Guardian offered having calmed himself down somewhat. "We can have teams setup to get both her and her children. We have been training some of those rescued previously for this type of mission. I think it is time to use them. There could be some causalities on a mission like this, but those who volunteered for these teams are willing and ready."

"Okay," the High Seat answered. "Go ahead and get the pieces in place for this rescue mission. We can't afford mistakes on this one. And we can't kill or seriously injure anyone guarding those we are trying to rescue. This is an information war as much as anything, and we don't want to give the appearance of atrocities of our own, trying to right one being committed against us. I know that makes this harder, but for now, that is how we need to play it. Do we have any other business to discuss?"

"Yes," the Seeker answered. "We should discuss next steps with Gabriel. As some of you know, he has acknowledged his gift and is currently in the early stages of his training. I have not been able to truly determine his loyalties. If he has any connections with a ministry, I am pretty certain he hasn't reported back his dream gift. That would likely get him classified with a mental defect. But at some point, we need to let him get closer to the truth if he has a chance of achieving his potential."

The High Seat outlined her idea of what to do next. After some discussion on the council, it was agreed to.

∞ ∞ ∞

Gabriel was already appreciating the closer location of his grandmother Isabella's home. She had a large house and the area he was provided to stay in was situated in a private way. He wasn't sure how she managed the energy quota for something of this size, but when he asked, she simply said to not concern himself with this, and he was to use whatever temperature control and water he felt he needed. On top of that, she didn't even want to discuss the topic of how much she wanted in compensation for him staying there. She told him that being able to see him more often was more compensation than she would ever want.

It was a very strange phenomena to be appreciated like that by someone who was largely a stranger other than the biological link. Gabriel saw that the family connection mattered here. He still was trying to understand what it meant to him, but he could see why his extended family would have been upset to have him left in the capital versus returned to his family when his parents had died.

Gabriel liked the authenticity of the work on his uncle's farm and felt he was slowly earning the trust and respect of those around him. Gabriel looked at the time. He had left straight after work and came back to clean up, versus socializing some as he normally did. He planned to head into town tonight in order to make his weekly visit to the Deerbarrow Inn. Gabriel finished cleaning up and said a quick goodbye to his grandmother as he headed out the door.

The walk to town was uneventful. Fortunately, his grandmother's farm was closer to town than his aunt and uncle's was. Upon reaching the outskirts of Deerbarrow, he started seeing some papers strewn on the ground. Even up here in Xenon, he had seen very little evidence of using paper. To see it spread all over the ground was an unusual sight. Gabriel looked closer at one of these papers, then stopped suddenly when he saw what it was discussing. The paper was denouncing the Ministry of Scientific Compliance with a story of how an unjust arrest had been made for the petty violation of saying the word "God."

The story said that there was no attempt made to advocate for a religion, just an inadvertent slip of the tongue in the privacy of her own home. As a result, she was likely to be executed in the coming days and her children were going to be shipped off to the capital, not even able to be taken in by their remaining family. They even had photos of the small children with their sympathetic looking mother making this look even more provocative. Gabriel took a quick photo of the pamphlet with his handheld and continued walking. Once he had walked well past the papers, he logged into his Oversite client and attached the photo and a brief update on what he had found, sending it as a priority to his case officer. His main role here was to look for the start of a resistance, and this was something obvious and actionable. If they handled it correctly, someone from a ministry would come by and discover these papers without it being traced back to him.

Gabriel continued his journey to the Deerbarrow Inn where he said hello to Wallis and then proceeded into the common room. He recognized several of the people here who greeted him with some familiarity, but still a bit of distance. There seemed to be tension in the air, but he didn't think it was directed at him. He walked up to the bar area and asked for a beer. He had been asking co-workers at the farm which drink would be a good one to start on if he were to try an alcoholic beverage. The ministry had suggested he only stick to one until he was more accustomed to it as it may impair his ability to keep his cover and affect his judgement. As he was walking away from the bar, he saw Tom walk in.

"So, you decided to try the beer?" Tom asked with a smile on his face.

"Yeah," Gabriel answered while taking his first sip. He couldn't help to slightly contort his expression when he tried it.

"It is a bit of an acquired taste," Tom said.

"It isn't too bad," Gabriel replied. "I think I will try to finish it. Did something happen? The room feels pretty tense right now."

"There were some fliers posted," Tom answered. "They were posted around town and had some inflammatory accusations on them."

"Have you seen it?" Gabriel asked.

"Seen it yes, but no one is going to be caught with a copy of it." Tom answered. "That is a good way of getting arrested for sedition, even if you were taking it to a ministry official to be turned in. I am sure it will be eventually discovered, and some surveillance footage will identify the person who posted them. No idea if what it said is true though. Was pretty outrageous if it was."

"What did it say?" asked Gabriel.

"Mainly it just said they are going to execute a mom from another portion of the Xenon sector in a few days for a minor violation of the Adherence to Myths Act. Not only that, but they were going to ship her surviving kids to the capital instead of giving them to her extended family." Tom answered in a very low voice. "I don't know the person accused of being involved, but word will get out if she was someone who was trying to make a stand, or if the pamphlet is true. Going to be a lot of people upset if turns out to be true. But if they remove the kids, that will be a new escalation. So far, those arrested have had their children given to the care of relatives if anyone came forward. Your case was different in the capital, but in this sector that at least has been the way it has been handled."

"I can see how that would make people upset here. Even to me who grew up in the capital, this seems excessive. Do you think anyone will do anything about it?" Gabriel answered in the same low voice.

"Hard to say," Tom answered. "There isn't much that can be done. It isn't like there are a lot of tools the people of Xenon have that could make much of a difference. There has been an uneasy truce for the last several years. If this is true, that truce may be strained. People will be upset, but will they do anything? No idea on that."

"You don't seem that outraged on this," Gabriel offered. "You seem to be taking it better than the rest of the room is."

"I usually wait for the facts before getting worked up," Tom answered. "Just because something is published, doesn't make it true, regardless which position that it advocates for. For all I know, this could be a ministry pamphlet designed to entrap. Enough of that. I am here to relax and watch you struggle to drink the rest of your beer!"

Gabriel smiled and then inwardly groaned as he saw he had only consumed about a quarter of his cup. The taste was becoming less bad the more he continued to sip at it. He also noticed that drinking the beer seemed to reduce the distrust he had sensed around him. Sure, he was nowhere close to being accepted like someone who was raised here, but it was like the symbolism of him embracing their culture was an olive branch of reaching across the divide to being accepted.

Gabriel stayed long enough to finish his beer as he mingled around saying hello to the other patrons he had met while he had been staying in the inn. They were polite and friendly, but none was as forthright as Tom had been relative to the somber mood in the room.

Gabriel headed back toward his grandmother's house. He passed the place there had been fliers on the ground, and they were no longer there. He wondered if there had been a ministry response to collect them, or if someone else had picked them up to distribute them. His question was about to be answered.

"You there!" said a uniformed officer. "What are you doing at this time of day on this road?"

The officer was wearing the insignia of a Ministry of Scientific Compliance agent. Gabriel was pretty sure that his presence and mission had not been provided to the local ministry officials. He had been given a way to identify himself if it became necessary, but that was to be done only as a last resort. This officer was probably just responding to the pamphlet escalation that he had observed and reported.

"May science and reason guide your day sir," Gabriel replied. "I am on my way back to my grandmother's house where I live. I have been at the Deerbarrow Inn tonight and am headed back before it gets dark."

The ministry officer looked at Gabriel with suspicion. He raised his scanner and proceeded to run an identity check on Gabriel to confirm who he was and that his living location story matched up. Gabriel was glad he had followed protocol and updated his domicile location with the ministry when he moved, or this could quickly get out of control.

"So, you are living with Isabella and are working on Kelby's farm?" the ministry officer asked. "I know most people who live here, and I don't know you. And your accent isn't from around here either."

"Yeah, I recently moved back to Deerbarrow after growing up in the capital. I was originally born here," Gabriel explained.

"Says much the same in your file here. I am looking for some paper pamphlets. Did you see any on your walk from town?"

"Not that I am aware of, officer," Gabriel answered. "Don't see much paper anymore, so I think I would have noticed if there had been some."

"I'm going to need to search you. We've been finding them spread all around this area," the officer stated.

Gabriel was thoroughly searched. All he had on him was his handheld, so the search was uneventful. The officer looked like he wanted a reason to detain him but finding nothing, he reluctantly let him go on this way. Gabriel left a bit concerned that he had slightly misled the officer. He hadn't seen any pamphlets leaving the inn but had seen them going to it. If there was surveillance in place here, that would raise questions later, especially since he had briefly paused to read what was said. Either way, he had escaped unscathed and if there was follow-up, it should help his credibility locally rather than harm it, provided he wasn't arrested.

∞ ∞ ∞

Quintin entered the room, quickly aware that he was likely the lowest ranking person present. After his handheld buzzed, Quintin quickly skimmed the follow-up report Gabriel had just sent.

"Deerbarrow is the third report of pamphlet propaganda we have had today," Xavier offered. So far these have all been contained to the Xenon sector, but I would not be surprised if it spreads to the adjacent sectors soon."

"Do we know yet where these are originating from?" another official asked.

"We have only found one posting that was put up in the range of a surveillance device." Xavier answered. "Let me show you the footage and tell me if you can make anything of it."

Quintin watched as the image of a largely deserted street was shown in low light. Xavier told them what portion of the image to watch. Quintin blinked and what was previously an empty wall was now a pamphlet. One frame the pamphlet wasn't there and the next it was.

"I even had our technology team fully scrub this image," Xavier explained. "I'd welcome any ideas you may have."

Quintin watched again as the same phenomena occurred. The pamphlet was not there, and then suddenly it was.

"Did someone compromise Oversite and edit out the footage?" Quintin asked. "This seems like the most probable answer. Although, I am not sure how anyone could do that with the security protocols we have in place."

"If they did, they were very skilled," Xavier replied. "The technology team indicates there is no evidence of tampering. I'm not saying they are wrong, but they got there somehow. We will keep digging into this further. But that is not why I called you all here. I need a threat assessment of the likelihood anything will happen as a result of this."

"I just got a new report in from a key contact, and he assesses the mood as tense but skeptical," Quintin offered the group. "Once word reaches them that this is not a false report though, it is likely that the sector will get more volatile. I would not be surprised if an attempt is made to rescue the woman and her children. The change in protocol you ordered sir, did get this prisoner to the containment facility successfully. Rebels may become bolder and try to rescue her at this location."

"That is a good point," Xavier answered. "Let's increase our security footprint at this facility and also move the children to a more secure location."

"Have we considered releasing both back to freedom as a way to invalidate the pamphlets?" offered one of the participants.

"Considered it, yes, but we can't give into the pressure," Xavier answered. "We have been awaiting a major change moment for the Xenon sector. If we approach it correctly, this could be the transformative event we have been needing to fully unify the nation. Then we can identify and put down the resistance elements once and for all, by bringing them out into the open."

CHAPTER 9

Gabriel began his evening exercises with the lily. He had improved in his ability to enter the dream state through meditation. Raelynn said when he became fully capable in this skill, he would be able to transition in mere moments instead of several minutes. His typical time to enter was improving, but he still felt he had a long way to go before he could transition that quickly. She had explained that if you can alter your life to be in an inner state of peace, being able to shift your perspective was nothing more than a mental jump as opposed to a gradual buildup to getting there. Many never improved faster than he currently exhibited, but those who were strongest could do as she had stated.

Gabriel was having more trouble than normal attaining his focus today. He had read a ministry report from his case officer seeking explanations to the sudden appearance of pamphlets that the surveillance systems were unable to detect. The ministry seemed to be focused on the technological possibilities of someone altering the digital footage of the posting areas. Gabriel was coming up with some alternative hypotheses, but none he wanted to be the messenger on to the ministry. He had no interest in explaining how he had attained the ability to enter a dream state and alter the placement of items in the real world.

And beyond that conundrum, that also begged the possibility that this Way of the Lily may be tied somehow to the budding resistance movement. Gabriel was wondering if the path to growing in the dream state gifts would lead him to finding the resistance leaders. But all he had currently was knowledge attained from his dream state. He could not report that without bringing great risk to himself and his own credibility. He needed independent evidence gathered in the real world that could make these connections if we wanted to report it. So many thoughts were swirling in his head. It was no wonder he could not get to the dream state tonight at any typical speed.

Gabriel reset his thoughts and again refocused to the lily in front him. He finally managed to clear his thoughts and found himself in a field of lilies. Raelynn was waiting for him with a slightly bemused expression on her face.

"I am sorry I am late," Gabriel said apologetically. "I had more trouble than normal clearing my head tonight. I am sorry if I kept you waiting very long."

"No worries," Raelynn offered. "It gave me more time to make my sweater."

"What is the lesson plan for tonight?" Gabriel asked.

"I was thinking we could work on traveling through your memories, as a means of traveling within time," Raelynn answered.

Gabriel immediately saw a potential pitfall with doing this. If he traveled back to a memory when he got his mission instructions, he could expose his role and operation. He had to make sure that any exercise stayed well clear of that possibility.

"That sounds interesting," Gabriel answered. "What do you have in mind?"

"Many people with the gift can move within their own timeline of memories with some practice," Raelynn explained. "Those who are especially gifted can move beyond their own timelines and explore in areas where they did not exist. I think we should start on the simpler method. Before we begin this, I want you to remember this time and place. When you are ready to return, redirect your focus to now and here. If you focus hard enough, you will return back to the current time. If I attach to you when you do this, I should be able to stay with you whenever you go. Remember these instructions in the event we get separated."

"I will," Gabriel promised as he showed an intrigued expression on his face.

"The interesting thing about this," Raelynn continued, "is you can spend what feels like a very long time exploring and yet return to the present like no time has passed. I'll warn you, that the longer you stay exploring, the more tired you will become, so I wouldn't recommend taking a super long excursion before you get a feel for the cost it will have on your body.

"What is the likely limit?" Gabriel asked.

I once heard of someone spending the equivalent of years exploring the past. When he finally returned, he could barely move for weeks. People just thought he was sick, but the reality was he had overdone it. Also, don't try to alter anything in your timeline. Most people can't do it, but don't try in case you can. You never know what impact you can make on events that should have already happened, not to mention it could kill you to try."

"I understand," Gabriel answered while considering the risks of doing it incorrectly. "How far back do you recommend I go?"

"The when doesn't really matter, provided you don't try to change anything. I would recommend starting with a pretty vivid memory and then we can explore from that time context," Raelynn explained.

Gabriel began to direct his thoughts. He wanted to pick something from his past, but not from a time that it would compromise his current mission. He let his thoughts drift back to when he graduated from the Ministry of Education.

Gabriel peered through the fog, then saw himself. He was looking down from the stage. He had taken top honors in his school and had been accepted to the training program at the Ministry of Scientific Compliance. He looked into the audience and saw his classmates and various dignitaries from several of the ministries. This was a moment of great pride in his life. The image was the one he remembered. Turning to his right, he saw Raelynn watching with him.

"This was my graduation ceremony," Gabriel offered. "I received top honors in my class, which allowed me to get into the ministry training track program. It was a very big honor."

"Yes, you look very proud," Raelynn replied. "I find it strange watching this and not seeing families of the graduates sharing the event with them. It seems emptier that way to me."

"I had my classmates with me and there were important people from the government in attendance. It did not diminish the event to me in any way," Gabriel answered in a slightly defensive way.

"There are definitely differences in Xenon versus the capital. Let's look around the event and see if you can make any observations you didn't consciously make the first time around," Raelynn suggested.

Gabriel proceeded to walk around the auditorium. The more he looked at it, he realized how few people he actually knew. While he was on friendly terms with his classmates, he didn't have a close relationship with any of them. It was hard to get too close to them if he was actively competing against them.

He looked around briefly to see if Emily was present for this event. She was from a different school sector and hadn't met her until later in his life. He was slightly surprised to see a younger version of Xavier present in the back of the auditorium. It looked like he was talking to a younger version of the Scientific Compliance ministry head. Gabriel knew there were several government officials present, but at the time he didn't really know who these people were and what impact they would later have in his life. It was interesting to see them present at a monumental event in his life. Gabriel walked closer to them and was surprised that he could make out their conversation.

"As I was saying, sir," Xavier was speaking, "we have a few graduates here today that show some really good promise for our ministry. I have had my eye on one of them especially, who was originally born in the Xenon sector. I am hopeful he will provide help to our cause in that sector someday. You know with such primitive beliefs Xenon has relative to families, he should have an easier time up there than others we have tried to send. We will first have to get him through the training academy. There are a lot of people who do not succeed in passing that gate…"

Gabriel had a quick realization that they were likely talking about him. He wasn't sure if Raelynn heard any of that, so he decided to move along and see what else he could discover. Gabriel scanned the faces of those in attendance to see if there was anyone else that he may recognize. He was nearly through the crowd of faces when he did a double take on one doing a great job being inconspicuous. There was no mistaking it, it was his grandmother Isabella quietly looking on. She had a mixture of sadness blended with pride. Sadness knowing that she would likely never get to share her life with him, and pride in seeing him grow up and achieve some of his goals and dreams. He watched her take one final look at the stage and discretely exit the building.

Without thinking, Gabriel took off after her. Face recognition and tracking systems were not as advanced then as they were in current time, but there was still a lot of risks she must have taken in coming to the capital. If the wrong person stopped her and her identification was not properly authorized, she could have had a very unpleasant experience. Plus, how would she have been able to come here? It was nearly impossible to get a travel pass, and being the spouse of a convicted malcontent, her ability to get outside sector travel approval would have been difficult at best.

Isabella walked with confidence and purpose. From his trade craft class, he could not help but to complement her demeanor. She showed no suspicious behaviors and blended in well with the flow of people in a way to not attract any attention. She exhibited the behavior of someone out doing some casual shopping. She stopped at a couple of market booths and appeared as if she were considering getting some supplies that were common to buy. He noted that she didn't buy anything, as it would have created a record of her presence in this sector.

Isabella stopped at a store front, then decided to go inside. Gabriel followed just before the door closed behind her. Inside she greeted the proprietor, made a carefully worded statement, and was ushered into an area of the store that was not the common customer area. Some furniture was adjusted, and a rug was moved showing an opening in the floor, appearing to lead to a hidden opening of some sort. Gabriel followed her down and noticed the opening closed behind him. He saw a small glow up ahead and continued to follow her toward this light.

Isabella continued past the light and went to the wall, pressing on it to reveal a hidden passage, before she closed it behind her. She slipped through it as he quickly followed. Inside he saw a tube-like device that she seated herself inside of. Gabriel was just starting to walk up to join her when he saw a flash of colorful light and she was gone. The light that was barely illuminating the space he was in suddenly was gone, and he was in a pitch-black place without certainty of how to get out.

Gabriel's initial feeling was fear, but he quickly calmed himself as he allowed himself to consider the situation he was in. "Raelynn are you still near me?" he called out.

What he heard in reply was a slight echo of his unanswered question, followed by complete silence. She was no longer with him. He was trapped in a dark recess of the ground in a different time. Gabriel continued to calm himself in order to better contemplate his situation. He recalled Raelynn's instructions before he left, and let his mind focus on the time and place he had left before he came here. Focus didn't come quickly as he fought to remove the questions and implications of what he had seen from his mind. When he fully succeeded, he felt a sudden influx of warmth and slowly opened his eyes. He had returned to the lily field where he had left from.

"I am glad you made it back," Raelynn calmly stated. "I was worried there for a minute that you would forget the instructions I gave you before you went exploring."

"I thought you were going to stay with me?" Gabriel said with a slight accusatory tone.

"I tried to," she answered, "but you took off so fast, by the time I followed you out of the auditorium, you were out of sight. I can use my gift to follow you to the time and place, but if we get separated there, I won't exactly know where you are. My gift is not capable that way. I am sorry if that gave you a fright."

"Once I calmed myself and remembered your instructions, it worked out," Gabriel answered. "That was a very strange experience going back in time like that. It was one thing to remember my own memories but venturing out beyond them was something unlike I thought possible."

"You look troubled," Raelynn stated. "Did something give you a surprise?"

"Yes, my grandmother Isabella was there," Gabriel answered after a brief pause before explaining all he had seen and how he had got himself back.

"Does it surprise you that your grandmother would do all that she could to come to your big event?" Raelynn asked. "I would not be surprised if she was also at other big events in your life, from what I know about her. You are, after all, her only direct living family."

"I can see that she would want to attend, yes, but what I don't understand was the way she got there. And that it happened in color when she disappeared. Does that mean that she used the power of dreams to travel somehow?" Gabriel asked. "This opens so many questions. There are so many aspects of this that run counter to everything I have been taught, and I don't know what to make of it."

"We often see things we don't immediately understand when we travel back in time," Raelynn answered. "Time often brings clarity in the face of confusion. My advice is to reflect on this journey. You did well tonight. I think it is time for you to return. It would be good for you to see how tired your body is from this activity so you can better judge your limits in the future."

After this comment, Raelynn faded out and was gone. Gabriel had an initial temptation to go back to his graduation and try to gather more information on what happened, but quickly talked himself out of it. He remembered his promise to Raelynn to not go beyond his training on his own. Gabriel focused himself to return to the waking world, exiting the field of lilies.

∞ ∞ ∞

Gabriel awoke from his meditative trance and took in the surroundings around him. He was back where he started in his grandmother's house. He glanced at the time on his handheld and was surprised that just a few minutes had passed since he had entered the dream state. Yet at the same time, he had a vivid recollection of his dream state experience he had just encountered. But was it real? The ability to translocate objects had been enough evidence to convince him that some strange powers were real in his dream state, but it was a bridge too far for him to fully believe that he could traverse through time and interact with events that he didn't even experience within his own memories. But the detail and the memories were so real. How could he substantiate them? Asking his grandmother directly presented problems. Even if she admitted to the flow of events he observed in his dream, would that provide enough evidence for him to believe with certainty what he observed was real? What evidence could be found that could be independently verified?

The more he reflected on this, the more his thoughts kept coming back to the store that Isabella had entered before she transported herself out by whatever method she had used. If he could somehow find this store, he could determine if this secret passage was real, and from that, provide evidence of the truth of his dream.

Gabriel pulled up Oversite on his handheld and logged into the map view program. He pulled up the auditorium that he had his graduation in. Making sure his door was securely closed, he activated a feature in his handheld that projected the street view into a three-dimensional format that he could navigate through in a similar manner that he had in his dream. While the memory was still strong, he retraced the path Isabella had taken. Some of the landmarks had changed in the intervening years, but enough was similar to then that he was able to follow what he had experienced in his dream. He came up to the storefront she had entered. It looked more run-down than he had seen in the dream, but Gabriel had a strong belief that this was the same place she had entered. He tried to enter the store in the virtual reality simulation, but there did not appear to be data enough to support a simulation in the files for this. He would need another method to explore this location.

Gabriel exited the map program after noting the address and coordinates. He then did a data search on everything about this store. It looked like it was no longer in use as an active business. Per Oversite records, it may be abandoned, but you couldn't always tell. There was information of active business activity there in the time frame that he had graduated, so that didn't rule out anything he had seen in his dream.

He needed to somehow get inside that building. Gabriel decided to make an investigation request to his case officer, Quintin. He sent a report that he had overhead a reference to the name of this store and felt it was suspicious that someone in the Xenon sector would be aware of it. It was probably nothing, but he wanted to chase down a lead. He asked if he could get a team to check out the address and to observe by drone while providing tasking instructions if he wanted something to be looked at closer. This would probably create more questions on who his source was, but he could claim it happened without his handheld on him. He didn't think he could get by with that excuse very often, but thought his request was routine enough sounding that it was worth trying.

He was surprised that he received an almost immediate reply that a team could be deployed, and if now was a time he could observe. Gabriel messaged back that he was free for the rest of the evening and didn't expect to be disturbed, as his grandmother had gone to visit someone.

Thirty minutes later he had a three-dimensional projection displaying through a special set of glasses. He watched a live stream as the store was entered. There was no one present in it, and it appeared the storefront had not been used in some time. The team was carefully doing a normal sweep of the store, scanning it for contrabands. Gabriel steered the drone into the back room. He was surprised that the room layout so identically matched the image he had seen in his dream state. This was clearly the same place, and one that he had never visited in person in the woken state. Gabriel waited until the team checked the back room. When they were getting ready to leave it, he sent a message asking them to move a table and rug and check for anything suspicious under it.

After a brief delay, a hidden door was discovered with a ladder heading down to the darkness below. The team was suddenly showing some excitement. What was turning into a routine check without any significant findings, was quickly turning into something with far more potential. Gabriel waited until a temporary light source could be put in place in the passage going underground. Once it was illuminated, he could see the outline of a large underground cavern. It was clearly the same place. What he had dreamed was real. He requested that they look for any secondary hidden passages. This could be a way to travel unseen, or a place to hide people.

Gabriel heard the sound of the front door being opened to the house. His grandmother had likely just got back. He quickly messaged to his case handler that he had to exit quickly so he wouldn't be compromised. He asked to leave the stream of video available so he could look at it closer later and let him know whatever was learned. Exiting out of the virtual imaging, Gabriel quickly situated his things in case Isabella decided to say hello, while his mind struggled to process the implications of what he had learned.

CHAPTER 10

Gabriel woke earlier than he needed to, anxious about potential consequences to him from the store raid in the capital the night before. Beyond worrying about personal exposure, he was still troubled trying to deconstruct another real-world confirmation of his new-found dream gift.

Since he was up early, Gabriel decided he would spend the time logging into Oversite to determine what else happened on the raid and provide the cautionary advice to not make the raid stand out if it wasn't already too late. He first saw a congratulatory message from Xavier thanking him for the notice on the pamphlets and encouraging him to keep learning more things like this promising storefront that had a suspicious feel to it. Gabriel thanked him for the note and said he would do his best to not let the ministry down.

His next message from Quintin was the investigative summary and a link to where all the footage was stored. It did not appear they had found the secondary passage he had observed in the dream state. There was a lot of speculation what the cavern space was used for or had been used for. The active thinking was that it was used to shelter fugitives or people without travel permits. They didn't know if there was a network of underground passages, but several people could comfortably subsist in this area undetected for quite some time.

Quintin indicated he had installed passive surveillance in the underground entrance and on the building itself. Quintin also provided instructions to the inspection team to get out quickly, so it did not seem like more than a standard sweep. Quintin included other adjacent businesses in the inspection to not have it stand out. Gabriel felt thankful that Quintin already addressed his concerns and was on top of things.

This message calmed Gabriel down quite a bit and he decided he should go ahead and get dressed for work. He picked out a new outfit and proceeded to put it on. As he grabbed yesterday's pants and proceeded to transfer the contents of the pockets from that pair to the ones he was currently wearing, he was surprised to see a folded piece of paper in his hand. Gabriel opened it carefully to read what it said.

Gabriel,

Injustice is the currency of tyranny. The current regime deals in injustice, and those who see this are morally bound to oppose it. Your parents believed this as do others who endeavor to be patriots. If you have interest in joining the side of justice, wear a lily petal on your shirt after you get out of work and take your normal way home. Leave your handheld at home today.

No sooner had he finished reading it, it disappeared from his hand replaced by an ash type substance. It was like it had disintegrated shortly after he had touched it, but it could have also been a translocation trick made to appear that way. This could be the break he was waiting for, he thought excitedly.

Gabriel quickly logged back into Oversite and sent a very quick note that he was at risk of being unable to report for an unknown time giving a quick summary of the note he had read. Now running behind schedule for work, Gabriel quickly logged out of Oversite and set his handheld on the table. He went to where his lily plant was and tore off a couple of the petals and put them in his pocket. Quickly drinking down his breakfast shake, Gabriel walked out the door with a renewed sense of purpose in his step.

∞ ∞ ∞

Gabriel found himself distracted as he progressed through the work day. He had no idea what was in store tonight but couldn't shake the feeling of excitement as he looked forward to whatever would await him. It was possible that nothing would happen. It could just be a test to assess interest on his part to see if he would wear the lily petal. Either way, he would find out soon.

Gabriel decided to not stay real late today to allow whatever was going to happen to occur. He said his goodbyes to his aunt and uncle as he stepped out the door. Gabriel reached into his pocket and pulled out the lily petal, attaching it to his shirt button. Gabriel thought it would stay secure and be visible enough to be noticed.

Gabriel had an uneventful walk back along the path to his grandmother's house. When he was a little over half-way home, he felt a strange tingling sensation, and everything went completely dark. He wasn't in the dark in an unconscious way, it was just dark, like someone had suddenly extinguished the sun. Gabriel made some careful exploratory steps and quickly came to the realization that he was no longer on the path he had been walking on and was instead in a new unknown place. It was cooler than it had been a moment before, and there was a musty scent in the air. He also seemed to be in a fairly enclosed area, maybe the size of a small confinement cell. He could feel walls as he extended both arms, slowly reaching around until he found the other two walls without having to move very much distance. The space behind him had what could possibly be a door structure, which after trying to ascertain its form Gabriel did not think had a way to open it from the inside.

"Hello?" Gabriel called out. "Is there anybody out there?" Gabriel's volume increased some on his second question when he did not get an immediate reply on his first question.

Gabriel was pretty sure this had something to do with the note he had received, but still wasn't sure what was expected of him in this space. Gabriel decided that he would give a few minutes before trying to find a method of escape. Existing in full darkness was an odd sensation, but thanks to the dream traveling he had done recently, Gabriel did not have a sense of panic. The best he came up with while brainstorming ways out was to enter the dream state and seek Raelynn's advice on a technique on getting out of the place if it came to it. This was probably wishful thinking since he couldn't see and didn't have a full lily plant with him, but it provided a rationale for staying calm none-the-less.

It seemed a few minutes had gone by when he heard the faint sound of someone walking in the distance, slowly growing louder. The sound seemed to be coming from what could be the door structure.

"Hello? Is someone out there?" Gabriel called out once again.

"Sorry, it took me a few minutes to get to you. Just hold on a few minutes longer," an unknown voice answered. "I need to scan you to make sure you can be safely released to meet with those who reached out to you. You don't have anything electronic with you, do you?"

"No, I left my handheld at home like I was asked." Gabriel replied. "I am not aware of anything else but am very curious if you find something. I have heard rumors that the government is getting really creative with surveillance equipment. But I don't think I have anything on me to answer your question."

"No implants either?" the voice asked. "I don't want to give you a health problem when I give you an EMP burst. Sometimes those who have been imprisoned are implanted on release. Some will destroy the host if they are disabled."

"Now you are making me nervous," Gabriel replied. "I have been in confinement, but due to the nature of my infraction, it wasn't on the list to warrant a tracker implant. At least that is what I was told. Not saying they didn't give me one without telling me. Do you have a way to check that?"

"We can detect most models, but if there are some new models we haven't discovered yet, I can't guarantee that we will find them." He replied. "Sounds like it is pretty low risk of you having one. Either way, I will do the full spectrum scan before triggering the EMP burst. If you want to back out now, it isn't too late, but once you come through that door, it will get progressively harder to leave."

"I'll admit I am nervous, but go ahead and do your scanning and burst," Gabriel said. Do I need to do anything to help? Anything that gets me out of the dark faster would be most welcome."

"Oh, I didn't leave the light turned on? Sorry about that. I can fix that right now," the person replied.

Gabriel quickly closed, then squinted his eyes as a dim light turned on. It wasn't very bright, but it was much better than being in complete darkness. He had surmised the room layout pretty well. He saw the door opening, but there was not an obvious way to open it from the inside. It had a high ceiling, but he was fully enclosed. He thought the walls were rock, like you would find in a cave or cavern. The walls were lined with a metallic mesh, likely copper. He had heard of this technology but had not before seen it employed. It was used to prevent wireless signals from permeating the space. Since he had been told he was about to be scanned, this was likely an entry point that a visitor could be safely scanned and rendered a non-risk before being released to whatever was beyond the door.

Gabriel heard a series of strange beeping noises coming from above him. There was some sort of sensor sticking down from the ceiling completing the scan process. This went on for a few minutes before it stopped. It then switched to a beeping cadence followed by a loud bang type sound. Thankfully, he didn't fall over dead, which made him even more glad the ministry had decided to not implant him ahead of this mission. That would have been a bad outcome. Either he would be dead or would have had to turn back on his first good lead. Gabriel's thoughts were interrupted by a clicking sound coming from what he believed was the door.

The light on the other side of the door was not much brighter than what was illuminating the inside of the room he was in. He was a bit surprised to find the person there to greet him wearing a mask complete with a visible speaker. This indicated there was likely a voice modulator that could be used to pitch a voice differently than the way the person spoke it. He, assuming it was a he, was also wearing a loose-fitting outfit that covered the full length of the person's body and didn't give away many body features at all.

"I apologize for my appearance," the person stated. "We take great steps to keep our membership on a need to know basis. This protects each and every one of us from accidentally revealing key parts of the organization. The local governing committee will know of your identity as will I, who will be your main contact. Beyond that, no one else in the organization will know, unless it is mission critical that it is revealed.

Even then, you will have approval rights to reveal yourself to others or not participate in the assigned mission."

Gabriel couldn't help but noticing a mask and robe hanging up outside the door.

"Is that for me to wear?" Gabriel asked. "And what shall I refer to you as? Given the precautions, I assume your real name is not used, but do you have something to address you by?"

"So many questions which shall be addressed," the masked person answered. "Yes, I would recommend you develop a habit of putting this on. There isn't anyone here currently who is not authorized for your identity, but it is a good practice to follow from the start. Our rule here is that you select a voice modulation and always use that setting. It makes it easier to recognize someone when they are in disguise. Those that have been already assigned are disabled on your modulator, so don't worry about taking someone else's voice. If you turn that dial right there, you can see the choices until you find the one you like. Regarding your second question, we usually refer to each other by the title of our role. My role is teacher, so you may call me Teacher."

"What am I to be called?" Gabriel asked after nodding to denote comprehension.

"For now, you will be referred to as Initiate. In time, that title may change," Teacher answered.

Gabriel nodded his acknowledgement as he worked to figure out the settings on the voice modulator. Gabriel experimented with several options before selecting one that did not annoy his hearing but was markedly different from his usual voice.

"I think I would like to choose this one," Gabriel said.

"Very well, I will get you configured for that code," Teacher replied. "Once I sync that to the system, any mask may be used. The mask will learn your voiceprint and automatically modulate to this voice. If a non-configured person tries to use a mask and speaks, it will alarm and will identify the masked person as an intruder. And you must speak to activate the mask. We don't have much in the way of technology down here, but this is a necessary piece of it. If you come to a different location, you will need to be setup for a voice modulation there as well.

We only have a small local network here, and other places do not have anything that could be risked connecting or be infiltrated by a government system. We are pretty low technology here, but I think you will find we make do just fine."

Gabriel took a moment to process what he had been told. This indicated there were multiple cells associated with whatever organization this place represented. They were definitely trying to stay off the grid and seemed to project some hostility toward the government. Beyond that, he really hadn't learned anything actionable. But he was here, and it was a very promising development relative to his assignment from the ministry.

"The note seeking me out didn't have much in the way of details on it," Gabriel offered. "I have a lot of questions. I really am interested in what my parents were involved in and I have a lot of frustration with some of the actions the government has taken. But what is the purpose of this place, this organization and how do I fit in that plan? Will I get to resume my life in Deerbarrow or are you expecting me to live here for the foreseeable future?"

Teacher made a slight chuckling sound through his mask.

"Patience, Initiate," Teacher gently corrected. "Your questions will be answered to your satisfaction. You are not expected back at work until the start of the new week, so you have a couple days in which you will not be noticed missing. We left a note on your behalf to your grandmother that you will be away for a couple of days, so that should assuage the main concern that may escalate your absence. The rest of your questions will be explored as you meet the committee to determine your commitment and willingness to serve this organization. If you fail the test, then you will leave with questions, but no real harm to your person, provided you are not hostile to our cause. More on that later. Follow me, and we can get this process started."

CHAPTER 11

Quintin reviewed the communication that Gabriel had sent him. It was good news that Gabriel had been contacted by a subversive element. This could be the break that everyone hoped for. He didn't like how short of notice he had received and needed to make a call very quickly on if he was going to deploy extra surveillance. Xavier had asked to be informed on any significant developments, so he decided he would try to get ahold of him quickly this morning to make sure that he would make the right choices on how to handle this.

Quintin stepped out to ask his assistant to see if he could be worked into Xavier schedule, and was surprised to see Xavier walking up to his office.

"Good morning, sir," Quintin said. "I was just about to try to get some time with you."

"I am glad you are on top of it," Xavier answered as he walked into the more secure confines of Quintin's office. "I just saw Gabriel's latest report and think we need to discuss our surveillance options. This is something we definitely don't want to mess up. It could be the break we have been waiting for."

"I agree," Quintin replied. "I take it you have a preferred option? With all the field assignments you have had in your career, I would very much welcome any direction you wanted to provide on this."

Quintin wasn't sure he wanted this level of oversight and micromanagement, but having Xavier make some of the decisions should provide some protection if anything went badly. Not that it was a guarantee that Xavier would remember that he made them, but he at least had a reputation in the ministry of being someone who treated subordinates fairly and didn't sacrifice them in order to advance his own career.

Xavier began to recite the facts as he understood them, asking Quintin to add or correct any that Xavier had not fully stated correctly. Unsurprisingly, he had the full picture as had been reported, and there was very little that Quintin felt he could offer. It was clear that Xavier was not just providing cursory oversight. He was in all the details and might as well have been running the operation.

"I think we need to do something to track his walk home from work," Xavier stated. "If this meeting goes badly, this may be the last we ever see Gabriel and having a clue where he disappeared could be all that we have to show for it."

"I agree, sir," Quintin replied, not wanting to give anything resembling objection. "Gabriel was concerned that active tracking of him would risk compromising him, and I think he has a valid concern."

"We suspect they have scanners who can detect active surveillance," Xavier offered. "However, it we keep sufficient distance I think we can risk using some miniature drones. Do you agree?"

"It is a risk worth taking, I agree," Quintin replied. "I will offset their following distance significantly to hopefully be outside of local scanner ranges. Maybe put one drone ahead of his path and one behind?"

"Make it so," Xavier ordered.

Quintin quickly pulled up the drone tasking software on his workstation and programmed the orders as had been agreed.

"It is done, sir," Quintin stated. "I will let you know right away of any developments.

"Any developments," Xavier said emphasizing the word any before abruptly exiting Quintin's office.

As the day passed, there didn't seem to be anything amiss or out of the ordinary. Quintin kept a passive eye on the drone footage even though it had parameters setup to notify him should anything of significance occur. Quintin didn't think whatever was going to happen would happen at Gabriel's work unless people there were involved. Either way, he kept the two feeds up throughout the day.

He noticed Gabriel had left a bit earlier than he normally did, but it wasn't out of the ordinary. It was different watching him through the live feed versus trying to use his handheld to piece together his day. Gabriel was halfway home, and nothing had occurred yet and there didn't appear to be anything abnormal on the path he was on. Quintin looked away for a brief moment to take a drink of water. When he turned back, Gabriel was gone. The drone viewing system started beeping a warning that the notification parameters had been met and attention was needed. Quintin quickly backed up the footage until he saw Gabriel in his feed. Then slowly stepping it forward, frame by frame, until suddenly Gabriel was no longer there. One frame he was present and the next he was not.

Quintin had an immediate sinking feeling in his stomach. Had he compromised Gabriel? Were the drones compromised and somehow circumvented? This looked so similar to what he had seen on the escape footage where people were escaping on their way to confinement. Quintin quickly tasked the drones to do a wider sweep for anything that was a lifeform, to see if he could reacquire Gabriel. Once they reached a radius of a full kilometer, he reluctantly called off the sweep and left the drones monitoring the path where he had been before he had disappeared. Not feeling really confident, Quintin nervously picked up his messaging console and proceeded to contact Xavier with the news.

∞ ∞ ∞

Gabriel followed the person named Teacher through a poorly lit maze of what appeared to be an underground passage. The robe he was wearing offset the cool temperature in these passages. There was no obvious signage marking the way to go, and there were multiple choices of direction available in this underground labyrinth. About ten minutes into the walk, Gabriel thought the chances were very poor that he could make his way back to his starting point without a guide. Teacher came to a stop and made some movements that his body obscured. He then saw a door open into the wall, revealing another passage. Gabriel thought this must be a hidden passage of some sort should someone discover this area by accident or by intention. Gabriel followed Teacher through the opening before it was pulled shut behind him revealing another set of passages.

"Not much further," Teacher offered as he continued ahead beckoning Gabriel to follow.

After a minute or two more of walking, they approached another door that opened to reveal a small wooden table and chair in the middle of an otherwise unremarkable room. It had no windows in it. There appeared to be water in a pitcher and a cup to drink from set out. There were also some metallic looking utensils of some sort on the table. Looking around the room with a more detailed glance, he saw what was likely a few cameras setup with speakers.

"I apologize for asking," Teacher said, "but I have been instructed to ask for you to remove your mask, robe and to empty yourself of anything you may be carrying such as your bag or anything you may have in your pockets."

Gabriel was not sure the purpose this served. Since he had come this far, he wasn't going to make a big deal of something this minor, even if it did seem like an intrusion. Gabriel complied by taking his carrying bag and setting his shake mix kit and container inside it. He also removed the small multipurpose knife he now carried, which he had been finding increasingly useful working on the farm. Turning his pockets inside out, he found the remnants of the lily petal he had brought. The one he had worn on his walk seemed to have fallen off. He started to place the petal in the bag and was told that he was to keep that. Gabriel shrugged and put it back into his pocket.

"I am sorry to ask, but I need the necklace you are wearing also," Teacher interjected.

This caused a pained expression on Gabriel's face. Reluctantly he reached to unclasp it. He opened the pendant and took a time-consuming look at an image there which was he and Emily together. Sighing, he placed it inside of the bag.

"I think that is everything I am carrying unless you need my clothing also?" Gabriel asked with a tone of restrained anger in his voice.

"No," Teacher said. "I think what you have given up meets the instructions I was given." I will see this is returned to you later on. I need to leave you here now so you can interact with the committee. Good luck to you."

Gabriel wasn't sure why he was being wished luck but figured something was about to happen that was important. Gabriel redirected his energy to focusing himself for what was to come. He could not afford to be mentally distracted if he was going to earn the trust of whatever this meeting represented.

Teacher exited the room and Gabriel could hear the faint sounds of the door latching behind him. He was pretty sure that he did not have a way to open it if he wanted to escape. He was for all purposes a prisoner here until he could pass whatever test they presented to him. As he sat here contemplating his newfound captivity, the light level in the room began to drop. It faded down slowly until he could barely see an outline of his hand when he put it near his face. It wasn't as dark as it was right before he was scanned, but it was pretty close.

Minutes went by, seemingly extending into a lot more. He was not sure. Time passes strangely in the dark with nothing to note the passing of day. There was no technology to show the time. There was just quiet and emptiness in the dark. Gabriel thought he had advanced in his meditation skills, but this was an eerie disquiet, sitting silent in his thoughts with no end in sight. But there must be a purpose to this. Gabriel was tempted to try to enter the dream state but was afraid of the implications of doing that. He would hold out for a while longer before trying to make sense of what was going on that way.

"Who are you?" a commanding voice broke into his thoughts, enveloping the room with sound.

"I am Gabriel Carasa," Gabriel answered after a short pause.

Minutes passed without a reply. Gabriel was not sure why they asked him what they must already know, but nevertheless, he would play along.

"Who are you?" The voice repeated again breaking the silence of the room.

"I am Gabriel Carasa," Gabriel answered wondering if they were having technical difficulties with the microphone in the room. "Can you hear me?"

"Your words are heard but your meaning is unknown. Who are you?" the voice asked a third time.

Gabriel thought for a moment. He must be saying something wrong. They didn't want his name. They wanted something else. Did they want some deep philosophical answer of the essence of who he was? For some reason, he didn't think they were looking for that. Then the proper response came to him.

"I am Initiate," Gabriel answered.

"And so, you came into the world with nothing, so shall you come before the Order with nothing." The voice answered. "First you were of your parents who were of this Order, and now the Order must judge if you are worthy of new life to be reborn. Drink the water of cleansing."

Gabriel squinted in the dark, feeling for the pitcher and cup for the water. He remembered the cup was not filled, so he did his best to pour water into it. Taking the cup to his mouth, he drank. The water was unlike any he had tasted before. It was almost as if he was drinking a taste of life. It was refreshing and quenched a thirst he didn't realize he had. Gabriel drank the cup of water more quickly than he expected, then waited. Some amount of time passed again before the voice spoke.

"You have been cleansed. But are you nourished? The trials are many. Do you have the strength needed to sustain yourself through them? You do not. Eat the meal of nourishment, so you may survive the trials ahead."

Gabriel was confused what he should eat. He didn't recall seeing any shake mix, and he had given his up to Teacher. He then started to smell something he didn't recognize. It wasn't a bad smell but was one he did not know that stimulated his senses. He followed the smell and determined that a new circular object had appeared between the metallic utensils he hadn't recognized. The circular object had some items on it that appeared to be the source of the new smells. One of the objects he recognized from the crops that were grown on the farm. He had heard of people eating unprocessed food, but it was not a lawful act. This wasn't the health formulated meal that he had eaten his entire life. It was something different. He didn't feel right trying to eat it, but his mission required he infiltrate the resistance. Could it be they ate unprocessed food? That was a new thought. But no, he needed to figure out a way to pass this test. He noticed the light level had increased slightly and could now better make out what had been placed before him. It occurred to him that the metallic utensils were probably eating implements, so he decided to try to use them in order to consume the food. One looked capable of stabbing items, so he used it to stick into a long orange colored item and picked it up. He carefully brought it to his mouth and bit off a piece of it.

It was unlike anything he had experienced before. The meal shakes had flavors to them but grew monotonous. But this bite he had taken, lit his senses up. He chewed tentatively at first, similar to how he would chew a piece of gum which was a popular item for kids to consume. He noticed the item slowly get smaller in his mouth and he decided to swallow. Slowly, he tried another item in front of him and was surprised with its pleasantly unique taste. He worked his way through the many choices, until he had consumed them all. His body and stomach felt satisfied and wanting for nothing. He was full.

"You came with defect and were empty. But now you are cleansed and full. Revel in the feeling of life. Live with joy. Strive for justice. And hope for peace. Be one in the embrace of the Order of the Lily. You are alone no longer but are now part of an ancient order. One grounded in faith, in righteousness, and the love of life."

The words, Order of the Lily, were not what Gabriel was expecting to hear. All the work that Raelynn had done with him was focused on the Way of the Lily. Was it the same thing? Maybe it was a militant sect within this religion? It was all equally punished under the law, but was it tied together? Was this a part of the resistance movement? At the same time, the ceremony or test was very powerful. His senses were keenly awakened, more than he had ever experienced in his lifetime. Taste and smell had been stimulated in ways he did not know possible. His mind racing was interrupted again by the mystery voice.

"We offer you fellowship and purpose. What gifts do you bring that may serve the Order? Is your heart set with a noble purpose? Will you give up of yourself to serve others?"

Gabriel was unsure of the expected response. They had taken all he had on him except the lily petal when he came into the room. Was there a significance to that? There were so many answers he could give, and he wasn't sure what the right one was or if there was a clearly wrong one. Gabriel decided to take a chance to try to get to the answer.

"Is my heart set to a noble purpose?" Gabriel asked. "I hope it is. I want justice in the world. Oppression and injustice demand to be opposed. The person who was arrested for referencing a religious figure by accident should not lose her life. That is wrong and it should be stopped. Will I give up of myself to serve others? I will do my best. I have tried to do for others, but I freely admit I was not raised to value this. I did it for Emily before she died, I would like to think. But for others I will work to do better. I can promise to pursue growth in this, but I will need help to stay on the right path. As for gifts? All I brought in here that I was allowed to keep was this lily petal. I gladly offer it to the Order as well as use of the dream gifts it represents, as basic as they currently are. Beyond that, I am not sure what other gifts I have that can be offered. If I have something else you need, please ask it of me."

"The gifts you freely offer are acceptable and will be called on for the betterment of humanity and for the benefit of the Order," the voice answered after a long pause. "Since you claim to have gifts of dreaming, you will need to be tested so we can assess your current usefulness. We would prefer to not know who your instructor is in dreams, but we would like to know when you attain any new level of skill. The one who you know as Teacher will assess what you know. Arise, you are no longer called Initiate. You are now called Novice. As you complete certain tasks you may rise in title. Teacher will explain all this to you and answer any questions you may have that he is permitted to tell someone with the name of Novice. But to your question of nobility of purpose, do not fear, that woman will not die at the hand of her accusers. As have we with others before her, we will see her freed. With your help, we will continue to make right those who have experienced injustice and pursue a world where one's faith, beliefs, and words do not condemn them, but instead one is judged on their actions and their humanity."

With that, the lights were turned back on in the room to a normally visible level, and he heard a click of the door indicating Teacher was likely coming to get him. Gabriel's mind was racing. It was clear he had participated in some sort of religious rite or initiation. He also was told that this resistance group was responsible for freeing those accused of taking religious actions. Gabriel wondered if others had been escaping. He made a mental note to ask Quintin about this. It may be important to areas he didn't have a lot of knowledge about.

"Congratulations!" Teacher stated. "I have been informed you have been elevated from Initiate to Novice. Not everyone who comes named as Initiate leaves with a new title. You must have made a good impression on the committee. Especially with your past being what it is, I was surprised they accepted you so quickly."

"This is all moving so fast to me," Gabriel said. "I am not really sure what just happened. It was like I knew what I was supposed to say but I don't know where I got the inspiration to answer as I did. I want to help, but I am not sure how I am supposed to do that."

"Right now, you require extensive training before you can be of use to the Order in a more active capacity." Teacher explained. "I am told you have some talents in dreams. That will be very helpful, and I need for you to continue to learn from the person who is currently teaching you. I will help you learn other skills we will need of you. I will also teach you the history of our Order, and more importantly its teachings. You have a heart for doing what is right, but you lack a map on how to get there. This we must remedy, and it will take time. And unfortunately, due to the secrecy we are forced to live under, the learning must be mostly done here which presents difficulties."

"Can any of this instruction be completed in the dream state? I get a lot of my current training this way." Gabriel offered.

"Unfortunately, I do not have the gift to be able to do that," Teacher said. If you grow strong enough in your gifts to be able to enter my dreams then maybe it could be done, but very few people are gifted in that way. For now, we will target time on weekends. I have the ability to translocate, so I can manage to get you here if we setup a schedule for your training. And besides, senses are diminished in the dream state, and part of your training you need to experience in a woken state. No, you will need to train here. I am thinking we can get you started now and based on how that goes, maybe again in a couple of weeks. I will need you to wear a lily petal again to say you are still able to come, and we can use that as a signal to meet. Also, I think progressing your training in dreams is really important also, and I do not want to take away from that by having you here too frequently."

"I am sure we can work all that out," Gabriel said. "I am anxious to get started on this and get some questions answered."

Teacher chuckled. "You are very goal oriented, aren't you? Very well, follow me. We have a bit more spacious area just down this way that will make a much better place to learn. I have your things there including that necklace you seemed to value. Also, you can get back into your mask and put on this new robe style that matches your new name. You need to get into that habit in case someone unexpected stops by."

CHAPTER 12

$\mathcal{G}$abriel found himself on the walking path to his grandmother's house. It was very strange being in one place one moment then just appearing in a different place the next. Moving an inanimate object was one thing, but to move a person like this was something that made him squeamish.

There was a lot to think about from his recent experience. Teacher had continued to interact with him, but it seemed like most of his time was spent reading books related to the Order somehow. These texts focused on the tenants of justice, service, faith, joy, love and self-sacrifice. Gabriel was expecting to be given a lot of information about the history of the dream gift and some of the more noticeable traits of its application. When he asked Teacher about this, he was told that there were important building blocks that must be set in the proper sequence. If you try to build a structure without first securing the foundation, the structure would be feeble and likely fail in its purpose. In the same way, unless he could first establish a strong moral and righteous foundation in his life, he could not expect to gain the full intended benefit of the other gifts.

Gabriel couldn't help to notice that these tenants deviated some from the government primary stated tenants of science and reason. Sure, the government claimed to support justice and service, but the reality was that justice was secondary to the societal engineering goals that had been established by key science thinkers. Protecting the rights of an individual were secondary to the overall goal of society. If he looked at this objectively, doing right by an individual did not matter if it conflicted with something society as a whole required. His whole assignment in Xenon wasn't about justice. It was about control. Control of a culture protective of beliefs different than the central goals of those in power. And relative to service, it was about service to the goals of the collective, not to those who would benefit from help. Once you were not useful to society, your time was largely up, and the government would stop providing resources to sustain an unproductive citizen. But the teachings Gabriel was studying emphasized providing for those who were unable to provide for themselves. Building others up when their life situation had them down. This was a revolutionary concept, one that would completely undermine the framework coming from the capital if it could take hold and grow.

Faith was clearly the polar opposite to reason. Believing without having a proven scientific basis for said beliefs was the type of nonsense that caused the Scientific Reformation to begin with. Those who believed in myths got in the way of progress and were put down when they became disruptive. But this Order valued faith. He hadn't got very much time to study what specifically they meant by valuing it, but it was one of the core beliefs he was supposed to be grounded in. It was clear they had their own belief set, but they also supported the right of others to believe differently. The key was the freedom to choose to believe in the way they wanted to, and not have it dictated by others. Gabriel could see the potential harm with an unfettered allowance to believe in any crazy idea you wanted to.

And then there were joy and love. Joy seemed to be about getting the full measure of enjoyment out of your life – About experiencing all your senses, and not suppressing them due to some arbitrary rule. You didn't want your experience to come at the cost of another, but things like taste and eating unprocessed food seemed to fall into this category. Laughing, playing, and unproductive leisure were valued to provide the fullness of life and to provide balance. From the government's viewpoint, many of these activities were wasteful and caused choices that did not make good use of the planet's resources.

Love seemed to be the most foreign of all. Gabriel thought he had experienced love in his life but was starting to have doubts he had fully met the standard he was studying. He grieved for Emily, but why? Was it because of what he no longer had, or because of what he could no longer give? And what about the attitude toward children and family? To love someone solely because you contributed to their genetics was a concept that Gabriel was still struggling to understand. And he hadn't even gotten to self-sacrifice yet.

All these thoughts were swirling in Gabriel's head. What he needed to do though was focus on what he would report to the ministry. He needed to explain his disappearance and reappearance in a way that didn't expose his knowledge of the dream gift he had been developing. He did now have actionable intelligence on plans to help that controversial prisoner escape. Granted, he didn't know the when and where but knowing it was planned was significant. And now he needed to avoid his handheld even more with the guidance he was given. Staying connected with the ministry was going to be more difficult.

Gabriel approached his grandmother's house. She didn't appear to be home, for which he was grateful. Gabriel went to his room, communicated the thoughts to his case officer then completed his required meditation session. The meditation time was preferred to be done with others, but it was allowed to do by yourself if it didn't happen all the time. Gabriel was feeling exhausted and found himself unable to focus as his thoughts swirled around in his head from the past two days. He considered reaching out in the dream state to Raelynn, but he didn't think he could focus himself if he wanted to. He was spent, and shortly after completing the minimum of meditation requirements, drifted off into a deep and dreamless sleep.

∞ ∞ ∞

Joseph Lazerof cleared security as he made his way to the morning assembly point. You would think that security would recognize him by now and not waste as much of his time as they did today, but that is what you get when underqualified people get selected for menial posts. If it wasn't for all the capital personnel that were around the past few days, he would have given them a piece of his mind. But that could wait until all the visitors left. Revenge was something best performed by the patient. Joseph had taken careful note of who had given him a hard time. In a few days he would report him for a serious breach of protocol.

Yeah, that would be a fitting response for the failure to recognize his importance in the containment facility.

He was important here after all. Not everyone was allowed direct interaction with the prisoners who were due to be executed. These were some of the scum of society who couldn't follow the basic laws around avoiding religions. But he got to show them by watching over their final misery and then taking them to be ended in a room that gassed them until they died. Yeah, it took an important person to do that.

Joseph looked at the crowd gathered around the assembly area. It looked like someone important was here today. Wanting to make a good impression, Joseph checked his uniform and appearance, making a few adjustments to improve his look. You never know when an opportunity to impress someone could get you a better posting. Not that his current posting was bad being as important as he was, but maybe he could do something with a bigger credit allowance somewhere else if he was noticed.

"Good morning," a voice announced. "I am Commander Wilcox and I want to give an update on today's plans before the morning meditation time."

The voice was loud, confident and belonged to someone who was likely from the capital based on his accent and demeanor. Seeing the markings on his uniform, he was by far the highest-ranking person present at the facility.

"We have a high-risk prisoner who was transported in by flight transport three days back," Wilcox continued. "Since this is her second offense, she has been tried and deemed to be irrecoverable in her value to society. As such, her sentence is scheduled to be carried out per the law no sooner than twelve hours from the time of her conviction. Since this trial occurred a few hours ago, we plan to execute her eight hours from now. We have intelligence that suggests a resistance group may take some action to try to free her before justice is administered."

Joseph thought it was ridiculous that someone could get past all the security here, but they seemed worried about it so he decided he could play along.

"In response," Wilcox continued, "we have taken additional precautions to ensure that the criterion of the law is successfully carried out. You will be issued weapons today to carry in addition to your normal defense mechanisms. Any attempt to attack the security here or rescue the prisoner is to be met with deadly force. We cannot allow anything to get in the way of following our duty to the law. Your section leader will have your specific instructions following meditation. Any questions?"

Seeing none, he walked away and let the person leading meditation begin reading the chosen text for the day. The meditation topic was the same drivel it always was around saving energy and following the ways of science, not that he was prepared to state that opinion out loud. That would be a fast track to be a prisoner here.

"Anything else I am supposed to do?" Joseph asked his section leader as soon as meditation was completed.

"Pretty standard routine for your placement, other than the deadly force orders," he answered. "You will need to check-out a weapon to carry like the rest of the section."

"Understood, sir," Joseph replied. "I'll go get my weapon and relieve my partner now."

"Go ahead," his section leader answered. "And expect a lot of radio status checks. By the book on this one, a lot of eyes watching and listening both here and far away."

Joseph did his best to not roll his eyes as he walked to the weapon area to get a weapon. He was relieved that he was going to be able to do his normal role with the prisoner when securing for justice. The extra agents were likely going to be covering the outer perimeter which left his normal team to do their regular roles. At least he was familiar with his job and would not make a fool of himself doing something he hadn't practiced very much. And he was very good at his regular job.

Joseph moved to his assigned position and formally relieved the outgoing guard who had the post he was to take over. Joseph wasn't accustomed to handling the extra weaponry he had on his person today. Sure, he had completed his annual qualification on it, but weapons were not typically used within the prisoner perimeter, in case a prisoner got their hands on one. But the normal prison population was isolated today away from this high-profile prisoner. She really didn't seem like much of a physical threat to make a violent act.

The weapon execution orders were unusual. Joseph didn't see much difference between using his weapon and the chamber that used a gaseous termination substance. The weapon would likely be more painful during the act, he considered. The ministry didn't usually revel in inducing pain in its prisoners, especially once a sentence had been issued. It was more like apathetic indifference. Someone who they needed to extract information from may be another story but removing someone who no longer had value to society was typically done in a relatively painless manner, provided he didn't rough them up too much before punishment was administered.

"You ready to die?" Joseph asked with a smirk on his face as he saw the prisoner in her cell.

The prisoner was in some sort of meditative state. He thought he heard her voice quietly conversing in some sort of religious devotion. Either way, she didn't answer his question.

"Too good to talk, eh?" Joseph challenged. "Don't worry, you still get to die."

He probably should have struck her for the religious activity and ignoring him but all that would probably do today was create some unwanted commotion. Today he needed to look competent in his job in case he made a good impression. Not everyone approved when he pushed the prisoners around. He really wanted to ask her what made her so important, but with all the cameras and extra monitoring, he figured nothing but bad could come from asking questions he wasn't briefed on already.

"Status check for Lazerof," came a status request just minutes after he had relieved the other guard.

"All clear here, sir, just like it was five minutes ago," Joseph replied not bothering to mask the annoyance in his voice.

"Understood. Stay vigilant," came the reply on the radio.

After making a quick weapon check, he paced a few steps down the corridor. Pausing suddenly, he thought he heard a sound that was not the typical sounds coming from this area of the prison. It may be one of the visiting agents doing a physical check on him, but he tensed up and readied his weapon in case this represented a real threat that he was instructed to look for. He looked past the corner of the hallway and found nothing there.

Relaxing slightly, he turned and found himself face to face with a person dressed in a similar style uniform to his own, but it was not someone he recognized. He thought he knew all the people who worked here, but it was possible that someone had started recently that he was not aware of. Also, he was not carrying the newly issued weapons which Joseph found very suspicious.

"Identify yourself!" Joseph called out while he lifted his weapon up to challenge the other person until his bona fides could be established.

"Guard first order, Smith, doing standard security check as ordered!" the voice confidently replied.

"Do not move or I will fire," Joseph commanded. "I don't know you. I need to confirm your identity with my section lead."

"I just transferred in," Smith replied.

"I didn't see any communication," Joseph answered with growing suspicion. "And where is your weapon?"

"I am not qualified on it yet," Smith answered.

"Likely excuse," Joseph muttered. "Section lead, I have an unexpected agent calling himself Smith. Please confirm identity or I will fire on him."

The stupid radio wasn't working, Joseph concluded after not getting a response. The person saying he was Smith stood there patiently not exhibiting anything resembling threatening behavior. Joseph suddenly felt a woozy sensation. Before he could sound the alarm, his world went dark.

Joseph's eyes opened. He found himself without his weapons, occupying one of the cells in his section. He had no idea how he had gotten in here. In a panic, he looked out of the cell, and to his chagrin, found the prisoner was missing. Her cell still appeared to be closed and locked, but it was empty. Security rules had kept him without a means to open the cell up, so someone else must have helped with that. He called out loudly but there was no answer. Joseph checked and surprisingly found his radio was still on his person. He pressed the call button, and this time he did not experience interference.

"Lazerof to section head," he called out.

"Section head here," the voice replied after a brief pause.

"We have a code five in the prisoner wing," Joseph announced. "I appear to have been drugged or something and the prisoner is not in her cell. I have been locked in an adjacent cell and am unable to investigate further. Please advise."

"Your situation is understood," his section leader responded testily. "We are already busy searching the complex for places the prisoner may have gone. Don't expect to be let out anytime soon. I have a feeling that you will happy to just occupy that cell by the time the investigation is done."

Joseph cringed at the last comment. So much for impressing the visitors. He couldn't wait to find out who had screwed up his opportunity. They could be added to his revenge list.

∞ ∞ ∞

Quintin watched the pandemonium unfold in Xavier's office on the big display. One moment they had the prisoner in custody and the next one they didn't. There was a lot to try to understand relative to what had happened. There was clearly a security perimeter setup and it was being run by one of the top officers they had in the ministry specializing in this type of operation. But the perimeter was penetrated, and even with all the cameras setup and other technology in play, it wasn't immediately clear how the resistance had managed to break through and extract the prisoner.

Gabriel's intelligence warning had been accurate. There was a clear pattern emerging where there was some sort of technology in use that scrambled the visual feeds to hide the escape of prisoners. The guard who reported the prisoner missing reported a similar drugged sensation that Gabriel had. Quintin made a request that one of the monitors go back and replay the guard footage. He wanted to see the exact sequence of the disappearance.

Quintin, and now others in Xavier's office, watched as the guard named Lazerof made his way through his rounds. You could hear the check-in with his area leader. Then he saw the emergence of another person dressed as a guard. Lazerof had pointed his weapon and asked for identification. He tried to confirm identity with his section lead, but his communicator did not appear to be working. Then someone came up behind him and injected him with something that caused him to drop to the ground nearly instantly. They removed his weapon and locked him in a previously open spare cell. Following this, they went to the cell the prisoner was at. Looking around where a very full view of the camera could make out the person's features, he spoke.

"While you would execute an innocent with impunity, we now show mercy to one who has killed many. We seek freedom. Freedom to practice our faith peacefully, freedom to exist, and freedom to raise our families free of ministry overreach. Overreach whose intent is to corrupt our young minds to be mindless puppets of a tyrannical system whose very foundation is built on lies."

With that, a curtain like barrier was raised and when it fell to the ground, both the infiltrators and the prisoner were gone.

"Oversite," Quintin commanded replaying the video feed right before the curtain went up, "identify attackers."

Quintin's console processed for a few moments then put up personal profiles of the two attackers on the screen. These were two escapees from prior *Adherence to Myths Act* transports. Not only were they escaping but they were coming back to break out others. This news was not going be received well in the ministry.

Xavier appeared to be communicating with someone of importance based on the deferential tone he was using. The discussion appeared to be growing more and more animated with Xavier appearing to be advising against a course of action. At the end, Quintin heard Xavier say, "Yes, Minister. I understand. I will issue the orders immediately."

Xavier had a conflicted expression on his face as he addressed those in his office.

"The ministry has decided it is time to send a strong message to the sectors due to escapes of those in violation of the *Adherence to Myths*

Act," Xavier stated with a forcibly neutral expression on his face. "Our attempts to be reasonable have been met with rebellion. This can occur no longer, and we will respond with more strength than ever before. Our job will become more difficult in the outlying sectors, so I am counting on each of you and your teams to step up to meet whatever challenges arise."

Quintin looked around and saw the group was very focused on every word coming out of Xavier's mouth. Something big was going happen.

"Effective immediately," Xavier continued, "the oldest direct descendant will pay the sentence for anyone who escapes and does not serve theirs. This will be administered regardless of age or position in society for those who live in the outlying sectors. Quintin, please send orders that the oldest child of this woman who has escaped is to be executed immediately using whatever weapon or method is most quickly available to complete it. Ensure it is recorded and the footage will be used to communicate on the news outlets the consequences of defying a justly administered sentence."

"I'll get right on it, sir," Quintin replied wondering if he should do now or wait until Xavier finished speaking.

"Further," Xavier continued, "we will be deploying additional agents to the outlying sectors. No longer will residents of these areas abide by a different set of laws than the capital follows. Their children will be removed from them at the same interval that is done in the capital, and there will be no tolerance for skirting the daily affirmations and meditation requirements. Failure to comply will result in not just reduction of credits, but in progressive discipline including confinement and ultimately execution. We have plans already drawn up for this possibility. We are ordered to proceed with implementing them immediately."

A shocked silence permeated the room. Those who had worked as ministry agents within the territories in question emitted a sense of worried uncertainty relative to what was about to take place. But within the room were some who did not have this broadening experience. Their countenance shone with a gleam of zealous anticipation of the glories that were to come, in finally bringing the whole of the sectors into the full light of the true path of understanding. They were ready to be heroes for the cause of science, irrespective of what consequences may come.

CHAPTER 13

$\mathcal{P}$hillip was pretty perceptive for someone who was only seven years old. Well, he was actually closer to eight. After all, his birthday was only a couple of seemingly long months away. He and his older sister had been taken into care of a child services worker named Ivy since their mommy was having some trouble. His dad wasn't still alive, so Ivy had been asked to help. She seemed nice enough and said kind sounding things, but whenever he asked about when he could see his mommy next, she said something like maybe soon or we'll see what works out. Then she would offer him a toy to play with, or some sort of new game on a handheld. The game was one that his mom had said he wasn't allowed to play when he had asked, so he felt sort of naughty when he played it. But it was fun and took his mind off of things, so he played it anyway.

What he missed most though was the ability to play outside in a large open space with his friends. When he wasn't going to school, he would play and run around outside. His mom told him that as long as he stayed around one of the neighbors she knew and didn't get into any trouble, he could do that. He got lots of exercise, got dirty and had lots of fun. For some reason, he wasn't allowed to go outside like that anymore. He had to stay inside the building or play in the small space outside Ivy called the courtyard. When he asked if he could play with his friends, it was back to the maybe soon or we'll see what works out.

That left playing with games on the handheld, playing with the not fun toys, or playing with his sister. His sister was nice enough to him, but she just wasn't fun. She cared about girl things and never wanted to go get dirty or run around. But since she got here, all she did was stare at her doll and look sad. She kept telling Philip to be strong, to not forget their parents, and to find their aunt and uncle if they managed to get a chance to leave. She even made him recite their aunt and uncle's first and last names, and where they lived. Phillip was so bored he even asked Amy to play with him in things she cared about. She just wasn't interested. Something was wrong with her, but he always thought girls were odd, so maybe it wasn't so strange after all.

Phillip's mom seemed really stressed out before Ivy took them, so maybe she just needed a break. Sometimes people went away for breaks. He remembered that she had said something like, God help me, one day when she looked worn out, and then he saw a horrified look on her face. But right after that she smiled and laughed it off like everything was ok. He wasn't sure what she said meant, but it was probably a naughty word that he wasn't allowed to say. His mom and some of his friends' parents were funny that way. They got all upset if you said a bad word, but they said them when they forget you were close enough to hear them.

The more he thought about it, his mommy started acting strange right after that event, almost acting afraid. She gave Phillip an extra-long hug that night and kept using different words to say how much she loved him and Amy. He even thought he saw Amy and his mom having a serious talk. His sister was nodding serious, like she was getting the most important job in the world to do. The next day after he got up was the last time he had seen his mom. She gave him a big hug and let him go off and play with his friends. When he came back to the house, Ivy was there waiting for him with his sister and a couple of people wearing uniforms of some sort. They even were holding weapons which looked really cool. He asked if he could touch them and asked what they needed them for. They didn't really say much, and Ivy said that it was to keep them all safe. Phillip didn't understand what they needed a weapon to be safe for, when everyone was nice to each other where he lived. But he was mostly feeling left out because he never was allowed to touch or hold the weapons. Some people had all the fun and it wasn't his day for it.

Amy didn't act like she liked Ivy very much. She probably had a good reason for it. She probably missed her friends and wanted to see mommy like he did.

Today was different than the other days he had been staying with Ivy. There seemed to be a lot more people with uniforms that came by to visit today. They wouldn't talk with him either, and none would let him hold their weapons.

"I need you and Amy to stay in this special room today," Ivy said in a way that made Phillip not want to go in the room.

"I want to play outside today, even if I have to go to that boring courtyard," Phillip announced.

"Maybe later," Ivy answered. "For right now, I need you to stay in here. I even brought some toys in here for you to play with."

Phillip was frustrated. This was setting up to be the most boring day ever! Someone came in holding some sort of circular thing.

"What kind of a toy is that?" Phillip asked curiously.

"It is a special kind of necklace," Ivy explained while approaching Phillip. "I will put it around your neck."

After Ivy left the room, Phillip tried to get it off his neck, but it didn't want to release.

"You probably shouldn't touch that," Amy said. "It will probably hurt you really bad if you take it off. I don't trust it."

Amy wasn't being fun again, but she seemed to know what she was talking about, so Phillip decided he didn't want to get hurt by it. But there was nothing else to do in this room. He sure did miss home.

After sitting in the room for a long time, someone new came into the room. He seemed nice and wasn't wearing clothes like all the people with weapons did.

"I am going to try to get you two out of here so you can see your mother," he stated.

Phillip liked the sound of that. He knew this person was a stranger, but this stranger seemed nicer than the ones he had been forced to listen to so far.

"I can't wait to see her," Phillip answered excitedly.

"Did they really put those around the necks of children?" the stranger muttered to himself before continuing with a now sad look on his face. "I am sorry, there is something I need to have with me before I can bring you. Please don't tell anyone I stopped by. I will return as soon as I can."

Phillip felt sad he had left without taking them as he watched him carefully leave the door. Amy didn't say anything, but she looked even more sad if that was possible. Ivy and some others came into the room suddenly, all worried looking. This time they didn't leave.

A while later, some people with uniforms and weapons came into the room and pointed the weapons at Amy.

"Not in here," one of them said.

"But the orders said…"

"I said not in here, let's do it with less eyes watching."

With that, Amy was led out of the room like she was in trouble. Phillip wasn't sure what she had done wrong. A few moments later he thought he heard a loud noise like a banging of some sort. For some reason, Phillip felt sad suddenly. He wished his sister was with him. He missed his mommy. And for the first time since he had been taken away by Ivy, his brave façade broke, and he began to quietly cry, trying without success to quench the feeling of emptiness that was slowly enveloping him.

∞ ∞ ∞

Gabriel watched the news release on his handheld before he was about to depart for work. It was flagged for mandatory viewing in the general channel. Since he was supposed to mostly leave his handheld at home, he figured he should view it. At a minimum, he could be informed should anyone discuss it. Queuing it up, it was not what he expected to see.

"Early today," the narrator read, "a convicted violator of the *Adherence to Myths Act* violently escaped confinement in Xenon killing multiple guards in the containment facility. She is considered highly dangerous and is currently at-large. An active warrant for immediate execution has been issued if she is found. Per section 3.24 of the Xenon criminal code, her oldest child was executed in her place as shown now.

This law has not always been enforced, but recent events require a more diligent application of the law."

Gabriel had never heard of such a law on the books and had studied them closely in his prior role in the ministry. He was pretty sure he would find it if he looked and it would be backdated to appear on the books, one of the advantages of a paperless society. It was likely issued in response to the escape, Gabriel thought.

The footage next jumped to show the sentence that was given. It showed a small girl who was holding a doll being shot with a weapon. Her body convulsed, then fell to the floor. The doll finally fell out of her hands, discolored in her blood.

Gabriel was aghast with what he had just seen. This was clearly endorsed by the ministry, but Gabriel could not see what possible upside this would have. Sure, it may keep blatant escape attempts from occurring, but if they had sent him here to find the resistance, his job just got way easier. Anyone who wasn't already sympathetic to the resistance would likely be so now.

Gabriel pressed play on the other message. This one was not graphic like the first one. It simply announced that all children ages six through age seventeen would be transferred to the care of the Ministry of Education, as was the policy in the capital and surrounding sectors. This transfer would begin in three days. A Ministry of Education official would visit every impacted residence to facilitate the transfers. Failure to support the transfers would result in arrest, with swift and severe justice administered for any resistance given.

Gabriel did not expect this to go smoothly either. The population in Xenon was generally compliant in their actions. Their thoughts were a different matter, but they did not go out of their way to initiate open opposition to ministry edicts. They found ways to subtly circumvent policies, but overall, they existed in a sort of truce. They pretended to go along as long as the government pretended to believe they went along. This would be one area that they could not pretend. Families were their prized assets to be protected at all costs. Water, energy and credits were not what was important to this population; Family was. And this latest edict was hitting at the heart of what they most cared about.

Gabriel was about to get more of a chance to be part of the resistance than he ever imagined. And when he honestly looked within himself, he was no longer sure which side he most identified with.

∞ ∞ ∞

The High Seat looked around the table getting ready to call an emergency session of the governing council of Kayden to order. The energy in the room seemed to be tense and volatile. Inaction would not be the result of this meeting. The question was what action would be taken.

If she or someone else had only foreseen the possibility of there being proximity-based detonation devices on the children. These could be dealt with, but only if the right expertise was present, otherwise the kids and those near them would be incinerated in a local explosion. And unfortunately, it would now be even harder to rescue the remaining child. It still was astounding that young children would be used as pawns like they were in this instance. Notifying the mother who escaped had been one of the hardest things she had done, but leadership carries heavy burdens and this one was hers to bear.

She had expected some sort of pushback after the rescue, but the ministry response escalated things to a whole new level and this could not stand. And then the brutal murder of the daughter was beyond anything she thought possible. They called it justice, but this was not justice. This was tyranny propagated by evil people, fearful of having their power threatened. The government mindset already didn't value life that didn't contribute to their way of thinking, but the girl was only ten years old. What had she done to justify this outrage? She had committed no crime. But the ministry had determined that the value of her life was best spent in sending a message. All this for making accidental references to old religious ways which had been ingrained in upbringing for generations.

Seeing that the last of the expected attendees had arrived, the High Seat called the meeting to order. The Reader provided the opening text.

"And a great upheaval will be thrust upon the people. As fire strengthens iron, so shall a new challenge strengthen the people. But it will be at a great cost, for fire also burns away that which is weak and without substance. Go into this time with clear minds and strength of purpose, for he who is uncertain will wander and be lost before being consumed. Protect the people. Prepare the way for the one who can bridge the divide. In this dreamer comes the way for the salvation of the people. *The Lily Chronicles*, Chapter 2, section 3."

"Thank you, Reader," the High Seat stated. "I think you all know why this meeting was called today. We have three days if we are to believe the ministry announcement, after which they will start to remove our most precious assets. I am surprised they didn't start this immediately, but they probably don't have the level of officials and agents in place in order to pull this off yet. Chief Protector, would you walk us through the options that have been developed to respond to this."

"Thank you, ma'am," The Chief Protector responded. "We are pretty limited in our options. The first option is to do nothing and let the ministry execute its edict. If this occurs, we expect individual resistance in each family, with many parents being arrested or killed, and the children still taken away. Those who are not native to this area, we expect mostly full compliance and cooperation. Most of them already voluntarily give up their children to the care of the Ministry of Education. We also expect this group to be sympathetic to the ministry effort to gather children and will inform on neighbors and others should some sort of resistance activity occur."

"I think we can safely say we do not plan on doing nothing," the High Seat stated. "Walk us through our options for resisting this unjust edict."

"Certainly," the Chief Protector replied. "We have some plans for a direct confrontation, but we would be greatly overwhelmed both in numbers and available weaponry. We managed to save some weapons when the confiscation happened many years back, but honestly, the newer models which we have very little access to are much more effective. We have so few weapons, that while we could use them to mount some targeted insurgency raids, we would not be successful in any sort of open conflict."

"I understand," the High Seat replied with resignation. "What is your recommendation making do with the best available use of what we have?"

"At the council's prior direction," the Chief Protector continued, "we have been completing underground excavations. This was done in case we required a large holding area for either people or supplies. We have a group of dreamers with this talent who have been working on this project for many years now. We believe we have enough space developed to tightly house about eighty percent of the sympathetic population, and if we bring in more dreamers, we could exceed that within the matter of a few weeks. Kayden has been carefully building food supplies and we have available water sources either through naturally occurring means or with dreamer assistance."

"Can people really survive down here for prolonged periods of time?" someone asked.

"Those who we have rescued from the abhorrent Myth's Act have been existing there already." He answered. "I am not saying it is great, but living is better than dying. We also have, through this infrastructure, developed a method to access the protected nature preserves. This area isn't as widely surveilled as the human living areas. In the event that the underground strategy becomes either unsustainable or alternative methods for restocking food supplies need to be developed, this could provide a fallback location for the people. We do not think the government currently has good technology for finding underground alcoves, but it will be a matter of time until they do. We do have multiple underground places spread throughout the northern sectors and even have developed some of them to reside under firmly capital-controlled regions."

"So, our response is to go and hide in holes in the ground?" asked the Seeker. "There must be more than that we can do. This is a people who live off the land in the open spaces. Can we expect them to hide indefinitely in the recesses of the ground?"

"If it keeps their families safe, they will go," the High Seat said sadly. "But there will need to be a plan for more."

"If I may?" asked the Chief Protector. Following a nod from the High Seat, he continued. "What I described to you was just intended as phase one. The rest of the population counts on Xenon for food exports. No other regions currently participate significantly in this activity. We are just bringing in the last of the harvest of this season's crops. There is no reason this needs to get to the ministry processing centers. And it would greatly strengthen our food reserves."

"But wouldn't someone just make use of our farms and continue crop production?" the High Seat asked. "I can't believe the food reserves are that low."

"My sources believe their food reserves are much lower than you would think," the Chief Protector continued. "Granted, the Ministry of Nutrition could probably synthesize something resembling food, but their own studies concluded that the same level of nutrition would not be achieved, and a long-term diet would result in decreased health response. With all the restrictions on chemicals and energy usage, we keep up with supply but there is typically very little excess. Losing a full harvest would create a lot of leverage, probably more so than open fighting would. And how well do you think outsiders could do if asked to take over our farms? If we left our equipment in a state of disrepair, and they tried to hold to the impossible energy and water quotas that we supplement with dreamer intervention, they may grow some things, but won't grow enough."

"How does that get us back to the surface?" the Seeker asked.

"We may need to supplement this effort with targeted guerrilla campaigns and put out a lot of communications explaining our side of the story to put pressure on the government in their more loyal sectors," he continued. "This will not be a short or painless effort, but it will be one we can have hope of a winnable culmination. If you have a different approach that can provide as good of chance of success, I would love to hear it. Sadly, we have very few options and none of them are what I would consider good ones."

The High Seat and the rest of the council processed his comments with sort of a shocked silence. Sure, they had done some scenario planning, but it was one thing to talk through outcomes in a thinking exercise, it was quite another to put a plan of this nature into motion. Seeing no one else speaking up, the High Seat brought the discussion to a head.

"Does anyone have a better plan to propose than this one? Or any major suggestions to improve this one?" the High Seat asked. Seeing continued silence, she realized they had consensus. "Ok, then we will proceed this way. We have a lot of work to do in order to pull this off in the next three days. Let's work though those details now."

About three hours later, they had worked out the semblance of a plan. The first priority would be evacuating those known to be sympathetic to the resistance. Second, would be those who valued family ties and had been native to the area for many generations. Those remaining would need to be vouched for before someone would approach them. It was unfortunate that some deserving would be left behind, but security was paramount, and casting the net too wide would endanger everyone's safety.

"Any other business we need to discuss?" the High Seat asked with a feeling of exhaustion creeping in on her.

"Yes," interjected the Seeker, "we need to have a plan for Gabriel through this."

"What do you suggest?" the High Seat asked.

"He needs to complete his training," the Seeker answered. "Having him either left behind or massed with those evacuated will not be conducive to him becoming what we hope he can be."

The High Seat looked at the Chief Protector. "Do you think we can house what we need to if we avoid the training center?"

"I think so," he answered. "We may need to block off some of the connecting passages to further isolate it, but I think we can do it without jeopardizing our ability to house those who will get evacuated."

The Seeker nodded her approval. "We will need to keep the one known as Teacher assigned to him, and I will need to continue to allocate time to train him in the dream state. This will divert key resources from the other effort, but I can't emphasize enough the importance on this development continuing. The prophesy calls on us to both protect the people and to prepare the way. We cannot trade one at the expense of the other."

"I agree," said the High Seat. "We will also need a way to continue to train those who are identified with the gift and can eventually add additional students here."

Seeing agreement, the High Seat sought any other business and called the meeting to an end. A lot was about to change, and she hoped she had what was needed to lead the people through this time of struggle and upheaval.

CHAPTER 14

Gabriel arrived at work in the midst of a lot more chaos than he had ever seen before on the farm. Typically, the pace was purposeful, but overall patient. That was not the feeling he was getting today. It appeared that there was way more work that needed done than time to do it. He expected a sullen dejected atmosphere from the communique, but it was not what he saw here. No one was exhibiting overt cheerfulness, but what he saw was a unity of purpose matched with urgency. He looked around for his uncle or aunt, but they were not in sight. He did see his cousin Tom and decided to check with him if he knew where he was supposed to be working today.

"Glad you are here Gabriel," Tom interjected before Gabriel could say anything.

"So, what is everyone hurrying around for?" Gabriel asked.

"The harvest is believed at risk, and we are running around like crazy trying to get it brought in," Tom answered. "Whatever magic you used to weed that entire field on your first day, we sure could use something like that again right now!"

"I am glad to do whatever you need me to do," Gabriel replied wondering at his choice of words. "What needs done?"

"We have our harvesting equipment tied up on the north fields," Tom replied. "Unfortunately, we need harvesting done on the south fields for whatever we can save, even if done by hand. Grab a wagon, a garden fork, and some baskets. Come with me and I'll get you started on what you can help with."

Gabriel went to the supply shed and quickly grabbed the supplies he was told he would need. Tom barked out some quick instructions to some other workers and jogged to catch up with Gabriel who was headed to the south fields.

"What is the worry with losing the crop?" Gabriel asked curiously.

"There isn't a weather event coming that we know about," Tom answered. "The biggest worry is this three-day notice thing that got broadcast this morning. If we have a ton of ministry officials here watching, who knows if we can get the crop in. People are pretty worked up about the announcement, and some of the local people who are influential have suggested we speed up getting the harvest in before this occurs. There may be another purpose, but it has galvanized everyone in a way that gets minds off of what is going on."

"It wasn't a response I would expect to see," Gabriel answered thoughtfully. "But I will do my part to help."

Something else was going on, Gabriel was pretty certain. Something different than the story that Tom had told him. Tom had three kids in the age range the ministry was taking, and Gabriel either expected him to be maximizing time with them or working on a plan to hide them. The expediated harvest could be part of that, and he didn't think he was being told the whole story. Either way, whatever the plan was, it involved rushing in the harvest. Gabriel would do what he could to further build trust. Plus, this seemed to be important to Tom, and on a personal level, Gabriel didn't want to let him down.

"Ok, here are the fields I am hoping you can help with," Tom said while pointing to what he had in mind. "You will be by yourself for a while, so do what you can until we can send you more help. This crop is harvested under the ground, in the roots. You take the garden fork like this and dig around the plant. You see these round things? We want all of these removed and put in the basket. We have several fields of them but start on this field and get as far as you can. If you fill up the cart, just pile them beside the cart and we will get someone to come by and ferry it for you. Now you try, so I can be sure you understand how to do it."

Gabriel took the fork and pressed it into the soil a bit away from the plant like Tom had showed him. He pulled up on the plant and exposed the round, brown colored circular objects. They came in many shapes. He picked them off and placed them in the basket one by one. He scraped through the dirt around the plant to see if there were any he had missed and found one more.

"Did I do that correctly?" Gabriel asked.

"Perfectly," Tom answered. "You really are a natural at this. You will get faster with practice. Really sorry to dump you out here, but I need to get back and help my father with the rest of the work. I'll try to get someone to come check on you later today. It has been a really crazy day!"

"Tom, are you going to be ok with the announcement that came out today?" Gabriel asked with sincerity.

"I am still trying to process it to be honest with you," Tom answered. "I can't imagine not seeing my kids for years. I know you were raised that way, but I am trying not to think about it right now. Thanks for asking. I do need to run."

Gabriel surveyed the field in front of him as he saw Tom jogging off. There was no way he was going to dent this field going one plant at a time. But he didn't understand the harvesting process well enough yet. Gabriel proceeded to complete several more plants by hand, fully filling his basket.

Gabriel took a moment to visualize the process of harvesting this plant. The challenge would lie in identifying the part below the surface of the soil. He would almost need to lift the whole plant and surrounding dirt up in the air, shake off the dirt and the crop and the green part would be all that would be left. Then separate the crop from the green part. It was multiple steps, but something he thought he could do in the dream state if he tried hard enough.

Gabriel looked around the area for a lily plant. He knew there were a lot of them around the farm. After a couple minutes of walking, he was rewarded, and proceeded to dig it up so he could be nearer to the field he was working in. Looking around to make sure he was still alone, he set the plant in front of him and willed himself to a calm place, emptying his mind, while visualizing the lily like he had been practicing. His mind did not calm quickly, but it eventually did.

Gabriel opened his eyes, now surrounded by a field of lilies as he had seen several times before. He waited for what seemed like a few minutes in case Raelynn would arrive. He was mildly surprised when she didn't, but maybe she was caught up in the hysteria like what was gripping the farm he was at. He knew he wasn't supposed to do anything new without her, but this was really something she had showed him before, albeit a few more steps were needed.

Since she had not come, he willed himself to the field he was working in. The field looked the same, albeit without color, and just as overwhelming as when he was in his normal woken state. Gabriel focused his mind on the plant in front of him, and visualized raising it up, surrounded by the dirt below. He then slowly released his hold on the dirt and watched it slowly fall from the plant. Sure enough, there were multiple round objects attached through the root structure. Gabriel focused on the round objects and visualized them in his cart. They disappeared and he was holding only the top part of the plant. Gabriel released his mental hold on the plant and watched as it fell to the ground. He walked over to the cart and with satisfaction saw the crop he had just harvested in the cart.

"Well, done!" a voice behind him stated. "I was wondering when you would use this talent again. This is a bit more complicated than removing weeds, but it looks like you worked out how to do that."

Gabriel turned and saw Raelynn standing behind him.

"I waited a bit for you, but you didn't come right away. I figured since this is something I had sort of done before, I wouldn't mess anything up by doing it on my own. I hope that is ok?" Gabriel sheepishly answered.

"Sorry, I couldn't come right away," Raelynn answered. "Evenings are usually better for me and there has been a lot going on this morning. But if you are going to do crop harvesting, you can safely do that, but please don't try to do the whole field at once. With all the extra steps, you may have trouble sustaining what is needed to do it. Better to start smaller and work yourself up to it."

"Ok," Gabriel answered. "I can work with that. Maybe a row at a time?"

"Sounds like a good place to start," she answered. "See how you do."

Gabriel focused his will on the full row in front of him. He worked the steps in the same sequence he had done with the single plant. Raelynn was right. He was finding it harder to keep control over the process, but it was not unmanageable. He felt he could likely do more than that if he needed to, but it was a comfortable level and he could still make quick work of the field. Gabriel translocated the crop to the cart and released the full row of plants. The cart was over half full and he had hardly spent any time on it.

"How did that feel to you?" Raelynn asked.

"Pretty good," Gabriel answered. "I could definitely feel that it took more effort to do the whole row at a time, but it felt manageable."

"Then stay with that amount at a time. I bet your uncle would be very appreciative if you cleared all the fields like this," Raelynn suggested.

"Wouldn't that raise a lot of questions?" Gabriel asked. "I haven't gone out of my way to draw attention to my dream gifts. The weeding was theoretically possible for a person to accomplish in a day. Fields of harvest would not be."

"Your uncle knows that your parents had similar gifts," she stated. "I think you were sent here hoping you would use your gift to help where it wouldn't get drawn attention to. How many people know you are here working?"

"Just my cousin Tom," Gabriel replied. "In fact, the rest of the workers seem to be focused on the north side of the farm, opposite where I am now."

"I think this instance would be a good time to help," Raelynn advised. "I would suggest doing the full harvest then quietly finding your cousin, aunt or uncle to say you need to head to check on your grandmother. They will keep it quiet, and you can probably help your grandmother the same way if she is having trouble bringing in her harvest. Your family is pretty sure you have special gifts. Hiding it from them will not serve any purpose. They will protect you in it, even with their lives if necessary. That is their way. Just as I would protect knowledge of your gift with my life."

The last comment really got Gabriel's attention. There was a loyalty here to each other. A loyalty that transcended selfish motivations. He had people who would give their life to protect him, for no other reason than he was family. If he were to risk himself, what better cause would there be to risk for someone who would do the same for him.

Gabriel nodded, "Ok, I will do as you say."

"Be careful," Raelynn said. "I am sorry I can't stay and watch. But reach out your thoughts to me if you have an emergency that requires my help."

And with that, Raelynn was gone.

Gabriel paused to contemplate the conversation with Raelynn. He could help, and he wanted to, even if he didn't fully understand the reason why. He hoped he wouldn't regret it as he focused his mental energy at the next row as he began to harvest it one row at a time. Gabriel quickly filled the cart he had brought and started a pile next to it that continued to grow. Finally, the first field was completed. Gabriel found himself slightly tired, but overall feeling able to keep going. He walked to the next field and completed the process, starting a new pile in a similarly accessible place.

Six fields later, he was finally completed. Gabriel directed himself back to the lily field, and then back to a woken state. It had seemed like he had been working for hours, but the sun was not too far different from where it had been when he started. He was getting better at reading the time by the position of the sun in the sky. Maybe two or three hours had passed? He was not certain, but it was probably close to that. Gabriel consumed something to eat and drink to refresh himself. Once he had taken the needed steps to replenish his energy, he headed back to find Tom.

Looking around, he couldn't find Tom anywhere. He was probably helping on the north side harvesting work. Gabriel decided to check the house, and as reached it, saw Isadora scurrying around gathering some items. The photo he had seen of his parents prominently displayed was no longer it its usual place, as were some other items he was used to seeing missing.

"Oh, hi Gabriel," Isadora exclaimed coming to give him a customary hug. "If you are looking for Kelby or Tom, they are in the north fields working on the harvest. Tom mentioned he had asked you to help on the south fields."

"Yes, I have been busy out there this morning," Gabriel answered. "With all that is going on, I think I need to go check on my grandmother's farm, to make sure she has the help she needs today. Can you tell Tom that I think I got done what he was hoping I could help with?"

Isadora gave Gabriel a knowing smile. "Thank you for doing that. We will make sure that others believe someone came by with equipment to help."

"It is going to be a lot of work transporting all that crop," Gabriel said. "You may want to get someone working on that if that step is important."

"Thank you so much Gabriel," Isadora stated. "It has been such a blessing having you help us here on the farm. No matter what happens in the days ahead, know that we all love you and care about you, and have been so glad to have you back in our lives. Now go. Check on your grandmother."

With that, she gave Gabriel a big embrace and sent him on his way.

Gabriel walked the path home with a bit of confusion in his mind. If he didn't know better, it was like Isadora was getting ready to leave to go somewhere. Maybe this was the big response. Maybe the rebellion would go into some sort of hiding, possibly underground into caverns like he had seen. Maybe they needed the crops for food supplies to subsist on. Gabriel pondered all these things when he suddenly was encompassed in darkness, back in the knowing confines of the place where Teacher resided.

CHAPTER 15

*Q*uintin had been assigned to lead the announced collection of children in Xenon. Normally, the Ministry of Education would come to claim children when they reached the requisite age, but this was done in the regions that believed in this process, which made it a non-violent and typically uneventful activity. To make this easier, a protocol was used to make the attachment less strong between the parents and the child. Mainly it consisted of a medical implant that was given at birth to the parents. It did not harm the nurturing characteristics of the parents, particularly the mother. But it was able to neutralize the possessive instinct that was still seen in the northern sectors. A bond was most strongly built when the child was a baby, and while the parents were programmed to nurture and care for the child's well-being, anxiety about someone else caring for their child was largely non-existent. When the time came for the child to be given to the care of the Ministry of Education, the implant triggered a response of indifference and finality.

Research had determined that an implant put in after the early bond had been established provided some efficacy but was not enough to overcome the parent child connection. Those native to the northern sectors had refused the implants which was going to create challenges with Quintin's newest assignment. There had been ministry discussion on making these implants mandatory in the northern sectors, but the feared backlash at the time resulted in an educational campaign only, but not a requirement. Very few had asked to have the implant, and these were mostly people who had relocated from outside sectors.

The Ministry of Education was not equipped to execute a removal of this magnitude. The Ministry of Scientific Compliance, however, did have enough manpower to enforce something of this scale, and had volunteered its services to ensure that the recent communication would be enforced. Quintin, who had real experience in this sector, now had a great opportunity to prove himself and possibly aid his advancement.

It had taken the full three days to gather the ministry troops and officials needed for an operation of this scale. Quintin had recommended a large force for this, expecting risks of uprising and violent responses at some of the homes. He was pretty sure if an example was made of a few early resisters, then the rest of the population would come in line. But if they didn't, it never hurt to be fully prepared.

Quintin watched as the last of the troops got off the transport vehicle. His team was now in place. One final review, a good night's sleep, and he would begin the planned operation. Based on the number of people and how far they were spread out, he thought this operation would likely be finished in a couple of weeks. To be safe, he had communicated a longer expected timeframe to cover any subterfuge the population tried to exhibit.

"Sir," his assistant interrupted, "the extraction team leaders are all assembled as you requested."

"Yes, I need to review our final plans. There is no room for mistakes on this one," Quintin answered before following him into the meeting room. The room was full and there was a large amount of people present.

"Good evening," Quintin addressed the crowd after making his way up to the podium. "My name is Quintin Conlon and I have been put in charge of the mission for which you are assigned. I know you have all been issued a briefing packet, but I wanted to address any questions before we begin the operations tomorrow morning."

"Sir," someone asked, "can you clarify the use of the proximity detonation devices?"

"Yes," Quintin replied, "we expect resistance both from the parents and the children. I want all children taken fitted with these proximity collars. If they try to run or demonstrate sufficient unwillingness to follow instructions, they are to be detonated. I don't think it will take it happening more than once per pickup bus before we get compliance."

"Sir," another spoke up, "do you think that it will actually be necessary to detonate? And I was hoping you could elaborate on the force response when taking the children from their homes."

"Yes, I think it will be necessary to detonate or it would not be in the orders. There needs to be an early strong response. If we allow any sort of conflict, it will only enable more of it which will put our teams at great risk. We are still outnumbered significantly in this sector, even if the people are not as well armed as we are. We do expect households to act stupidly to try to keep their children and need to make some examples or we will risk the entire mission.

"Will we have to maintain a long-term security perimeter to the holding area we are bringing the children?" asked an older looking team leader.

"For a short time period yes, but we will be distributing the students to Ministry of Education facilities across all the reliable sectors which will reduce this need over time," Quintin replied.

Quintin looked around the room. The feedback he was seeing wasn't an excitement at the mission, but he didn't see any open hostility either. They would do as ordered.

"If there are no other questions," Quintin stated, "then we will get started first thing tomorrow. I will be accompanying one of the teams tomorrow to observe and make any adjustments based on the situation on the ground. You are dismissed."

Quintin had been able to pull off a tremendous effort to have troops deployed in the three-day time period with a workable plan in place. There had been a lot of discussion on what to do with the children who were taken, and the decision was made to relocate them away from Xenon. Some advocated grouping extracted children together to offset any risk of corrupting existing students. This option was held in reserve only for those students who proved to be disruptive. There was also the option to deem children not a good fit for society, but any decisions on this were being given a full year to assess, as to not miss any valuable talent that could be emerging.

Intelligence feedback Quintin had received indicated that there had been a lot of activity in Xenon following the announcement of the new program. No ministry officials had been harmed or abducted in this time that he was aware of, which surprised him quite a bit. There seemed to be a sense of urgency about, but none of his contacts seemed to understand what was driving it. He thought Gabriel would have the best chance of actual intelligence based on the resistance contacts he had made, but he had not checked in to even read his messages, let alone provide an update for almost three days now. He was likely involved in something but was not in possession of his handheld which had maintained its location.

What Quintin's active contacts had picked up was an urgency about bringing in the crop harvest. But that wasn't all that unusual. If there was an unfavorable weather indicator or high-risk event, the population would rally together and ensure they expediated the harvest. For some reason, they still cared a lot about providing food to the entire country. Their credit allowances were predicated on it, but the passion seemed to exist beyond that. Maybe they were fearful that if something happened with the children removal, that food would be in short supply. Maybe they were just trying to use the extra help of their children while it was available since many did help on the farms. Beyond that, there seemed to be an eerie calm, one that preceded a possible storm.

Morning came and Quintin selected a team at random to accompany. Each team had a certain number of living locations assigned to them based on Oversite analytics, which listed places where target aged children were registered to be living. With him was a standard extraction team of four and a representative from the Ministry of Education to act as the communicator. There would be a singular warning by the Ministry of Education person, and if any hostile act followed that, those resisting would be killed. That was the plan anyway. Quintin wanted to see how well it worked in reality.

Quintin's team arrived at the first planned house. Inside was supposed to be two adults and three children in the targeted age range.

Oversite detected all assigned handhelds inside. Quintin nodded to the Ministry of Education official to begin.

"Open up in the name of the Ministry of Education," the expressionless official called out with surprisingly loud volume projection. She wore a plan dark suit as was common attire in that ministry.

Silence met the announcement.

"If you resist or show violent intent, you will be killed. We are coming in," she continued in the same monotone voice.

She took out her ministry access card and electronically unlocked the door. She motioned to the extraction team to go on in to round up the occupants inside.

The extraction team drew their weapons and proceeded in a two by two formation with each partner covering the other. Quintin pulled up his handheld to view their visual feed inside the house. After about five to ten minutes of persistent searching they returned to the entrance.

"I am sorry sir," the lead officer stated. "There is no one inside. We checked every possible hiding place. They must have left."

"Do another sweep," Quintin ordered. "This time look for hidden passages in the floor. Pull up the floor if you must. We have seen evidence of this type of hiding place in other areas recently. Meanwhile, I will check the broader surveillance log to see if can get a clue where they may have gone."

Quintin initiated Oversite for the footage of this area when the handhelds were last moved. He had an active camera with view outside this house. Syncing up the time stamps he saw when they went inside the evening before. All five of them were present. Since then, facial recognition had not picked up any footage matching their imprint. It was like they had disappeared.

"Sir," the lead agent interrupted Quintin's thoughts. "We have significantly damaged the flooring structure and see no evidence of any passages underneath the house."

"I am not getting any evidence of them leaving, so they must have gone somewhere," Quintin replied thoughtfully. "Either way, we have wasted enough time here. Let's move to the next house on our list."

Eight houses later, each result had been the same. No one was at home. Surveillance had shown people entering the home but not leaving it, yet no one was there. So far, they had way more questions than answers, and more importantly, no children for the Ministry of Education.

The next house on their list housed a Ministry of Transportation family who was not native to the area. This family had one child in the target age but had only just met the age requirement. Either way, it had come up on the planned extraction route.

The Ministry of Education official did her monotone announcement at the door and was greeted promptly by a younger woman who was likely in her early twenties.

"Come on in," she offered. "I have been waiting for my summons to give up the little one. I was wondering if it would occur following the announcement a few days ago."

The team tentatively came inside and found a small child looking curiously at them.

"These are some nice people from the Ministry of Education I was telling you about," the mother shared. "They are going to take you to school like your mom and dad went to when they were about your age."

With that she reached down, gave him a short hug and lightly pressed him in the direction of Ministry of Education official.

"Don't worry," she quietly said to the Ministry of Education official. "My implant is working, and you don't need to fear any of the crazy responses you have probably already experienced today. This isn't the first child I have given to the care of the ministry. We each need to do our part to ensure the best are developed in the cause of science, don't we? Plus the extra credit allowance we have received has been appreciated."

"Thank you for your service, ma'am." Quintin answered.

"Come this way young man," one of the agents instructed. "We need to get you seated and fitted with a special collar for the trip."

The small boy started walking toward the transport vehicle. Then he stopped for a moment while he was getting fitted for the promised collar. He turned, taking in a final look at the woman who had borne him, who would likely never see him again. He knew he should be feeling something, but instead he just felt a calm indifference coupled with mild curiosity at what his next stage in life would bring. Turning away, he touched his new collar while listening carefully at the importance of not trying to remove it.

"I think I have seen enough," Quintin informed the group. "Continue on as per orders, I am headed back to the command center."

Quintin was not far from the base and was able to get back quickly. Reports coming in indicated his experience was being shared by the other teams as well. Quintin quickly reviewed the analytics before his handheld interrupted him.

"Good afternoon, sir. I was just about to contact you with an update," Quintin offered.

"Is it my imagination, or are the numbers collected significantly less than expected?" Xavier asked.

"You are quite correct sir," Quintin replied. "I was out with one of the teams this morning. Most addresses were found abandoned, except those with ties to the government or those not local to the area. Much of the population appears to have gone into hiding. We have been reviewing surveillance and there was nothing to suspect that targets were not at home, but when we go inside, no one is there. If we have collected twenty percent of what we expected to today, I would be shocked."

"That does not bode well," Xavier replied. "I thought when I sent you up there, you would be more on top of this situation than you appear to be. Eighty percent of the population can't just disappear."

"We hardly dented our planned sequence. We have been spending extra time looking for hiding places, and tracing down any surveillance histories and leads," Quintin said with a slight defensive tone in his voice. "I am leaning toward recommending altering the plan to sweep every house, versus just the ones with registered children present. They have to be hiding somewhere, and we need a full sweep, not one with holes that we miss since our focus is too narrow."

"That will take additional time," Xavier said processing what Quintin had reported. "But that can't be helped. Anyone you do interact with will need to be interrogated, which will consume additional time and resources. I approve your plan. But let's divert resources away from the ministry heavy neighborhoods and focus on the rural areas where the true locals to this sector reside.

Quintin considered redirecting and decided it was a good change in plans. He was mildly upset he hadn't randomized the collection points in his initial plan. This would be a good alteration moving forward.

"Also," Xavier continued, "anyone we interrogate in the rural areas, we need to ask about the location of the harvest and food stocks. The Ministry of Nutrition is in a tizzy that this season's entire food harvest has gone missing. They are probably exaggerating, but anything we find out on that topic is of great interest at the moment. We do not keep an infinite reserve of foodstuffs, and if we can't find out where the missing harvest went, that will put population at risk of all sorts of problems."

"Yes, sir. I will pass orders to be on the lookout for information of this nature. Thank you for your understanding, sir," Quintin said formally.

"Don't thank me yet." Xavier snapped. "This has turned into something way bigger than I sent you up to take care of. Expect me first thing in the morning. I think I will need to take overall command of the sector activities. Keep executing the sweep you recommended. I expect timely updates and results."

At that, the line disconnected. Quintin yelled at the nearest person to him to get him some intelligence he could act on now. The person scurried around frantically but in his inner being he knew that it was for show. There were no easy answers to be found.

CHAPTER 16

The High Seat watched the events unfolding around her with a tentative satisfaction. Nearly every dream gifted person in the northern sector was involved in the busiest three days in her memory. Those qualified to translocate people were the busiest of all, as that could only be safely done by the most gifted of all dreamers. Those with a more rudimentary gift of translocation were being focused on transporting food stocks and resources that the evacuated population would need to subsist on for the coming months, if not years.

The caution her organization had employed had been effective, and her instructions had been followed for those wanting to be relocated to the living caverns below the ground. She had not provided any details on where evacuees would be relocated to in her communication but had asked that each family stay quartered in a single bedroom, and to put a marker on their door if they wished to be evacuated. This was passed through couriers across Kayden's trusted network. Some of the population had a reasonable idea what would be involved in their new living arrangements. Regardless, the High Seat was very careful to undersell the living conditions. It would be spartan, and due to surveillance systems would allow only rare exposure to the outside. And once you got there, you were in it for the long run. No one could be allowed to leave until leaving did not jeopardize those remaining.

Those who wanted to protect their children, marked their doors. It was understood that it would be folly to send the children only and stay behind. Those who did would be imprisoned and most likely executed. She also was surprised how many grandparents and families without children marked their door. It was like it was contagious, the fear of what could come made them want to stay part of the community they knew, even if they were uprooted from their homes.

A week ago, asking people to go into hiding would have been generally dismissed as mad ravings of someone not grounded in reality. While the population in Xenon generally rolled their eyes at each new ministry edict, each had felt largely safe if you followed the rules to a certain level of compliance. But the ministry communication had changed the entire outlook of a community. Executing an innocent child for the crime of nothing more than being born to someone who had defied the law, galvanized the population in unified fear and prompted a desire to oppose this tyranny. And any who were not convinced by what happened to the little girl, got there in a hurry when seeing the mandatory confiscation of children order that was about to be implemented. If the government had just continued its slow process of gradual change, they would have eventually achieved the compliance it desired. But their patience had been exhausted, and in the High Seat's opinion, a great mistake had been made.

The Chief Protector entered the makeshift command center that had been setup. His face revealed a distracted expression and some level of concern.

"Anything new to report?" the High Seat asked when she saw him enter the room.

"We are still mostly staying ahead of the ministry extraction teams," he answered while pointing at a map of Xenon that was on the wall, "but they have spread out their forces more randomly. They have already succeeded in getting some children from some of our more rural areas we did not expect them to visit so early."

"We knew that we would struggle to stay ahead of them," the High Seat said with some resignation in her voice. "Are there any options we have to slow them down or speed us up?"

"All dreamers are fully engaged," he answered. "Anyone who can translocate people is doing it and those who have dream gifts other than translocation are operating the transport tubes to shuttle everyone away to the staging points. I really wish we had more transport tubes. That is not going as fast as I want it to."

Almost anyone who had any semblance of dream gift could be trained to operate these vehicles. These had been designed to detect someone who had activated their dream gift and translocate the vehicle to a programmed coordinate location. The High Seat used a similar shuttle system to transport herself to the council meetings, but that vehicle was much smaller. Larger shuttles had been developed to support resistance activities where you needed to move an entire team to a defined location together.

"We have to make do with what we have," the High Seat replied. "I have been doing some surveillance in the dream state, and higher leadership is taking over the ministry response. This will likely make our work harder."

"That explains the change in where the extraction teams were sent," the Chief Protector replied. "That can't be helped now. We will just have to work harder."

"Let's adjust and try to make our dreamers who are translocating more mobile to adjust to the moving extraction teams," the High Seat stated. "Let's use dreamers to feed intelligence and try to better stay ahead of them."

"I will get right on it," he replied. "I am worried we don't have enough people to keep fully up, but every little bit we can do to save another child is vital."

"We have what we have," she answered. "We are in a desperate race. We can't let up."

The High Seat estimated it would take a few more days to complete the evacuation activities. About fifty percent of the target population had been translocated to the hiding places. There would be time later to better organize the people distribution in the settlement areas, but the initial priority was getting everyone to safety. And getting everyone to safety was already in jeopardy.

∞ ∞ ∞

Xavier was impatient to leave for Xenon, but he had received an urgent summons to address the Great Scientist Council. This wasn't high on his priority list, but one did not ignore a summons to appear in front of the council. They rarely all met in person, but his supervisor had informed him that all were present today in a non-virtual manner.

Xavier was escorted into the council chambers. All the seats appeared to be full and he noticed that all eyes immediately went in his direction when he entered. Previous times he had addressed the council, he was not sure anyone was paying attention and aware of his presence. This dynamic seemed to be quite different today. Xavier continued to find it mildly entertaining that not one member of the council had a scientific specialty in their educational background. Not that he would ever voice this aloud, but it was amusing, nonetheless. The original council had been populated with mostly science minded people, but over time, they had transitioned into the most skilled at politics or managing the bureaucracy of their respective ministries.

"We have taken too light of a hand with Xenon," the Minister of Transportation stated when he saw Xavier come in. "It is about time that we put them back in their place. Don't you agree Xavier?"

"Yes, Minister," Xavier replied. "We definitely need to get this sector under better control."

"I do hope you take a very firm hand against these rebels when you get up there," the Minister of Education said. "The family structure has been the bane of my existence for quite some time. That is a tradition that is long overdue for elimination. I hope you make enough examples of the population to adjust their thinking."

"I will do what is needed," Xavier answered wondering about the high level of outrage. "The population of Xenon appears to have implemented some preparations for a crackdown. I expect this will not go quickly, but we will not hesitate to take any action that is needed to achieve our objective."

"I know the council is not concerned as much as I am, but with the harvest disappearing we are in dire danger or running out of foodstuffs," the Minister of Nutrition interjected. "If we cannot recover it, we will barely make it to the next harvest before running out of food."

"Then we will just have to make sure we produce more food then," the Minister of Energy interjected. "You are just worrying too much.

Besides, I am sure the food that was stolen will be found. Xavier will see to that."

"But if the local population doesn't continue to support growing crops?" The Minister of Nutrition asked.

"Then we will use automation and general labor pool people to flow up there and take over the crop production," the Minister of Scientific Innovation replied. "You are way too worried about this. What is most important is gaining a purity of thought regarding scientific principles."

"And if we have a new labor pool on the farms up there," the powerful Minister of Energy Conservation offered, "then we can prove that our new energy targets for farming are achievable and won't have to listen to all the reasons why it isn't possible."

None of this discussion seemed to be particularly relevant to Xavier's current purpose for being there. He now saw where the strong response had come from to crack down on the northern sectors. In fact, seeing this strong anti-northern vitriol increased his respect for his minister who had seemed to provide latitude to moderate the response from what it could have been. Not that the current response was mild at all. Ultimately, he wasn't sure where his boss had allied himself on the new edicts and probably would never know. He had his marching orders to execute and would complete them to his fullest abilities.

"Why don't you go ahead and give us your update now?" the head of the council asked.

"We are actively underway on extractions of the children," Xavier answered. "We believe that much of the population has gone into some sort of hiding. Our teams have captured some children so far, but nowhere near the quantity we expected. We are responding by taking a more systematic approach to sweeping the sector. I am also deploying some teams randomly in case they are evacuating against our actions. This will take longer, but we will find anyone who is missing."

"This reminds me of a religious myth that was stamped out many years back," the aging Minister of Communications stated. "One cult professed the ability to mystically relocate objects as part of some religious rite. This ability is nonsense of course, but perhaps remnants of this sect were doing something to make it seem like they had this ability to spread their religious drivel to the population and rally them to support."

"Information on this would be helpful," Xavier replied doing his best to maintain a neutral expression on his face. "I do not recall reading about this within the ministry archives."

"That information wasn't something you wanted to be in possession of during the Scientific Reformation," the Minister said with a chuckle. "But a few years after, we did commission a limited study to better understand the myths that may still be practiced in secret. I will see if I can find that content and send it to you."

"Thank you Minister, that would be very helpful," Xavier replied while considering the significance of this offer.

"Thank you for your timely update," the head of the council stated. "We have conferred and believe you will be an effective voice for the council in Xenon in these perilous times. You will be given the title of Administrator of the Northern Sectors and have precedence to all other ministry officials in Xenon, Brendag and Villron sectors answering only to this council. You are charged to complete the extraction of the children, but even more so to bring the northern sectors into compliance, restoring the flow of vital exports needed for sustaining the country. This assignment will set for a duration of two years. Act with decisiveness and use whatever force is required."

"Thank you for this honor, ma'am," Xavier answered. "May science and reason guide you."

Xavier exited the council chambers. This was a great opportunity, but one riddled with many pitfalls. Xavier was pretty sure that he would be either moved to the top floor of the ministry in two years' time or be severely punished for failure. He preferred to avoid the second outcome.

Xavier traveled by air transport, arriving at the crack of dawn in Xenon. A hastily assembled party welcomed him, including most of highest-ranking members of the ministries in the Xenon sector. They had all received the communication announcing Xavier's appointment. Being answerable directly to the Great Scientist Council was very powerful backing. Career minded officials wanted to get on the good side of someone whose stray word could make or break their future in their respective ministry. Xavier made hasty greetings and introductions with the assembled officials, and asked if there was a place he could address them. He was ushered into a large conference room.

Behind the façade of the welcome, Xavier was able to detect an element of fear and uncertainty. The fact that he had to be appointed was an indictment of the job that they had been doing here. Plus, the high-profile failure of the escapes and not finding the children they were looking for weighed heavily on everyone assembled. When everyone looked to be mostly assembled, Xavier addressed the group.

"Good morning," Xavier said with the voice of confident projection. "There is a lot to do, so I will be brief. Our immediate mission is clear. We must complete the removal of children to the Ministry of Education. I know we have run into some obstacles on this front. Contrary to the reports I have been getting, they are not just gone. They are hiding somewhere, and we will find them and those who are circumventing the law by concealing them. We will be thorough in our search, complete in our interrogations of those people we do find, and we will complete our mission on this front."

"But this is just the beginning of what we are called to accomplish," Xavier continued. "We are in a battle for the hearts and minds of the northern sectors, primarily here in Xenon but also in the adjacent sectors of Brendag and Villron. We will be forceful when we must, pragmatic when we can, and ultimately, we must have a way to recover to move forward as a sector and as a nation. Gone are the days of two sets of laws, where we have one for the capital and one for northern sectors. We are one country and we will have one set of laws, and we will overcome those who oppose the ways of science."

Xavier stepped away from the microphone and was answered with a thunderous round of applause. Xavier nodded in acknowledgement of the applause and sought out Quintin in the crowd and motioned for him to come to him.

"Welcome sir," Quintin stated as an initial greeting. "Congratulations on your recent appointment. It is well deserved."

Xavier nodded in a dismissive manner. "Take me to your command center. You can give me a full update on where we are with the children collection activity there."

"Right this way. It is just a few rooms away," Quintin answered. "This building is the closest we have to a good ministry headquarters in this sector. I have been using it to coordinate the operation. I will assume you will want to take over this space. If it is not to your liking, I can show you the other options available."

Xavier continued to walk with Quintin, appearing deep in thought while not providing any verbal response to the offer Quintin had made.

"Here we are sir," Quintin finally was able to say. His demeanor was showing a bit of uncertainty after the rather cold reception Xavier had given him.

The room was laid out with many monitors and there was a team of about ten personnel monitoring communications and interacting with the remote teams. Recessed behind this was an office room with a partition up, providing a semblance of privacy. Xavier saw this office and immediately headed toward it. Once inside with the door closed, Xavier looked directly at Quintin.

"Please tell me some positive news," Xavier impatiently asked. "Give me some reason to not relieve you of your role in this messed up operation."

"Upon your recommendation," Quintin interjected, "we moved extraction teams further into the rural areas. I did a random spread of the teams and tried to mask their movement in case the hiding was somehow tied to where they thought our teams were going to be sweeping. I won't say we have had perfect success with this tactical change, but we have captured some children who are multigenerational families, not tied to a ministry in any way I can determine. I didn't focus on Deerbarrow yet, to allow our agent there more time to avoid detention, but the other areas around the sector have been hit randomly as I stated. We haven't got to all the residences yet, but they were prioritizing their evacuation approach to where we were telegraphing the placement of our teams. So, I would say our success rate has risen from near zero on target demographics to about fifteen percent since last night."

"Have you learned anything from those families whose children you have taken?" Xavier asked.

"We have had to make multiple examples of parents," Quintin replied. "Very few have been taken alive, and those who have been, are in a near comatose state. Some resisted, and some went numb. Those who have resisted are dead per instructions. Those who didn't, will take some time to figure out what they were told. We are actively working on it."

"Offer them a deal," Xavier replied in a matter of fact way. "Get their children back to them if they cooperate with what they know. You can keep them all confined so word doesn't get out. And later on, when we get what we need to know, we can still take the children away."

"Excellent idea sir," Quintin answered. "It is good to have you here. There is a lot to manage and your input is most welcome. I'll issue the orders as soon as we are through."

"Well at least we don't have a total failure on our hands. Let me get a lay of the land, and I will check back with you later on. You can keep overseeing this activity for now. Don't make me regret it." Xavier said with an ominous tone in his voice.

"Thank you, sir," Quintin answered. "You won't."

Xavier abruptly left the office to look around. He motioned for his assistant whom he had brought with him.

"Setup meetings with each of the senior officials of each ministry represented here in Xenon," Xavier ordered, "and arrange for me to survey the other two sectors under my charge within the next week. Quintin tells me this is the best place for a central command center. Make sure he is correct. If so, displace him somewhere else, but close enough so I can keep an eye on him and his team."

His assistant nodded quickly and proceeded to take charge of the area. Xavier's assistant invoking his name seemed to have the effect of creating urgency. Now he just needed to find some place to think while the logistics were handled. There had been some breaks overnight, but that was not going to be enough. This resistance needed to be broken, and it was going to take a ruthless approach. While he had not been an advocate of going down this path, the government was committed, and Xavier needed to ensure it had the best chance of success. Xavier inwardly smiled with anticipation to the script that was about to acted out. He was in the field again, and it felt exhilarating.

CHAPTER 17

*G*abriel awoke ready for another day of instruction. Well, maybe it was a new day. Gabriel really didn't have a good grasp of time where he was at. There were no electronics, no time pieces he had access to, and no sunlight to provide clues to the passage of days. There were chimes that sounded at specific intervals. There was a chime to eat, a chime to study, and a chime to sleep. These seemed to sound at a specific cadence, but you could never be sure.

What he was studying was interesting. There was a never-ending supply of books that needed to be read. And once he had read an assigned book or passage, he was mercilessly quizzed on what he had read by Teacher. If he gave a satisfactory answer, he would get another assignment. If he didn't, he would be asked to re-read and reflect for deeper meaning.

When he agreed to be accepted into the Order, he thought he would be getting more instruction on his dream gift, or how the resistance operated, but so far, the focus was all about expectations in values and beliefs. Plus, there was some strange busywork of turning pages in random books without reading them, while he was contemplating deeper meaning on Teacher's questions. Teacher had explained that he had a lot to unlearn so he should expect things to take a while, and as such had asked him to hold off on his dream training. He first needed to master the building blocks. Gabriel had met Raelynn in a dream shortly thereafter to explain this to her, and she nodded like she expected him to say that. He missed the interactions with her. Really, he missed interactions with anyone. This was the most solitary time he had ever spent in his life. While Teacher provided some human contact, it was not the same since he was staring at someone wearing a mask and speaking as a teacher versus as a friend. The solitary time combined with the books he had been reading, really gave him time for self-reflection. Time to look within himself to determine what he was and what he believed. And this was the hardest part of all.

Teacher said that once he completed his building block training, he would get to interact with some others who were in a similar place as he was in the Order. Any interaction beyond Teacher would be welcomed, and that served as motivation to continue with good speed and focus.

Gabriel spent a tremendous amount of time the last few sessions on a passage about selflessness. The angle taken in the writings was not about promoting the good of the whole versus the interest of the individual, as he wanted to gravitate to. It was more about seeking to do good for others for no other reason than doing good for them, even if it inconvenienced you or caused you to sacrifice something that you personally cared about. Or that is what he thought they were wanting him to understand. He had been sent back to reflect for deeper meaning on this passage several times already and was hoping he would get it correct at his next cadence with Teacher. He had already covered the basic study requirements in each of the other key tenants. He thought if he could finally master this one, it would mean he had accomplished a key milestone.

Teacher interrupted his study as he walked up on Gabriel suddenly.

"It is time to review this text," Teacher stated. "Have you gained sufficient wisdom?"

"True wisdom cannot be bestowed, it must be searched for, experienced and lived. I seek to take a step on this path with my actions, but there is never sufficient wisdom," Gabriel answered in the expected response he had learned in an earlier text.

Teacher nodded in an approving manner. "What is the ultimate gift of selflessness?"

Gabriel had been asked this question many times previously. Each time, he had been instructed to study some more. He tried giving away his personal possessions, giving his time, giving up career ambitions, and none of these appeared to get the satisfactory response. He had been contemplating what could be greater than all of these. And each time Teacher's response had been, "You would offer so little?"

Gabriel had been deep in thought on this topic and had finally had an idea. It may have some holes in it, but he was going to try a new answer this time.

"Is it to give up my life?" Gabriel asked with uncertainty in his voice.

Teacher paused and did not immediately reject his answer, which was usually a good sign. "It could be that you are close to the answer. In what way could this be demonstrated?"

Gabriel contemplated his question for a few moments then answered. "If someone I cared about was in danger of being taken by the ministry for execution and I knew their whereabouts…It would be like me not telling what I knew, even if it meant being executed instead. Or maybe taking an action to allow them escape, even if it meant I would be killed."

"But wouldn't your commitment to the law supersede your commitment to selflessness?" Teacher asked.

"I must first fulfill my duties to the Order before I can fulfill my duties to the law," Gabriel answered. He still wasn't sure he believed this, but it was the expected answer he was pretty sure.

"But aren't the laws just? Who are we to offer defiance to them?" Teacher asked.

"We are those trained in the Order to protect that which is just and oppose that which is not," Gabriel answered. "Those laws that are unjust are not binding. But not all laws are such. We work to teach the people the errors, so change can occur. We work to remove obstacles, so the people can experience the full way of love and life."

"You have learned well," Teacher said. "You have completed the study of the building blocks. Next, you will continue your growth in your dream gifts and higher teachings of the Order. Gather your possessions, and we will move you to a different library. Here you will split your time with more reading of texts and with time spent in the dream state developing your abilities. I will spend time with you as I have, quizzing you on what you have learned. You may also see other students sharing the space with you. Please do not inquire too much into their histories or identities. In today's times, we gain safety in our anonymity. But they will give you variety from the solitude you have experienced these last many days."

Gabriel expressed gratitude to the change and followed Teacher to the new location. He had thought there were a lot of books to read in the place he had been in. That wasn't even close to the amazing collection of texts stored in this room. There was row after row of books in a room that he could not see the end of.

"This room of books is amazing!" Gabriel exclaimed.

"This is one of the foremost libraries in the world," Teacher explained. "When the Scientific Reformation occurred, there was a big effort to destroy any book associated with areas of religious or supernatural thinking. A large effort was made by the Order in saving as many as possible. Each sector has their own library location. Some books are unique to only one library, but there are many others that are duplicated. We have taken steps to control the environment in this area to best preserve the texts. The very oldest books we have digitized, but only within local equipment stored here on the premises. It is very risky to connect anything that could notify Oversite and give away this location. The loss of this library would be a great loss to our history and teaching."

Gabriel nodded, still trying to take in the magnitude of what he saw here. "Are these all books related to the Order?" He asked.

Teacher chuckled. "No, these are books from all teachings, even those who we do not believe. While we would like to have everyone believe as we do, we also hold true that everyone should be free to believe and choose what they want to. We even believe that if people want to choose to not believe, that is fine also. But it is mostly about having the choice. We also have books that are not intended to be religious in nature, but due to some references within them, have been banned. We do not want to lose our literary history."

"But what good do these books do if they are hidden here where hardly anyone is allowed to use them?" Gabriel asked.

"A very good question," Teacher answered. "For now, our main purpose is to preserve them for when they can exist in the light of day. But we also use them to teach from. Most do not see them, but you are being given a great gift to learn from their knowledge. We have an ongoing effort to digitize these texts, so someday when society is ready for change, this knowledge can be once again shared with all."

"I have read many of them," Teacher continued, "but as you can see, reading all of them is not a realistic goal. I would like for you to start with books from the Order, focusing on dream gifts. They are in this section here. But you are welcome to explore and read anything that interests you."

Gabriel looked at the section he was referring to. They appeared to be indexed by different aspects of dream gifts. The shelf must have had several hundred books on it. Gabriel sighed internally. Just when he thought he was making progress on his training, he realized he had just begun.

∞ ∞ ∞

Gabriel should have been rusty getting into the dream state. He surprisingly entered it very quickly, even without an actual lily plant to assist him. With very little to distract, he was able to center his thoughts very quickly and pass into the dream world where the field of lilies existed. He entered this area and decided to wait here for a time to see if Raelynn was available to join him. He was not disappointed.

"Well, hello stranger," Raelynn greeted him after he had been waiting what seemed like a few minutes. "I take it you have completed the first phase of your training?"

"Yes, it took a very long time, but it is finished. I am allowed more advanced studies, and am able to resume my dream training," Gabriel answered with a smile on his face. He was very glad to resume his interaction with Raelynn.

"You seem more centered and at peace," Raelynn offered. "It gives me joy to see that. Can I safely assume that you had a much easier time entering the dream state?"

"I didn't think that was related, but yes, it was probably the easiest time I have ever entered it on my own, and I didn't even have a lily plant to look at," Gabriel answered. "I have been doing a lot of self-searching and thinking lately, and I feel more at peace than I can remember before."

"This was your most important lesson so far," Raelynn said. "Until you master yourself, you can never fully achieve your potential in the dream state. Both in getting here and what you can accomplish while here. Remember the lessons from who goes by Teacher, and they will serve you well."

"You know Teacher?" Gabriel asked.

"I may not know who goes by Teacher for you, but I have also had instruction by one named Teacher," Raelynn answered. "All those in the Order must pass though that gate under Teacher's instruction."

"But not everyone is asked to join the Order, are they?" Gabriel asked.

"You need to have some level of the dream gift in order to join," Raelynn explained. "There is a supporting order for those who share the beliefs but lack the gifts. They also get training, but it is not nearly extensive. Typically, what you just finished, is what non-dreamers are asked to accomplish. They are also educated some on things dream gifts can accomplish, so it does not surprise, should they observe it. What is most focused on are the moral tenants that you just finished. Educational programs have been conducted to counter the ministry sanctioned schooling, but that has been getting progressively harder to complete. I guess that is easier now that we have evacuated most of the population and children, but recently it hasn't been so."

The term evacuated most of the population got Gabriel's attention very quickly. So that is what he was seeing the beginning of when he was translocated into his training.

"Evacuation of the population?" Gabriel asked with a shocked expression. "That seems to be a pretty major change since I have been training!"

Raelynn smiled, "Yeah, I probably shouldn't have slipped that in like that. We evacuated nearly everyone when that 'we will take your children away' edict came down from the government. I think they were expecting some violence and excuse to clamp down on us, but it didn't work out that way. We just executed a backup plan and have been in hiding for the last several months. I won't pretend it is going super well, but it is way better than having families split up."

"So how has everyone been surviving?" Gabriel asked.

"Well, we have plenty of food for now, since we took the entire harvest when we evacuated. It has been amusing to monitor the government trying to follow their own guidelines for farming, which by the way hasn't been working for them. Those who have evacuated are staying in a similar type place to where I imagine you are, except are a bit more closed in and crowded."

"Is everyone safe?" Gabriel asked. "I can't imagine the government is not actively trying to find those who escaped."

"They are starting to look underground," Raelynn answered. "So far, we have stayed ahead of them. We have dreamers building new living spaces non-stop, to spread out the risk of being found. This probably won't last forever, but we are hoping we can gain leverage if we can hold out longer than the food supply on the surface does."

"Wow!" Gabriel answered. "I have missed a lot! I can't believe so much has been going on and I missed it all."

"You have been doing what is most important," Raelynn said. "If you are going to play a part in this, we need you to be trained as much as possible. You need to be doing what you are doing."

"I guess I understand," Gabriel replied sounding unconvinced. "I just feel that I may not have been doing my part."

"Your part is to grow in your gifts," Raelynn explained. "What we need most right now are those with the dream gift to help with the resistance that is ongoing. You have the potential to be very strong in that gift. Most dreamers who are already helping will not progress much further in abilities than they currently have. You on the other hand, have much more potential, one I hope will make the difference later. For that reason, you must continue to grow in your gifts, so we can use you when we need you most in the future."

Gabriel took a moment to process what she had said. He was being groomed for some later purpose, but one that he was not being told. He didn't like it that he was isolated from what was going on. He wanted to participate in the action and interact with the other people. Plus, he had the ministry to contend with. Who knew their opinion of him right now? Did they think him dead or maybe unable to report in? And if he could report in somehow, would he want to?

Raelynn interrupted his thoughts, "You seem less centered suddenly. I probably dropped a lot on you all of a sudden. Remember your training, and do not let the seemingly urgent nature of things get you unduly distracted. Handle each thing separately and with calm. Find your place of peace and focus inwardly on it."

"Thank you, Raelynn," Gabriel answered, "I will work on that right now."

Gabriel took a moment to refocus his thoughts and was able to take them sequentially in his mind. He did not need to have answers to these questions right away. He had time to decide his best path. He did not have unlimited time with Raelynn.

"I think I am in a better place," Gabriel offered. "I would like to resume our training if you are willing."

"Of course," Raelynn replied. "I would like that also. Now that you have access to the Order's library on dreaming, there is much there you will have questions on and will want to try. Before you try something you have not done, please discuss it with myself or Teacher. We will not limit you as much as before, but we can hopefully help you avoid common pitfalls that have caused great harm to those who acted without knowing what they were doing. As for my main request of you, I want you to explore in the past. In the library there are very descriptive books and pictures which can aid you getting outside of your own personal timeline if you find you can do that. When you read up on that, I would recommend you trying it. Until then, go back to times in your life to explore the things you did not see that happened near you. The world does not exist how we often think it does."

Gabriel nodded his acceptance, "Ok, I will do this as a priority."

"I also do not plan on accompanying you on this journey," Raelynn continued. "If you call to me, I will do my best to come find you, but always keep a visual picture of where you left from to be an anchor to pull you back, so you do not get stuck wondering through the past. You are no longer the baby you once were in your gift. Yes, you have a lot left to learn, but you can take some steps on your own if you are careful."

CHAPTER 18

*P*hillip woke up from sleeping in his bed. This was supposed to be a day of great excitement for him. He was finally turning eight years old. He had been bringing up his upcoming birthday to some of his classmates, but there was no sense of enthusiasm from them. A birthday to them was just another day. Sure, they knew when their birthday was, but that was about all there was to it to them.

He had started to explain how his mom and sister had thrown a party for him and invited all his friends, but his teacher had overhead, and told him to not talk about that. That was his old life and he was now part of the Ministry of Education and needed to learn to live by their ways. He really didn't like their ways very much, but as time kept going by, he had a harder and harder time remembering what the old ways were like before he came here. He could still picture his mother's face in his mind and his sister, but he was starting to worry if he saw them again, he wouldn't recognize them. He tried drawing a picture of them a few times, but they were erased by his teacher and he was told to stop thinking of them.

His teacher kept talking about being deemed worthy of living to contribute to society, whatever that meant. He had a few years yet, but when he turned thirteen, he would be tested. If he did well on his test, he would get to stay in school and continue to gain skills for a job in society. If he couldn't pass the test, he would be lucky to join the organ donor program, provided his body had sufficient match characteristics with someone important in a ministry. If he didn't have that, then he would not have value to society and would be ended, whatever that meant. The ecosystem could only support a population of a certain size, and you needed to provide value, if you were to exist in it. The more he thought about it, getting older meant he was closer to taking that test. All he wanted was to get back with his family but thinking about that too much would mean he wouldn't pass his test.

His classmates were all so serious and didn't hardly laugh or have fun. Maybe because he was new and they all had known each other before, but he wasn't sure. It probably was if there were only so many slots available when you turned thirteen. Having more people around to compete for them made your chances harder.

The other thing he didn't like was that they had made him use a new name. They said that it was for his own safety, but he wasn't sure he believed them. If he used a different name, how would his mom find him? But he learned very early on he didn't want to mess up and use the wrong name. They had made him change schools when he messed up the last time and made him be bored in a dark room for days, to help him remember to use his new name. Now he had yet another name to use. Today he was Robert. His memory of being Phillip had begun to fade as was his joy of experiencing life.

∞ ∞ ∞

Joseph Lazerof was thankful to still be alive, although it was ridiculous that he had to think that. After three months of the ministry interrogating him, he had been absolved of intentionally aiding the escape of the prisoner. He had lost his position in the confinement center. After all, how could he be trusted, if he couldn't handle the simple job of guarding a helpless prisoner, not that it had been his fault the prisoner had escaped. He was tired of being blamed for the gross incompetence of others, but he had finally been set free, and that was probably the best it was going to get for him. His hopes of getting a better assignment in a different sector were gone, and now he was just trying to show his worth as a general laborer. He had been told if he showed an aptitude at doing this work, he could move into a supervisor position, which would be an increase in credits and status over what he had been doing. And when he looked at his competition, he thought his chances were pretty good for that happening, provided those who made the decisions were smart enough to see how much more qualified he was than all the other lackeys.

Looking at his supervisor, he thought he couldn't do any worse job than he was. You would think someone from the Ministry of Nutrition who oversaw the farm production, would have a clue about how a farm was run, and could give good guidance to its operations. Well, he definitely was giving guidance – good guidance? Well, that was a different story. There was a manual that contained a listing all the regulations and steps needed to do the farming properly. That would be great if the manual was written by someone who had been on a farm before, but it was probably written by someone like his incompetent supervisor. The quotas for the water usage didn't seem realistic and the energy allowances seemed to be not grounded in reality, but his idiot supervisor believed his precious manual couldn't be wrong which meant asking for a variance for more of either wasn't going to happen.

Plus, there was all that strange equipment that no one really knew how to run, or how to repair if it didn't work correctly. Joseph had always had a pretty good mechanical aptitude and had been assigned to get the equipment working that was needed to complete the plowing and planting. He eventually did get it working. It wasn't exactly sabotaged in a permanent manner, but some key pieces had been removed. At least in this situation, a manual was a useful thing in determining what wasn't functioning correctly, but that was only because Joseph was able to understand it. Most of the people here wouldn't have been able to do that.

Joseph had gotten the approval to charge the planting equipment with the energy allotment needed to prepare a field and plant it. The equipment would disrupt the soil and then insert the seeds needed to grow the new crops. Joseph was assigned the job of driving the equipment. This also took some time to figure out. He thought it was very strange that this equipment hadn't been more fully automated. It seemed like you could have equipment scan the field and automatically complete the driving for you. But instead, this was still a very manual operation. Technology probably could be adapted to do this, but it was likely not deemed important enough to allocate valuable ministry resources on something so menial. Joseph had completed just under half of the field when the equipment stopped moving. It had depleted its energy bank. The calculated energy allotment for the whole field had only lasted for half.

"The planter is out of energy. Do you want me to charge it up again so we can finish this field?" Joseph asked his supervisor.

"The manual says the charge you used is enough for an entire field of this size," he answered. "You must have done something wrong."

Joseph was careful to fix a neutral expression on his face. "I don't think I wasted any movement with it. Maybe there is something wrong with the equipment?"

"The Ministry of Nutrition has a technical services line," his supervisor stated. "It says in the manual to contact them if the expected energy output is not achieved. Can you handle doing that?"

"I'll get right on it," Joseph said, trying very hard to not roll his eyes in view of his supervisor as he walked away.

A couple of hours of being passed around and put on hold multiple times, he had a repair ticket approved. In six to eight weeks a technician could be deployed. Apparently, there was a long wait for services, since several other farms had similar issues. Government efficiency in action. Joseph signed up. Joseph again asked his supervisor if he wanted to use additional energy to complete the field, but he didn't, instead deciding to wait for the technician to come.

So, one half of a single field was complete with about twenty more similar fields present on the farm. And now all the workers were literally hand planting the remainder of the first field to make up for the bad energy usage of the planter. At the rate they were going, they might have it planted before the technician arrived, maybe.

And there was the water. Well, the lack of water. Joseph was pretty certain that you needed water to grow crops. That usually came in the form of rain, but it had not rained in several weeks. It would take special approval to requisition water for irrigation, and as expected, his supervisor didn't want to make that request either. They now had a really small crop planted and nothing wanted to come up out of the ground. They couldn't use water and couldn't use energy. Hopefully the other farms had someone who had a better idea of what he was doing, but he was not confident they did. But Joseph did have a sore back, blisters on his hands, and a certainty that food products would soon be in short supply. But if that happened, maybe his supervisor would move on, and someone could finally recognize his value to do more than plant crops that would never grow in a dried-out field.

∞ ∞ ∞

Xavier reviewed the crop reports. There were a lot of positive words being given about how everyone was working hard and were following the farming standards to the letter. When he looked at the actual planting statistics, Xenon was sitting somewhere between ten and twenty percent planted, versus the hundred percent they should be at. And the sad thing was, he wasn't sure it was even that good. He was expecting a less efficient planting than those who had been doing it, but this was far below what he had feared. The only saving grace was that he had been told that Xenon had a very long growing window would support crop growth through much of the year, so it wasn't like they were missing a critical timing window. But some crops grew better in some seasons than others, which further complicated the mess that was developing.

Xavier checked the time and prepared himself for his next meeting. Kayleigh Anderson was his next appointment. She was the senior ministry official from the Ministry of Nutrition in Xenon. She had been in place about one and a half years and was just short of the typical timing an aspiring ministry official would transfer out and to a new higher-level position. She was a mid-ranking official in the Ministry of Nutrition. Common sense would say that the highest-ranking person in the sector that was responsible for nearly all crop production would rate higher than that, but that was not the case. This was a post that could be leveraged for advancement, but by itself she did not have a lot of authority in the ministry.

"Good morning, sir," Kayleigh said as she extended her hand in greeting. I appreciate you meeting with me this morning. May science and reason guide your day."

Kayleigh was younger than Xavier would normally see in this position, and she had a reputation for being career minded and ambitious. Xavier hadn't interacted with her very much since being here. His initial impression of her was that she was competent, organized and had a plan she was executing against. Xavier's focus had been mainly on trying to secure the children and as that area had stabilized, or at least wasn't adding new information anymore, it better allowed him to redirect his focus to his other main priority for being in this sector, food production.

"Without science and reason, all is lost," Xavier ritually responded extending his hand in response. "Thank you for coming. I have been reviewing the crop reports and am frankly concerned with how far behind schedule we appear to be. My assistant, I hope, told you I wanted to understand what obstacles are preventing us from being in a better situation?"

"Yes, she did," Kayleigh answered. "May I speak directly sir? My answer may not be very popular to hear."

"I am not very patient with any other kind of talk, Ms. Anderson," Xavier replied. "Please proceed."

"Thank you," she answered. "The first problem we have is very little knowledge of how to grow crops. The ministry has sent us low-level officials to run each of the farms. We also have taken general laborers from the pool to complete the needed work. Our ministry provides training to everyone on the standards expected to operate a farm, and for each major task. Each task has an expected energy consumption quota and a requisite water consumption."

"I am aware of this process," Xavier replied. "What does this have to do with lack of production? We don't have knowledge, yet we have a documented standard and are following it. I would expect some drop off in production, but not at the level of ninety percent!"

"I fear it may be more than that," Kayleigh replied. "I have been completing an inspection circuit of several of the farm operations around Xenon and have yet to see a farm that has completed ten percent of its planting. And to be honest sir, what I have seen planted and germinated, doesn't look like it will yield anything near we are accustomed to getting. The soil is parched, and what is there appears to be dying."

"That is not good at all," Xavier said.

"No sir, it is not," she answered.

"What is causing this when you visited the farms?" Xavier asked with frustration slowing building in his voice.

"Let me start with the planting. Each field that crops are planted in has a targeted energy allotment for planting. The equipment is charged with the allowed energy amount and they clumsily begin a planting operation. The most I have observed the energy quota supporting was two thirds of a field planting. Most farms are lucky to get half." Kayleigh said resignedly.

"That would mean that we should have at least half of the fields planted. So why are we so low?" Xavier asked.

"Each farm official when seeing that the first field did not get the required coverage, has stopped using the equipment and has called for technical support," Kayleigh answered. "Most of the expertise on this equipment has gone into hiding. Those we have, are operating on a very big backlog. When I managed to find and interview one of the technicians, he said that the energy quotas are based on perfect ideal conditions which we never see. Even after they fully tune the equipment, we won't be able to get the quota to meet the field requirements. They improve the efficiency, but it still doesn't work. As a result, the farms are afraid to overconsume energy and have redirected their labor to manual planting to offset the energy shortfall. Needless to say, this goes very slowly."

"So how did the prior workers get the fields planted?" Xavier asked. "Clearly they had a method somehow."

"They got energy waivers for one thing," Kayleigh answered. "They were pretty skilled at explaining why it was needed. Plus, the quotas were higher when they were here. The Ministry of Energy Conservation has been trying to lower the quotas for a long time and took the opportunity to change them when people could not competently oppose them. From what I could tell on the old quotas, we would probably average about eighty percent planting efficiency and that is with not being experienced in what we are doing."

"You are saying," Xavier interrupted, "that the reason we are not getting the planting done, is that we are trying to do the planting with unrealistic energy quotas, and we are afraid of asking for waivers?"

"That is the gist of it, yes," Kayleigh sighed.

"And the poor performance of the crops," Xavier continued. "let, me guess, we need to use water to irrigate, but the standard says we shouldn't need to water it, so we watch our crops die?"

"That is my assessment," Kayleigh stated in a resigned manner.

"And have you done anything to make changes to fix this?" Xavier asked.

"I have requested changes to the energy allotments," Kayleigh answered. "But I do not have authority to approve these, and with the increased scrutiny on any behavior that may be deemed as disloyal to the precepts of science, there are very few in my supervisory chain who are willing to advocate for this need. That is why I am speaking with you sir."

Xavier took a moment to consider the implications of what she had said. Xavier was worried that there would be a sabotage campaign by the native Xenon residents. They didn't need to sabotage at all. They just needed to let the government policies act unchallenged, and it would have the same impact as sabotage.

Xavier had the influence to advocate for changes here. Kayleigh was correct to ask his help. But how far was he willing to go? He was several months into an assignment that did not have a meaningful victory. Could he survive to serve his full two-year term if he handled this the wrong way? The more he thought about it, he really didn't have any choice. He needed to subdue the sector and get food production back up. As much as he didn't want to touch this issue, leadership came with a heavy burden to make hard decisions and make enemies at times when needed. It was time to see how strong his authority in this sector really was.

Xavier visibly sighed, "What do you need me to do?"

Kayleigh explained her desired approach. Xavier made some notes and provided some suggestions of his own. This detail would prove helpful for his next meeting which was a conference with the Great

Scientist Council. He was expecting incompetence based on recent planting results, but Kayleigh had really impressed him, even if she hadn't found a way to overcome the policies she was being asked to implement.

Xavier checked his appearance and surroundings after Kayleigh left before remoting into the virtual meeting with the Great Scientist Council. This meeting was using a technology that emulated a virtual presence in a common meeting room. It was a rare thing that the Great Scientist Council met in person with their physical bodies all in the same location. Prior to coming to Xenon, he had addressed the full council in person, but under normal conditions, they did a virtualized remote. This system allowed you fully engage your senses in your interaction with someone else in the room, simulating any sensory conditions such as smell, touch, as well as sight and hearing. Taste really wasn't deemed useful, but one of the minsters had expressed a curiosity in it, which got some researchers scrambling to figure out a way to include this in the sensory array. This technology was not widely deployed throughout the government, but top ministers did have access to using it. Xavier had requested a station for this assignment to allow him to minimize travel and improve his access to the council. He was somewhat surprised he was granted this indulgence. He suspected it was so everyone could have equal access to him, versus having to go directly through his home ministry.

Xavier waited to be formally admitted into the session. He only had to wait about five minutes, which must have meant they were very anxious for his report. Xavier linked into the meeting room and saw that all council members were present.

"Good afternoon," Xavier offered in greeting to the council.

The presiding officer nodded in recognition. "The council recognizes the Administrator of the Northern Sectors. Please present your report."

"Thank you, ma'am," Xavier opened. "First, I am pleased to report we have had no uprisings or violent resistance activity in the last month. The population that is present and visible in Xenon, Brendag and Villron sectors have been compliant, and have been following the same laws that are followed in Preath and the rest of the sectors. It has taken some time for the population to understand the changes, but we have dealt harshly with those who were not complying, and that has served to improve performance for the remainder."

"At least that is some good news," one of the ministers stated in a less than enthusiastic manner.

"About the only good news, I am afraid," Xavier carefully responded. "I say that because we have only accounted for about eighteen percent of the original population of these sectors. Most of those remaining had a documented connection with the government. Those captured who are native to the sector without the government connections, we have been able to interrogate. There appears to have been an expectation of evacuation for some we captured. They said if they wanted to be evacuated, they were to mark their doors and wait in a central room together."

"Did you determine what technology or means was being used to evacuate them, or where they have gone to?" asked another minister.

"We have not, but we have some suspicions on this," Xavier answered, thinking about the report he read on religions the Minister of Communication had given him. "We believe that this Kayden organization, yes Kayden is what the resistance seems to have named itself, has some sort of underground network. When I say underground, I don't mean just off the grid, I literally mean underground. Our belief is that there are one or multiple underground locations that people are currently living in. We have found some empty ones that have shown signs of a quick exit."

"Don't we have a way to scan the ground for these places?" the Minister of Transportation asked.

"I am told we used to have some technical expertise on this, but as mining was phased out to be replaced by reuse and recycling of existing components, so was this technology," Xavier answered. "This knowledge existed in the Bredag desert sector where most of the mining occurred. I have requested a high priority on resurrecting this technology and improving it. If the council wanted to lend their support to this, it would aid greatly in searching for those who disappeared. I have encountered some hesitancy within the capital to prioritize development of a technology whose use fell out of favor with scientific priorities."

"That seems like a fair request," answered the presiding officer. "We will add this to our agenda next month to come to resolution on it, if there are no objections from the council."

Xavier did his best to keep his face neutral. Another month seemed like an eternity and for something that was such a high priority. At least they were willing to discuss it.

"So, what about the food situation?" the Minister of Nutrition asked. "Are we as far behind schedule as my sector lead indicates? I have a mind to replace her if the progress reports are accurate."

"Ms. Anderson is doing an admirable job in my opinion." Xavier replied. "You have done well in appointing her to this position. Her and my challenge is directly related to the provided energy quotas for producing the crops. With all the experienced farm workers absent, the replacements are not skilled enough to complete planting and crop maintenance to the required energy and water targets. Most farms have been unwilling to inefficiently plant any fields after their first one, realizing they are doing it outside of optimal energy models. It would be against science in their mind, if they continued to plant crops using energy at a non-optimal rate. This belief is widespread, and further reinforced in the training they received before being sent to oversee the farms."

"We provided very clear standards on how to do the tasks," the Minister of Nutrition challenged.

"Yes, and without them, we wouldn't have the first idea where to start with new people doing the crop production. It is believed that most of the prior farm managers had additional efficiencies they had developed that were not captured in the standards. To be very direct if you would allow me, we need temporary energy quota increases and instruction to the leads to use the needed energy to get the planting done."

"There is always an excuse why the energy targets can't be met," the Minister of Energy Conservation said with frustration building in his voice. "Don't people realize that our resources are precious, and the impact on the environment must be weighed against anything that could harm it?"

"Yes, I appreciate that very much," Xavier answered. "I do not ask this lightly. If I understand the state of the food supplies correctly, if we do not get a planting rate to at least fifty percent in the next month, we will have to start allocating food to the population in a reduced supply. And right now, after twice that time, we are only at ten percent planted."

"Thank you for the update, Xavier," commented the head of the council. "You are well informed as always. We will take your recommendations under advisement and put this on the agenda for next month's meeting. That should give each of the ministries time to evaluate your recommendations. Keep up the good work."

Xavier was faded out of the meeting. While he was hoping for immediate endorsement, he was not that surprised the decisions had been delayed. Until there was a real problem that was seen, he did not expect to see urgency on the council's part. The sectors were compliant, and the laws were now evenly enforced. They largely had everything they had wanted. They had power and control if they ignored what they could not see. And for the time being, they had food enough to eat. The priority would come on the food soon enough. But unless they were prepared, it could rock the foundation of their society.

CHAPTER 19

$\mathcal{G}$abriel transitioned out of the dream state. He felt like he had spent years experiencing the history of his life, the ministry, and at some level of the founding of the nation. He was expecting to feel completely drained and lethargic, as this was the longest journey he had ever taken, but at most he felt a little sluggish. He had been told that long trips typically caused a drain on the dreamer, but for him there was rarely more than a minor slowdown upon return. Both Teacher and Raelynn said this was remarkable, but never gave more feedback than that.

He had asked if there was a way to read new books in the dream state without consuming actual time and was cautioned against it. Apparently physically moving books to read them risked changing the timeline continuum, versus just observing didn't harm anything. He had been doing some time shifting, searching for the authors themselves and trying to find periods in their lives when they were instructing others. This proved helpful in some ways, but when you couldn't ask someone an actual question, it sometimes proved problematic. So, he still lost time doing actual reading, but was able to move though this training at a breathtaking pace.

"What have you learned today?" Teacher asked, walking in on Gabriel.

This was the simple question Teacher asked regularly at this time of day. In the library Gabriel now had access to a clock, which gave him access to the actual time of day.

"I have learned much. I am grateful for each new insight and hope that knowledge fills me with a better experience of living life and an ability to improve the lives of those around me," Gabriel answered in the ritual response.

"When did you go on your journey today?" Teacher asked.

"For one, about fifty years before the Scientific Reformation." Gabriel explained. "In this time, there was freedom of expression and religion. Aldous Kendell lived then whose book, *Dreaming with Purpose* you suggested I read. He had some interesting ideas on impacting reality by invoking change on the past if you could find a seminal event that caused a chain reaction of outcomes. If you could influence this event just ever so slightly, he thought it was possible to change the course of what was to come, and what had already happened. Looking at how those around Kendell treated him, his ideas were not in the mainstream of where the Order was at. They didn't move to silence him, but he didn't have a following either. I found where he gave a lecture, and there were only two people who showed up. The lecture was fascinating, but not acclaimed."

"And what do you think about this concept?" Teacher asked.

"I am seeing problems with impacting a reality that precedes your existence. For example, if I went back in time to try to change something, but that change caused me to no longer exist, then I could never have changed it to begin with!" Gabriel replied.

"That is the key paradox relative to this study." Teacher answered. "I do know that some with the gift have been able to go back into time a few seconds and impact events at a very small level. This is usually very draining to the person doing it, but they swear they remember the prior outcome even though the people watching only remember the changed outcome. Naturally, this is very hard to collaborate, which probably impacted the credibility of Kendell."

"I can see the problems validating that for sure," Gabriel answered.

"So how is your translocation practice coming?" Teacher asked.

"I think it is going pretty well," Gabriel answered.

"Do you feel comfortable taking the test for translocation of real people?" Teacher asked.

"I think I am ready to test for it," Gabriel answered. "I have moved around the animals you had me practice on, and I did go back in time to observe several training events on this by noted experts. But if you think I need more practice, I will keep working on it. This is definitely something I don't want to mess up!"

"No, I think you are ready also. And to prove it, you can move me first," Teacher offered. "Move me from where I am currently at to be on the other side of the room."

Gabriel nodded and quickly got himself into the dream state. Lately, he was finding the transition to be nearly seamless with little to no delay. Focusing on Teacher, he took in his features and then imagined him to be in the new place in the room. Confirming he moved, he exited out of the dream state.

"Well done!" Teacher exclaimed. "And I didn't end up in the void or embedded into the side of the wall. What a relief!"

Gabriel chuckled at Teacher's displayed humor. He was usually so formal but seemed to be having some fun with Gabriel today.

"Now I need you to find and move someone you cannot visually see." Teacher explained. "In the sleeping area, one of the other students is resting. I need you to find him and move him to a different bed."

This would take a two-step approach. First, he needed to explore in the dream state, then he needed to translocate. Gabriel entered the dream state and visualized himself in the sleeping area. Sure enough, one of his fellow students was resting. Gabriel took in his description carefully and then visualized him sleeping in a different bed. He watched him move. Satisfied he had completed his task, he woke and told Teacher it was completed.

After walking to the sleeping area, Teacher rang the bell to wake up the student and to confirm he was intact. Seeing he was, he had one more task for Gabriel to complete.

"I now need you to translocate yourself," Teacher challenged. "As we have discussed before, this is best done over relatively short distances."

"Ok," Gabriel replied. "Would going back to the original room be sufficient?"

After seeing Teacher nod, Gabriel transitioned himself to the dream state, took in the black and white version of himself and visualized himself back into the room he started in. Opening his eyes, Gabriel saw that he had arrived at his desired destination.

A few moments later, Teacher walked in the room and gave Gabriel an embrace.

"Congratulations!" Teacher exclaimed. "You have completed your next phase of training. You are now to be called Affirmed."

"Thank you so much," Gabriel said with genuine gratitude.

"While your training never really ends," Teacher explained, "you have progressed enough where you could be of great help to the Order and to Kayden in other ways. I have an assignment if you are interested in hearing about it?"

"Yes," Gabriel said, "it would be very interesting to have a change of scenery. No offense to being here of course."

"This is potentially very dangerous," Teacher cautioned. "Your cousin Tom has been training with a team to find and rescue children from the Ministry of Education that belong to parents in hiding. Unfortunately, the children are spread all throughout the sectors, and we will need to infiltrate the schools they are in if there will be any hope of finding and rescuing them. This team needs a dreamer on it they can trust. It will be very dangerous, but if you are willing, the job is yours."

Gabriel gave this request some silent thought for a few moments before answering. While he really had been enjoying all that he had been learning in the library, it was time he stepped out and did something meaningful. He really liked his cousin Tom and would like to reunite with him.

"Ok," Gabriel replied, "I am interested and would like to join up."

"That is great to hear," Teacher said. "I will let them know. Go ahead and gather your things you have with you and come with me. I will help you meet up with them."

"Will I get to come back here more when this is over?" Gabriel asked as he scooped up his bag and put his meager set of possessions in it.

"I hope you will be able to," Teacher answered. "But there are other ways to continue your training. What I have done to help you is compile this list of key topics, authors and when and where they lived and am posting it on the wall here for you. Take a few moments to read it so you can later revisit it if you need to research a topic in time. Also, any book you read while you were here, you can go back and reread the same way. It is our way of having an access portal like Oversite without having Oversite."

"Wow! I never thought of it that way," Gabriel exclaimed while taking a cursory look at the list Teacher had prepared. "Now I am wishing I had read more books than I did."

"You didn't actually have to read them you know," Teacher hinted. "Are you forgetting the page turning exercises I had you do when you were looking for deeper meaning?"

"I can't believe I didn't make that connection!" Gabriel said. "I can go back and read anything I opened, can't I?"

"Yes, you can." Teacher replied. "While you didn't get though the entire library, you did complete the next few hundred books I would have had you study if I had time to teach you. I will also have some of the current students do this as well. I will note when each of the books on the posted list here were turned, so you can come back and visit them in your dreams. It won't be as meaningful as discussing them but will hopefully be there to help you continue to grow while you are away. Preferring the discussion is why I didn't suggest this method before."

"And I thought you were just trying to have me work on my meditation then, not realizing you were building a personal library for me to use," Gabriel said excitedly.

"It looks like you have everything?" Teacher asked.

"Yes, I think I do," Gabriel answered with a feel of finality.

Teacher motioned for Gabriel to follow and led him to an area of the space he hadn't been in before. He made an odd motion and a door panel opened, revealing some sort of cylinder like what he had seen Isabella use in his dream.

"This will take you to where Tom is training," Teacher stated. "The Order has kept this technology secret up until the evacuation. It lets someone with just a small amount of dream gifts translocate the vehicle to the programmed coordinate location."

"That is incredible!" Gabriel exclaimed. "How does it work?"

"This technology has been around for many generations." Teacher explained. "A dreamer with a keen sense of mechanical skills was able to determine a resonant frequency that could respond to someone in the dream state. By studying this phenomenon, he was able to harness the dream activity and magnify it in a way that the pod would be translocated to a programmed coordinate location. The original research, person's name, and time period are carefully preserved to only the highest members of the Order. There is fear this knowledge has potential to be used for ill purposes. But we do have engineering drawings and schematics to construct these. I will say these were vital to evacuating the population when we did."

"Wow, that is really amazing," Gabriel answered. "The distance problem with translocation was causing me to wonder how it was done."

"Using it is actually pretty simple," Teacher answered. "You press your hands on these two buttons to say you are ready, then you go into the dream state for just a moment. When it senses this, it will transport you to the location programmed in the console. I have preprogrammed it for your destination."

"Thank you again, so, so much for all you have taught me and shown me. I can't thank you enough!" Gabriel exclaimed.

"Remember to hang up and remove your mask and robe before you depart. Go in peace, Affirmed, and may your path be true and your actions just."

With that, Teacher closed the opening on Gabriel and was gone.

Gabriel briefly took in his surroundings then remembered to remove the mask and robe. He had it on nearly constantly, that it had become a part of him, and he felt strange with it gone. Gabriel situated his bag and body into the seat, and following Teacher's instructions, put both hands where directed and entered the dream state. When he opened his eyes, he realized with a sudden sadness and a keen sense of anticipation that he was no longer where he started.

∞ ∞ ∞

Gabriel looked around carefully where he had relocated to. It was a solitary room very similar to the one he had just left. He was thankful it was lighted as he looked for a possible exit. Surprisingly, the inside was marked with an exit symbol and what he needed to push to release the door. He carefully stepped out of the transport vehicle. After waiting a couple minutes, he decided to open the door.

The door released, and he looked out into the opening beyond. A pathway of some sort was present. He was clearly underground still, and the structure looked very similar to what he had been staying in for the last several months. Seeing no one to greet him, Gabriel decided to carefully explore ahead, hoping to find some evidence of life or a clue on where to go. He walked for a couple of minutes and he thought he heard voices up ahead. As he got closer, he was pretty sure one of them sounded a bit like his cousin Tom's voice. He could sense a tone that was both full of purpose, mixed with occasional periods of levity.

Gabriel peeked around the corner where the talking was coming from and saw Tom and some others dressed in a style seen commonly in Preath, doing their best to imitate the accent of that area. Not that he thought he had an accent personally, but it didn't sound natural of Tom to speak this way. He immediately noticed a couple of details that seemed off.

"I heard that you may want some help in how to act like you belong in Preath -- and from what I just saw, you need a lot of it!" Gabriel said as a way of announcing his presence.

Those present showed immediate concern having been taken unawares, but Tom realizing who was talking, relaxed the group and immediately went to Gabriel to greet him with a strong embrace.

"Gabriel!" Tom exclaimed. "I am so happy to see you. How have you been doing?"

"Well I haven't been weeding fields all by myself, so I guess pretty good!" Gabriel answered with a twinkle in his eye.

"Pardon my manners," Tom stated, I need to introduce you to the rest of the team. We got word someone may be joining us but didn't expect it would be you and so soon."

"I was surprised by the suddenness of it also." Gabriel answered.

"Well, you are here now," Tom said. "Gabriel, these are your team members. William and Alaine, this is Gabriel."

"Nice to meet you all," Gabriel offered. "Where are you all from, if you don't mind me asking?"

"Not at all," William replied. "I used to live just outside of Northfalcon, in the Xenon sector. Hopefully I will be able to live there again someday."

"What about you?" Gabriel asked Alaine.

"I'm from the Kaybeen mountains area," Alaine answered. "I probably could've stayed there too if they hadn't got all crazy searching through the mountains. Ministry people hardly ever bothered us there before, but they started searching like something crazy, so I decided I had better leave like the rest of the lowlands people did. So here I be."

"Well, I am glad you are here with us," Gabriel answered. "It is a pleasure to meet you both. Tom isn't sending you off to do impossible busywork tasks, is he? He has a bit of a reputation for that you know?"

"Oh, I haven't been able to tell anyone to do anything," Tom retorted. "We have our mission trainer to do that. We are just lowly trainees trying to learn to pass for someone who belongs in the capital."

"Well, I have some experience passing for someone there, which is probably why I am being assigned this?" Gabriel asked.

"That and your other skills, I presume have something to do with it," Tom answered.

"There is that." Gabriel agreed.

"If you are going to stand around and chat, you should at least do it like someone who is from Preath," a voice suddenly interrupted. "You are displaying too much joviality, which can look pretty suspicious the closer you get to the capital."

Gabriel turned around quickly, recognizing the voice.

"Grandmother!" He called out happily and was rewarded with a hug from Isabella. "What are you doing here?"

"Someone has to train you enough to make sure you come back," she said. "Since I have been to the capital quite a bit over the years, it seemed like a good choice to have me help with this. I won't be going with you, naturally, but it is up to me to make sure you are ready. I have managed to infiltrate the Ministry of Education a few times over the years."

Gabriel nodded knowingly, having remembered seeing her in one of his dreams when he had graduated. He wondered how many other times she had come to check in on him.

"I was told very little about the assignment before I came here," Gabriel offered. "All I know is that we are going to try to reunite some of the children who have been separated from their parents."

"That is a pretty fair summary," Isabella said. "But I will say this team's assignment will likely be the most dangerous. It would have been a lot easier if the ministry had grouped all the children who were taken together in one school area. Instead, they decided to spread them out across all the sectors. If we want to act to rescue them, we must do it a small bit at a time. If we succeed, then it will make rescuing the next children even harder as security is increased."

"Wow," Gabriel said. "That seems like it will be very challenging just to get into the schools, let alone getting the kids out. What makes our team's assignment the most dangerous?"

"Our primary mission is to get a child named Phillip to safety," Tom interrupted. "Remember the mother that escaped whose daughter they executed in her place?"

Gabriel nodded, remembering the provocative event that started this whole course of events.

"Well," Tom said. "The daughter Amy was only one of two children that were in custody. Her younger brother survived and was placed in a Ministry of Education school like many of the other captured children. Getting him to safety would be a huge lift to the spirits of the people in hiding. Not to mention a major hit to the government."

"So how do we know where he is?" Gabriel asked.

Isabella looked at him with a quizzical look in her eyes. "You are not the only person in the world who can trace historical events in their dreams. Plus, when we tried to rescue him the first time, we implanted a micro-beacon in him which can provide a real time location. You have to be within a hundred-meter radius or so to activate and pick up the beacon, but it should prove really helpful if we are going to make another attempt to rescue him."

"Wow, it sounds like a big honor to be selected for this team!" Gabriel exclaimed. "It seems like someone with more dream experience would have been better though."

"Your experience will be fine," Isabella answered. "Teacher would not have given you a positive recommendation if you were not ready and capable of this. Besides, you know the area, and can probably fit in better than most if you have to interact with anyone."

"What is everyone's role to be on this mission?" Gabriel asked.

"My role is to remove any of them proximity detonation collars that may be in use," Alaine offered. "I am not much use in other areas of this here excursion, so I will probably stay out of the way until needed for this task.

"I will pilot the transport pod, and with William will provide physical defense on this mission," Tom offered. "If we get into a confrontation, William and I have been training in weaponry and defense tactics and will try to buy time to get Phillip freed."

"And my role?" Gabriel asked.

"Your role is being the assigned dreamer," Isabella answered. "You can use your dream abilities to locate the general proximity of Phillip, and then transport the team to where they need to be. Once he is safe to move, you will translocate everyone out of there to the safety of a transportation hub hidden within the capital."

"You can also be the backup pod transporter," Tom offered. "I barely have enough of the dream gift to operate it, but if something happens to me, we need someone else who can get the team back. A good redundancy to have."

"I really want to try for this rescue within the next two weeks," Isabella said. "Phillip is being moved to different schools more frequently than I expected. I fear if we wait too long, we may have to re-plan a mission for a different location, which may not be as possible as I think his current location is. That is, if they don't take steps to execute him first."

Isabella began to outline the execution plan and the practice that she needed from the team before she would feel like they were ready. They needed to be able to work together as a team, plus relatively blend in in a highly tuned surveillance network. That would be a lot of work to accomplish in a very short period of time.

CHAPTER 20

$\mathcal{G}$abriel had just finished what he hoped would be his last rehearsal. His grandmother had been roleplaying several scenarios where different obstacles were unexpectedly encountered. These had ranged from one or more of the team members being killed or captured, all the way to a textbook extraction with no unexpected issues. Isabella believed strongly in leaving nothing to chance. A team that had fully considered contingency responses and practiced was much more likely to succeed together when encountering obstacles. They had also practiced criteria on when to abort and fallback plans should their transport exit path become compromised.

Gabriel had been able to get a lot of real-world person translocating practice, way more than he had gotten with Teacher. When he pressed Isabella for tips, he found out this was not her gift. She could travel in timelines in the dream state but lacked the ability to do other items often encountered in those with talent. He had to work within the training he had already received and just practice. He was getting a lot faster at it and could clear his team from one place to another in a matter of a few short seconds. This was good, but he thought had he been able to practice for a few more weeks he could approach something that would seem more instantaneous.

But time was not something they had, so he had to improve as fast as he could. His teammates had grown to trust his dream skills and grew more and more impressed each day as he continued to improve. He also had been developing a real, yes, a real friendship with each of them, especially Tom. This was a level of friendship he had never really experienced before. His relationship with Emily had many of the elements plus more, but it was still different somehow. When he was a student in the Ministry of Education, there was the tension of competition with classmates that precluded deep friendships. Alliances, yes, but friendships, not really. He truly felt he could trust each of his teammates with his life, which was probably good since he was about to.

This began to instill bits of conflict within Gabriel. If he was captured, he was reasonably certain he would undergo a lot of questioning but would likely not be harmed. But there was also a risk that due to the nature of the rescue, he may not be able to establish himself before he was fired on. He was not without risk. But it also surfaced a suppressed conflict that had been lingering in the back of his mind. Whose side was he truly on? Was he still true to his mission from the Ministry of Scientific Compliance, or was he true to the Order of the Lily and to Kayden, and for that matter to his friends and family? It wasn't as clear as it was many months ago. But hopefully, he wouldn't be pressed to make a choice anytime soon. The ministry charged him with infiltrating Kayden, and one way or another he was well on a path to do that. But would he be able to feed information to cause harm to those he now cared about? He was no longer sure. Isabella interrupted his thoughts as she began the debrief from the last simulation.

"You all did well responding to the unexpected roadblock," Isabella offered. "Gabriel, good work impersonating a ministry official and cowing the watcher when confronted. And the rest of you, good job not talking and looking deferential."

"You sound like my wife," Tom said. "Don't say anything and everything will turn out better!"

Everyone got a good laugh at Tom's comment.

"I think you are as ready as you are going to be." Isabella declared. "Sure, we would all like a few more months to prepare, but we know the job, you have developed teamwork, and time is not on our side. Let's get a good night's sleep and I can send you all off first thing tomorrow morning."

Gabriel awoke having slept reasonably well. Ever since he had completed his training with Teacher, he found himself more centered, with the ability to calm himself, which made the transition to real sleep much easier. Isabella had given Gabriel some clues to help locate Phillip, including an image from before he had been taken. Gabriel and the rest of the team were also given a recognition scanner that had image data on it of nearly all the kids who had been taken. This allowed them to passively scan the schools and public spaces. Any hits for a match would log locally in the device for future use. These were designed as a stand-alone device, and not designed to link up wirelessly to any networks to prevent the possibility of being announced to Oversite. This same scanner was prioritized to scan for Phillip and could activate the locator beacon should the user deem that necessary.

Gabriel used Isabella's map of clues and he believed he had located Phillip in one of the schools on the edge of the capital limits. He was glad this was not a school he had attended. He would have to get his bearings when he arrived to traverse the best path. Isabella had a hand drawn map of the city and had marked the school Phillip was being held in and the approximate entry point the transport would arrive to. The map was more conceptual than accurate and didn't have road names and other normal detail he would find in Oversite. But he thought it would be enough, and what he didn't know for sure he was hopeful he could do some dream state exploring to expediate finding it, so the team was not adversely delayed.

Gabriel got into a six-person transport pod that had been prepared. He had been trained on how to set coordinates and how to use it. He was able to send it to one of three different evacuation locations depending on what state the mission was in. For example, if medical care was needed, he would go to one location, and if it was a clean extraction, he would go to a different one. If all went badly, he would go to the third one in case they were somehow being tracked. Fortunately, he was not the primary person for this role but as Tom had said, redundancy was very important on a mission like this.

"Good morning!" Isabella said excitedly. "It is time to see if you learned anything. Is everyone excited to get going? I always used to get really excited before making excursions into the capital unannounced."

"Uh, sure," Tom said less than convincingly. "After all, what could possibly go wrong?"

"Now, now," Isabella admonished. "Positive thinking and attitudes. Confidence and swagger are just as important as preparation."

"Yes, I am really, really excited," Tom said with a monotone tone correcting his prior statement which got a laugh from everyone.

"That is better. Alaine, do you have your tools all packed and ready?" Isabella asked.

"Yes, ma'am, I does," she answered.

"You and Tom have your weapons carefully hidden in your Ministry of Education clothing?" Isabella asked William.

"Yes, we both have them and are ready. Hopefully we won't have to use them." William added.

"I share your sentiment on that," Isabella answered. "Tom, you know what to do. I hope that I see you all later tonight to celebrate a successful mission."

Tom, taking his queue, did a quick scan of his team members to confirm their readiness. When he had received the requisite nods, he engaged into the dream state and whisked the team into the heart of Preath -- into the capital city itself.

The transport pod came to a rest. The passage was small and dark, like what Gabriel had experienced in his last trip in a similar vehicle. Gabriel and the team quietly disembarked the transport pod, and listened for any evidence of people or anything that could compromise their mission. There was an alternate capital location they could use the pod to get to, but it would require going through a more heavily surveilled portion of the city, and over a longer distance. If they had suspicions of this location being compromised, they were to go to the alternate location. But all they heard was complete silence. When they opened the hidden door, there was nothing resembling a recent presence. Tom turned on a low-level illumination device so they could safely walk in the passage. Tom and William had their weapons drawn as they walked forward.

Each of the team members turned on an image recognition disruptor device. This wouldn't make them immune to surveillance but would render ineffective the automated face recognition technology, putting strange smoothing to their features which made matching them in Oversite difficult at best. This equipment was highly illegal but had been used effectively within Kayden previously. A person walking by or on a recorded video feed would appear normal, but the scanning technology for face identification was disrupted.

Gabriel looked around, taking in his surroundings. There was an odd familiarity with where he was at. He couldn't place it, but he felt like he had been here before. He dismissed the thought, convincing himself that all these hidden underground caverns seemed alike. But there was still a nagging in his gut that he couldn't shake. He was probably just nervous he told himself as he continued to follow Tom.

Just as Isabella had explained, there was a stairway at the end of the passage which they carefully ascended till they reached a trapdoor. Tom extended a remote viewer that peeked up out of the trapdoor and when deciding that it was empty, opened the door which found him and the team in some sort of room. Tom and William did a quick sweep of the building as Alaine and Gabriel stayed back. Getting the signal that the building was empty, Gabriel joined back up with Tom.

"Looks like some sort of store or business," Tom stated.

"Yeah," stated Alaine, "Isabella said it was in a business district. If we getta a move on, we are likely to be safe before people come out."

Looking outside, Gabriel could see it was still fairly dark outside, but the sun was just starting to think about coming up. The building he was in looked more and more familiar. Maybe he had visited this store before when he lived in the capital?

"Well, we have a long walk to get to the school," Gabriel said. "Shall we get to it?"

"Agreed," Tom said as he put his weapon back into hiding. "Let's get going."

Isabella had decided that the team should walk versus Gabriel doing translocation throughout the city. They held that out for the escape, fearing that if the Oversite systems detected abnormalities ahead of time, alarms may be raised, ruining the rescue attempt.

Together they were going to go into the school impersonating a Ministry of Education inspection team. Gabriel had seen many come through when he was growing up. The school administrators and teachers were typically fearful of them and gave officials a wide berth. Gabriel was imitating a mid-level official who would likely outrank any lead school official within the Ministry of Education. He was wearing the uniform of an inspector, which was very distinct. A bad result from an inspection would likely result in negative consequences for those cited, an outcome no one in a school wanted to encounter. Each inspector typically had a retinue of a few lower ranking personnel to smooth the way on the inspection.

Gabriel and the others followed Tom to the exit of the storefront. The street appeared to be quiet, and fortunately for the team, empty of people. Gabriel looked around carefully still having a nagging feeling something was familiar. Then it hit him as a troubled feeling reached the pit of his stomach. He had been here before. This was the place he had followed his grandmother when she had watched his graduation. This was the same place he had the ministry inspect and it was the same place the ministry had at one time put under direct surveillance! And to make it worse, it may still be being watched.

"I've got an uneasy feeling about this all of a sudden," Gabriel murmured quietly to Tom.

"That have anything to do with your special skills?" Tom asked with a concerned seriousness.

"No, it is just a feeling of unease, not related to that at all," Gabriel answered not giving the full answer the team deserved that he may have set them up without meaning to, but too afraid to tell them the truth.

"Probably just nervous. I know I am," Tom said with a light forced laugh. "Let's get moving. The sooner we get there, the sooner we can get back safely."

Gabriel wanted to argue, but instead nodded and began walking in the direction of the school, all while feeling ashamed for not speaking up about the true risk of their situation.

∞ ∞ ∞

Quintin was busy combing through the latest reports about Xenon. He had already swept the sector for children and had ensured full and detailed interrogations were completed on all people who were found remaining. He was convinced there was an underground network that was hiding the population and he was having next to no luck in identifying where it was and how to access it. There had been reports of sightings of people who were believed to be in hiding. So far, they seemed to just be observing the pitiful farming attempts and had not engaged in any sabotage activities that could be confirmed at least. He did notice that some of the parents that had their children taken away, subsequently disappeared. Even some went missing that he thought had loyalty to the government.

The dynamic in Xenon was nothing like he remembered when he was stationed here previously. It had the feel similar to the capital. He was already seeing way more vehicles than he ever saw before. A lot of government ministries wanted to know what was going on. The remaining sectors were starting to get edgy due to the reduction in food allocations that had been implemented. The difficult decision was made to start rationing before they literally ran out of food in order to buy more time for the farms to start producing again. And once this happened, there was a lot more eyes curious as to the progress on the farms with their own ideas as to what should be done in a different or better way. Curiously, it seemed to have the opposite effect on crop yield. But with Quintin's role he was not immediately worried about food allocation. Sure, he had to sacrifice some energy credits to keep his food quota, but he had not had to suffer very much as an important ministry official. He needed, after all, to be at full strength in order to best serve the ministry.

Quintin's contemplation was interrupted by an urgent alert flowing through his handheld. Quintin, not having anything else as pressing decided to give it immediate attention. He was getting the alert from a stationed surveillance drone. Looking closer, he realized it was from that storefront with the hidden underground passage that Gabriel had identified. He hadn't heard from Gabriel in several months. While it caused him some worry, it was not unexpected that someone charged to infiltrate a resistance group may go off the grid.

Either way, this drone alarm, if he remembered correctly, was only to alert him if someone was entering or exiting the storefront. He thought it was possible that someone short of food was foraging an unoccupied business for hopes of finding something to eat, but you didn't move up in the ministry by leaving things to chance and not checking.

Quintin pulled up the drone video link and saw a group of four people dressed in the attire of the Ministry of Education leaving the building. He submitted a request for an Oversite face identification, but it was having difficulty getting a facial reading to make a match. The system seemed to be malfunctioning at an inconvenient time. Quintin got the drone to zoom in closer, trying to make out the features of each of the people. The person in front he did not recognize, but when he zoomed in on the second person, he got a shock he was not expecting. Clear as could be, he saw Gabriel.

Quintin's mind raced at the possible implications of this information. Gabriel obviously knew that this storefront was being surveilled, or at least could safely hope that it was, based on some of his last interaction with Quintin. So, by showing himself, he could be sending a message that he was here to do something with the resistance. When Quintin thought about it, it was an ingenious way to make contact if he didn't have a way to do it via Oversite or a trusted contact. Gabriel was telegraphing something likely important but didn't want to blow his cover. Quintin quickly reached for his communicator device.

"Is Xavier available?" Quintin asked Xavier's assistant. "I have some urgent information he will want to make time for."

"Important enough to break into a meeting with the Minister of Scientific Compliance?" the assistant asked, figuring it would sufficiently scare Quintin's request away.

Quintin paused carefully. He was already on thin ice with Xavier already. If he played this wrong, it was a good way to lose what he had. But the implications of this contact were too much to ignore.

"As much as it scares me to say it, yes, it is that important," Quintin answered reluctantly.

After about a two-minute delay, Quintin was connected with Xavier.

"This better be important. One doesn't cutoff the head of your own ministry lightly," Xavier said with tension in his tone.

"I think it is sir. You wanted to be contacted the moment Gabriel made contact. Well, I think he has. Pull up the feed on the link I just sent you," Quintin said quickly.

"What do you mean by you think he made contact? Either he has or he hasn't," Xavier said back impatiently.

"He was just caught leaving a house he identified that we had a passive surveillance camera watching." Quintin replied. "He had three others with him, and all were dressed in Ministry of Education attire. Gabriel himself looked like he was attired as an inspector if my uniform memory serves me correctly. We used to enjoy watching our school administrators jump around with high levels of fear whenever they would come for an inspection."

"I've got the feed up now. They appear to be walking like they are going somewhere. Have you been able to identify who is with him?" Xavier asked.

"Oversite is having trouble identifying any of them. It is like they are circumventing face identification somehow or Oversite is having problems again," Quintin answered.

"Come over to my office," Xavier commanded. "We need to get a team on this immediately."

"On my way," Quintin quickly replied.

Quintin made a fast walk to Xavier's office. He made it there in time to see Xavier deploying the team on the consoles to increase tracking activity.

"Quintin, I want you to go into my office and pull pictures of all known acquaintances of our agent and see if you have better luck than Oversite matching any of them." Xavier whispered to Quintin. "I don't need to remind you that his mission and identity must not be compromised in this room. Don't screw up and act like you know who he is. Got it? Let me know the moment you match someone."

Quintin nodded and quickly went into Xavier's office to get started. He had developed an acquaintance tree based on Gabriel's reports. He hadn't had much time to keep up with it lately, but it was there, and he pulled up the file. Quintin pulled up still facial images of each of the three companions and pulled up the file photo starting with Gabriel's family members and those he worked with on the farm. About ten photos into the analysis, Quintin stopped suddenly. He had a match with the first one in the line. Tom Carasa was the name and he was from Deerbarrow. He was Gabriel's cousin and worked with him closely on the farm.

Quintin quickly went back to Xavier, and quietly whispered to him the news of the match.

"All," Xavier announced, "we have confirmation that this group we are tracking has been in hiding and at least two originate from Xenon. At this point, we must suspect they are tied with the resistance, likely the Kayden organization doing something not in our interests. Ideas?"

"Why don't we arrest them, sir?" one of the analysts offered. "Then we could fully interrogate them to find out."

"It would be a much more effective victory if we could catch them in the act of trying to do harm," Quintin offered.

"I agree, Quintin," Xavier quickly offered support realizing that he didn't want to burn Gabriel by trying to capture him. As much as he wanted to debrief him, his value inside the resistance was worth so much more than burning his use now. "Dressed as Ministry of Education inspectors.... hmmm.... what would give them reason to risk themselves in the capital dressed like that?"

"Is there something in a school that they would want?" Quintin asked. "Anyone dressed like that pretty much has free reign of any school they visit."

"Of course!" Xavier exclaimed. "They are hoping to rescue some children who were taken, or if not that, survey if a school contains any children that were taken. Since we spread them out across the country, it would make a coordinated rescue attempt difficult. Find out if any children in any surrounding schools were relocated from the northern sectors."

"Sir," another analyst answered after a few seconds elapsed. "I can access this question at any school in the capital, but when I try to find the answer to your question at the Beta-2 school, it comes up restricted. I lack access to find out sir. Says that it requires authorization from the Minister of Education directly. Otherwise, I have a few names displayed."

Xavier looked at his assistant, "Get me the Minister of Education on a private line right away in my office." Then turning to the analyst, "Find out all you can about the children you do have names of. Specifically, if their parents are in hiding."

Xavier motioned for Quintin to follow, as they walked into his office.

"I have a feeling about the school that is restricted," Xavier said. "Remember the kid of the woman who escaped that started all this?"

Quintin nodded.

"There were actually two kids," Xavier continued. "One was executed, but the other was put in the school system. I heard the Ministry of Education changed his name and tried to hide him. It would be a very big deal for the resistance to rescue him. If I am right, we need to stop it, but still protect Gabriel so he doesn't get blown."

Xavier's assistant indicated that she had the minister he wanted to talk to on the line.

"Good morning," Xavier opened. "I believe we have an attempted rescue attempt by the resistance in process and one of your schools is a target of it. Who are you protecting with security access in school Beta-2?"

"Let me check," the minister answered. "The name is Phillip but is going by Robert if my records are correct. He was the kid that didn't get executed when you made an example of the woman's daughter who escaped. I should have just executed him also, but some believed he may have future use, so we have been keeping him hid the best we can."

"That is what I suspected," Xavier answered. "I need your help. We have specific reasons we can't just take out the team before they get to the school. For this to work to maximum advantage, I was hoping you could help with a few things."

Xavier then proceeded to detail what he needed done. After some back and forth, the minister agreed to help. The importance of doing this correctly could not be overstated.

CHAPTER 21

The sun came up over the horizon and traffic on the street began to increase. Gabriel and his team moved steadily in the general direction of the school they were targeting. Gabriel expected to see more vehicles on the streets remembering his time in the capital, but the traffic was less than typical. His grandmother had discussed that energy reductions were being extended even to midlevel ministry members due to increased energy needs being redirected to Xenon's farming push. The only way they could get energy increases for crop production was if those increases were offset in other places. That meant not everyone could afford to use their preferred mode of transportation every day, especially if they were close enough where walking was reasonably possible. Isabella thought this would explain the lack of a vehicle normally used by an inspector on this sort of mission.

Gabriel looked around as they got closer to the target destination. He was beginning to recognize landmarks from his dream scouting and was feeling more and more confident he could get the team to where they needed to go. Just as the target school came into distant view, Gabriel stopped walking.

"Can we stop for a moment?" Gabriel asked the team. "I need to get a reading like we planned on Phillip's location. This shouldn't take very long. The school is just up ahead if you want to start considering our options."

"Sure thing," Tom replied. "Let's talk amongst ourselves like we are finalizing our plan for inspecting the school."

Gabriel focused himself so he could enter the dream state. This took a few seconds longer than normal as he struggled with the inner conflict having possibly exposed his team. If he was lucky by the time anything was noticed, they would be to safety with Phillip. He hoped Quintin had abandoned the surveillance altogether. It had been months after all. At least Gabriel rationalized it that way in his mind.

Gabriel shook these thoughts off and searched through the school in order to find where Phillip was at. He found him in his sleeping dormitory and tracked him as he woke, ate and went to his first activity period. He seemed to be following his normal schedule. If all went to normal plan, there would be an opportunity to rescue him as part of the inspection. It was not uncommon for inspectors to interview students and if he made it look random enough, he could pick out Phillip and have him away before anyone had realized what had happened. At least that was the preferred plan.

"He is following his standard routine," Gabriel announced after exiting the dream state.

"That will make things simpler," Tom stated. "Anyone have any reason why we shouldn't proceed?"

After a short period of silence, Tom began walking toward the school as the rest of the team followed.

∞ ∞ ∞

Phillip was not liking being Robert. This new school was so strict, and never seemed to let him do anything that was even close to fun. He just wanted to go home more than anything in the world. No one was friendly to him here. At the last school he was at, at least people would talk to him. In this school they made him wear this uncomfortable necklace. It seemed to be put on in a way that wouldn't come off no matter how he tried to adjust it. He was told to leave it alone, but he couldn't help touching on it. It felt like a rope that tied him to this horrible place.

Something was happening today that seemed out of the ordinary. When you are unhappy, something different is at least better than something the same. The teachers seemed to be all running around like they were crazy all of a sudden. Phillip heard something about an inspection. His teacher said that they all needed to give good answers, and anyone who didn't behave or embarrassed the school would be punished. Phillip didn't know what give good answers meant and he didn't want to be punished, so he mostly hoped that no one asked him any questions.

Phillip was finishing his second instruction period and noticed a commotion at the door. His teacher looked nervously to the door and instructed the class to greet the visitor as they had been instructed. At the door were some people, one wearing a strange looking outfit. That outfit was crazier than the other ones, with special colors and badges on it, and looked more like a robe than normal clothes. Phillip thought that it would be fun to wear if he were playing pretend.

"Good morning Mister Inspector," the class said in mostly unison.

The inspector gave an indifferent nod in reply. The inspector then made some pointing motions while talking to one of the people with him. The person nodded.

"The inspector would like to interview some students." He said. "The rest of the class needs to leave until we have completed."

Phillip watched as two students were selected in order, then had a sinking feeling in his belly when he was also chosen. Phillip was really worried because he didn't want to answer a question wrong and get punished. Phillip's anxiety increased as his teacher and classmates exited the room.

∞ ∞ ∞

Gabriel was pleasantly surprised with how well the plan had gone so far. They managed to get into the school without too much difficulty. He had shown his forged ministry identification badge, which was enough to get inside. Gabriel had not been scanned to confirm identity that he was aware of. He was not forthcoming with his name, and only flashed the badge to make it harder on the school to check his credentials and his cover story explaining that since he lived closer, he was filling in for the normal inspector due to the energy reductions seemed to be accepted. This seemed to mollify the person he checked in with, and they were given free reign of the school. He really thought that the purpose of the check-in delay was to stall enough for someone else to warn all the school teachers and administrators they were under an inspection. Either way, they had made it inside, and were doing a visual inspection of the school.

Looking at the time, Gabriel thought the students should still be in second period, and proceeded to look into the windows of some classrooms as we walked by, carefully steering toward the classroom he believed Phillip would be in. He also let his scanner check each classroom in case there were additional kids held here that were part of those in hiding. Gabriel looked in the window, and seeing Phillip inside, made motion that he wanted to go inside. Tom opened the door and led the way inside. Gabriel noticed that his scanner had made a positive identification on Phillip, and when he did a beacon check, further confirmed this was the correct child. They were in the right place.

"The inspector would like to interview some students." Tom announced. "The rest of the class will need to leave when we are doing this to ensure we get good feedback that is not biased in any way." Tom then proceeded to identify three students, including Phillip.

Gabriel watched as the class filed out. Gabriel then surveyed the room. He didn't like that there was only one exit, but he did see a window, and it looked like it was capable of being opened. There was always that way out if needed, and thankfully they were on the first floor.

"Let's start with you," Gabriel said to Phillip. "What is your name?"

Phillip looked back with nervous energy, afraid to say something wrong. "Ph---I mean Robert." He said.

"What is that horrible necklace around your neck?" Gabriel asked Phillip.

"I don't know. They said I can't take it off." Phillip answered.

"No one else wears one like that do they?" Gabriel asked looking at the other two very nervous looking students.

"No mister inspector," one of them answered. "But he is new and new people sometimes have to do different things than everyone else."

"Bring me his necklace," Gabriel said to Alaine. "I want to see what is so special about it."

Alaine went over to look at the necklace. From a distance it looked like it was an advanced detonation proximity model. It contained a remote switch and would auto trigger if it left the proximity ring that had been configured for it. In this instance, it was probably set for the school grounds. Alaine had the training to disable it, but it would take time.

"This is going to take some time to get off if you want to look at it," Alaine said.

"I do, so hurry up and get working on it," Gabriel said briskly. "I am not sure it is regulation. Make a note to check that too." He said in Tom's general direction.

Tom nodded to acknowledge the command and made a motion to interact with his scanner that looked like a handheld.

Gabriel looked at the other two children who were quietly watching Alaine work on the necklace removal.

"So," Gabriel asked, "what is the purpose of science?"

"To lead us to the truth, and to keep us on the path to keep our planet safe," the small girl dutifully stated.

"Nice words, but what does that mean in your own words?" Gabriel asked trying to appear as if he were conducting a normal inspection.

"I think it means," the girl stated, "that doing what science says, is what makes everything better."

"And how do we know what science says?" Gabriel asked looking at the other small boy he hadn't spoken with yet.

"We learn it from teachings of great scientists and do what the ministries say we need to do," the boy answered.

Gabriel made like he was marking a score sheet on his scanner device with the responses and made a subtle glance toward Tom to see how the necklace removal was coming. Tom indicated more time was needed. Gabriel took the hint and began to quiz them on the basic tenants of science taught from an early age. This went on for a few more minutes until he heard a quiet clicking sound. There was no corresponding boom that followed it, which was a very good sign. Alaine handed the necklace to Tom who showed it to Gabriel. Meanwhile, Alaine was scanning Phillip for any more devices. Frowning, she made a hand motion that there was another device she had found. Tom carefully set the necklace down on the opposite side of the room and returned to where Gabriel was standing.

"Interesting necklace," Gabriel stated. "Is there anything else unusual they make you wear?"

"I have to wear a special shirt under my clothes too, mister inspector," Phillip answered obediently.

"I want to see this special shirt," Gabriel commanded. "Show it to me."

Phillip unhooked his school uniform shirt to reveal a complex vest underneath. Gabriel didn't know what he was looking at, but Alaine indicated it would take some additional time. She didn't look happy about it, like it was something difficult to work with. Alaine began to systematically work on disabling the vest when a loud beeping sound permeated the room.

"What is that sound?" Gabriel asked the two watching students.

"That is the alarm we hear when someone bad is in the school," the small boy answered. "We practice going to a safe place when that goes off."

Gabriel was certain that this alarm was not a coincidence to their being here.

"Why don't you go find the rest of your class so you can go to the safe place," Gabriel offered. "We will keep Robert safe."

The kids politely nodded and left as fast as they could. Gabriel was worried he would endanger them needlessly and wanted them out of the room as quickly as possible.

"I think we are blown," Tom said reading his mind. "I don't like being in this closed in room. William, can you see if you can get that window open. We may need to have a fallback position until Alaine can get that vest off."

"I am on it," William answered as he went to the window. "Alaine, how bad is this?"

"This here vest is pretty advanced stuff," Alaine answered. "I can disable it, but it will take me a good bit. And honestly, we need to stand really still to do this safely."

"The window is open," William announced as he came up by Tom at the door. Both were getting their weapons ready and accessible, albeit still concealed, in the event they were needed.

Tom glanced through the classroom door's window. At the end of the hall he saw upwards of twenty weapon wielding personnel moving at a fast rate toward their classroom.

"We can't stay here a moment longer!" Tom said with high urgency. "There is a large force with weapons coming our way. To the window now! I think we can defend from outside the room better than from inside. William, lead the way!"

William nodded and quickly made for the window. Phillip stood there looking scared, with a very confused look on his face.

"Phillip," Alaine said, "we are gonna take you home to your mama. But it is going to be scary for a bit, because the people here don't want you to go. Do you want to come with us to see your mom?"

Phillip nodded as Alaine escorted them quickly together to the makeshift window exit. Alaine lifted Phillip through, handing him to William, then quickly followed behind. Gabriel started to follow, but saw a weapon being pointed at Tom through the door.

"Watch out Tom!" Gabriel yelled.

Tom turned just in time to have the weapon discharge, just missing to the side of his head. This allowed him time to get his weapon up to defend himself. Making a quick well aimed shot, Tom neutralized the agent that had just nearly killed him. The shot from Tom seemed to cause a pause in the charge from the force assaulting them. Tom, feeling a rush of adrenaline, laid down some cover fire and moved in the direction of the exit window.

"Quickly, get out!" Tom commanded to Gabriel.

Shooting sounds came from outside the door. Gabriel quickly climbed to the edge of the windowsill, and felt something prick at his arm, followed by a feeling of pain. Gabriel jerked suddenly and teetered on the windowsill, suddenly lacking the strength in his arm to get out the window by himself. William started to come to the window to pull Gabriel through, but Tom waved him off, instead directing him to lay down cover fire so he and Gabriel could get out.

The cover fire did not come in time. Tom had an obstacle he could have hid behind, but instead seeing Gabriel exposed on the window and already hit, juxtaposed his body between the weapon firing and Gabriel, and bravely lifted Gabriel the rest of the way through the window to safety. Gabriel fell to the ground suddenly, and then realizing that Tom was being fired on, stood up to the side of the window, reaching down his strong arm and pulled Tom through as William was now laying down return fire.

"Thanks for pulling me through," Tom said with what was an attempt at a smile. "They came on a lot faster than I expected."

Gabriel looked down at Tom's body noticing that he was not quick to move away from below the window, when they needed to get moving. He noticed a pool of blood growing around Tom on the ground, and with closer examination, realized that he had been hit several times. It did not look good. It should be him on the ground bleeding, not Tom. Tom had taken the weapon fire intended for Gabriel. Tom had acted with true selflessness, and for what? For saving the life of a miserable person who didn't speak up to keep his friends safe?

"Why did you take the fire that was meant for me?" Gabriel asked with sad affection.

"Didn't you learn anything from Teacher?" Tom asked with a heartfelt smile while making measured breaths. "It has always been my job to keep you safe. You are important to our people and most important, you are family, and a very good friend. Now go on. My time will end, but please come visit me often in the memories of your dreams. Don't visit in sadness, visit with joy of good times past."

And with that, Tom's body slumped as the remainder of his life left him.

Gabriel looked at Tom with a stunned paralysis. His friend was dead. His friend had given his life to protect his. His friend was dead. Grief coursed hard through Gabriel's being, reawaking painful losses and adding a new one.

Gabriel suddenly felt his body being shook violently.

"Gabriel, Gabriel!" William was yelling. "We can't stay here any longer. We need to leave. Remember our contingency planning and training."

It was one thing to roleplay a team member dying, it was another thing to live it. But William's words had the needed effect to shake Gabriel from his stupor.

"Alaine," Gabriel asked, "how close are you?"

"I need a few more minutes," Alaine answered. "I am probably about halfway done."

Gabriel reached down and picked up Tom's weapon.

"We can't leave until the vest is off and moving will make it just take longer." Gabriel stated. "Let's hold this area until the vest is off. Then I can get us all out of here."

William nodded agreement and took up a position on the other side of the window, closest to Alaine. William sent some weapon fire into the classroom to slow down any advancing force. Gabriel didn't fire but was ready to do so when William needed to reload his weapon.

"I need to stop this blood flow," Gabriel yelled to William over the shooting. "You good for a minute?"

"Quickly!" William replied while continuing to make timely shots. "I'll yell when I need you!"

Gabriel was starting to feel light headed. Gabriel took off the robe part of the uniform he was wearing and tore off something he could tie around the wound to staunch the blood flow. He knew he would need more care than that, but all he had to do was get the rest of the team to safety. He had failed Tom; he didn't want to fail anyone else.

∞ ∞ ∞

"What a mess!" Xavier exclaimed while watching the firefight unfold from the video feed. Using the drone that he deployed to follow Gabriel, he could see that Gabriel was lightly wounded and the explosive vest was nearly removed from the Phillip boy.

"We can't let the boy escape, can we?" Quintin asked.

"No," Xavier answered. "I had use for him alive, but there is no helping it now."

∞ ∞ ∞

Phillip watched the events surrounding him with a quiet awe. He had never seen someone die in front of him before. He just wanted to go home and he was scared. At least these people used his real name. He liked that. But Phillip's thought was stopped short as he felt a sudden sharp pain resonating from his chest, not having time to process it fully as his body disintegrated and all that was near him. Phillip's life was snuffed out with so much potential left unrealized and so many open fields now unable to experience the joy of his play.

∞ ∞ ∞

Gabriel finished tying up his arm, when he was rocked by a loud concussive blast. He felt a full overload of all his senses. Shaking the ringing out of his ears, he looked around trying to determine what had happened. With great anguish, he saw what was left of Phillip and Alaine spread across the ground. William had absorbed some of the blast, but appeared to be alive, albeit barely.

"William, are you all right?" Gabriel asked loudly.

Realizing that William was no longer laying down fire to keep from being charged, Gabriel fired a few times out the window without looking where his shots were going. Training kicking in, Gabriel pushed his grief aside and centered himself entering the dream state. Looking around, he translocated William, himself and what body parts he could retrieve to the planned jump spot well away from the school. Gabriel then continued the transport progression until he reached the hidden underground room below the storefront where the transport pod was waiting. Gabriel got William, Tom's body and what he was able to gather of the body parts from the explosion into the transport pod, keyed in the coordinates for medical care and then initiated transport back to Xenon. He had to save at least one.

CHAPTER 22

*G*abriel awoke, lying in a bed of some sorts. He must have passed out from the blood loss after fleeing the school. He had a vague memory of arriving in the transport pod and a rush of frantic activity as he and William were attended to. Looking around, he was hooked up to some sort of medical equipment and appeared to be getting fluids by intravenous methods. This wasn't like the hospital he had taken Emily, but instead was a room, likely underground, made up to provide medical care. He was surprised they had the ability to use this level of equipment on him, as there was probably a short supply of vital medical supplies. He was even more surprised when he only felt dull pain in his arm where it appeared fresh bandages had been applied. They must have given him some medicine for the pain.

He saw some stirring out of the corner of his eye and tried to adjust his head to see who was there.

"Hello?" Gabriel called out.

"You are awake," a familiar voice answered back. "We were pretty worried about you when you came in all covered in blood."

Gabriel took a moment to process the voice, before recognizing to whom it belonged.

"Is that you, Raelynn?" Gabriel asked.

"Well, you are not dreaming, so most people call me Annabel," she answered.

"William?" Gabriel asked with uncertainty in his voice. "Is he going to make it? He looked pretty bad."

Annabel was now within Gabriel's vision. She looked down with compassion. "We still are not sure," she said softly. "He is still alive, but with our primitive hospital setup down here, we are really struggling to give him the best care possible."

Gabriel could hear what was unsaid. She didn't think he was going to make it.

"It is all my fault," Gabriel said with a dejected demeanor. "I could have saved them, but I didn't."

"It looks like you did your part." Annabel replied. "You have been through a lot and it is normal to feel blame when you made it back alive and others do not. Your grandmother said you acted bravely under weapons fire. You risked yourself to warn Tom, and you pulled him through the window under fire after he was hit. She told me all that happened. Phillip and Alaine were a tragedy, but Alaine knew the risk. Someone in a ministry must have detonated that vest. They probably had a camera watching and saw that it was mostly off and decided it was better to have him dead than escaped. And then to be able to focus yourself after all that happened to bring both William and the remains of the others back, that was beyond what would be expected of anyone."

"No, you don't understand," Gabriel insisted. "It is all my fault. I knew from the moment we left the storefront where the transport hub was located, we were at risk. Yet I didn't say anything."

"How could you know that?" Annabel asked.

"Because I caused it to be under surveillance." Gabriel answered dejectedly. "I followed my grandmother in my dream you helped me with at my graduation and saw the transport and underground passage. I wasn't sure it was real what I was dreaming so I asked the Ministry of Scientific Compliance to send a team to look. It was real all right, but they must have left extra surveillance which picked us up when we came out. Like I said, it is all my fault, but I was too afraid to speak up. I could have saved them all!"

Gabriel realized that he had just exposed his connection with the ministry. But surprisingly he did not care. It was a relief letting the truth out, but at the same time, he felt more ashamed than he ever had before. These people had taken him in, loved him, and exposed him to a gift greater than anything he had ever imagined, and all he was capable of doing was stabbing them in the back for all their kindness.

"Asked the ministry?" Annabel asked sadly.

"They sent me here to infiltrate the resistance." Gabriel admitted sadly. "I am an agent for them still. But I am so ashamed. I know who I am now, and don't want any part of that life anymore. But I have failed you all. I am lower than low and wish that I had died instead of the others. It is all my fault."

Annabel's demeanor had grown seemingly colder as Gabriel admitted his secret. He could tell, what he had said had upset her. But he had to tell the truth. Annabel was one of the few people he had left that he truly cared about. But how could he face her anymore? How could he face his Aunt and Uncle when he was responsible for their son dying? And then to allow Phillip to die? An innocent boy who just wanted to be with his mom. A mom who had already lost her daughter and desperately wanted to see her son.

"I think I need to leave," Annabel said with tears forming in her eyes. Then she turned and exited the room.

Gabriel lay in quiet sadness, with grief and shame pulsing through his body. He was without will, without purpose and empty. Gabriel let his worn down and tired body go, drifting back into a deep yet troubled sleep.

∞ ∞ ∞

Gabriel awoke. Lights were off in his room and he was no longer hooked up to fluids. After his stunning admission, he expected to be confined somehow, but he was being left to rest in this room. Gabriel stumbled to find some sort of light source. There was a light cell next to the bed that he found and turned on. Next to the light he found a folded piece of paper with his name on it. He opened it up to read it.

> *Dear Gabriel,*
>
> *I know you must be really hurting right now. You are blaming yourself for the death of dear friends and family. Based on what Annabel told me, you are feeling very down and wish you had died in their place.*

But I want to tell you that their death was not in vain. We have known all the time that you may be working for the ministry you supposedly left. And knowing this, we slowly brought you into our circle and taught you our ways. For you are family. You are of Xenon. And we will not give you up easily. You have the potential to do so much if you are brought to the true path. Every member of the rescue team knowingly risked their lives for the hope of redeeming yours. And know this, as evidenced by your own statements, their sacrifice has not been in vain.

And while the price has been high, it would be knowingly paid again. For what is the ultimate gift of selflessness? To give your own life to save another. Is that tenant not a pillar of the Order? Is that not what those with you gave? And while Phillip did not make that choice, you only acted to save him. We suspect he was going to be killed in a few days' time anyway. And while it is tragic that he was murdered by the ministry action, it was not due to your hand.

Go back in your dreams. Review your actions and grow. No one will despise you here. Here you will only receive welcome and love. The Order of the Lily embraces you. The council of Kayden embraces you. And as Kayden's leader and your grandmother, I embrace you also. Welcome truly home Gabriel.
With Deepest Love and Affection,
Isabella

Gabriel sat stunned after reading the letter. He could not believe what he was reading. He was forgiven just like that? After all he had done to harm them. As touching as that felt, he was not ready to forgive himself. You could not just wash away the loss of someone you cared about when you were the one to blame. There was an empty hole within himself, and he knew of no elixir that could sooth the pain. And it was one thing for Isabella, his own grandmother, to forgive him, but could he really expect the forgiveness of the family members that lost sons, fathers, or spouses? Could he bear to look them in the eye and beg for their forgiveness, or would he rather beg that they exact justice on him for his actions?

Gabriel sat in quiet, yet somber contemplation. In his old life, he would be jumping for joy that he had learned who the leader of the resistance was. But he was not. It was now a secret he would willingly protect with his life. He would harm no one else within the resistance. He would live his life trying to approach the value of the lives of those who had given theirs. And he knew it was a debt he would never be able to fully repay. He had heard Kayden's call and he intended to follow it wherever it led.

Gabriel reread the letter several times. Isabella had suggested he go back and review his actions and grow. Maybe that would be a proper penance. To go back and see his friends die repeatedly. To watch his cowardice in not admitting he had betrayed them. Yes, he would review his actions while he dreamed. He would learn, and he would participate in the pain until he could take it no more. And then maybe he would grow.

CHAPTER 23

*G*abriel closed his eyes and centered himself, tuning out the heartbreak that he was experiencing. He felt he shouldn't have been able to enter the dream state so easily after what he had gone through. He entered the portal point at the field of lilies. Part of him hoped to see Raelynn here, but after pausing for a few minutes, she did not come. He was not sure things would ever be the same between them. He had violated a trust, and while she may forgive him, Gabriel thought she had expected more of him, and things would be forever different. This was a journey he needed to make alone.

Envisioning the time right before he and the team left for capital, Gabriel found himself looking at the final departure in the transport pod. His team was there with him. All looked nervous, but at peace, united in purpose to save Phillip. They trusted each other. They trusted him. He could see it in their eyes. There was no doubt in them. While Isabella had said they all knew the risk, based on the look in their eyes, no one believed the risk. He had proven himself to them, and they knowingly had placed their lives in his hands.

He watched as the transport pod departed, then watched as his grandmother put her hand up for a final wave, standing there a few moments more with a worried look on her face. She knew it was dangerous and showed visible concern for the team's safety. She had not displayed this emotion in front of the team, but she was showing it now.

Gabriel willed himself to the arrival location. He watched as the team checked for a risk behind the hidden passage. If only they had turned back then, all would have been saved. But they didn't. Gabriel didn't realize where he was at then. One underground hide-out looks like any other. No, he may have been able to determine his location with a more acute sense of observation and recall, but he did not know until the team had stepped outside and was exposed. He watched the team step outside. He saw the nervousness on his own face and heard the weak comment he had made about something not being right. If only he had shown courage. If only he had turned around and kept the team safe. But he did not. He allowed them to march forward, to march on with quiet abandon. To march to their doom. All while he had the power to save them but lacked the fortitude to do so.

Gabriel observed as his team entered the school. Instead of following the team, Gabriel looked throughout the school. He wanted to know if the school had been warned of the team from Kayden being there. If only they had not been warned. It would not change the outcome, but the fault would not have been his. Gabriel explored and observed a large force of enforcement agents entering through a rear point of the school, clearly out of view to his team. No, this meant they had been warned. That, or there were some strict protocols on doing an inspection that had not been followed. But the fact that they were here already, would mean they would have had to been sent before Gabriel and the team had even announced themselves to the school. No, they knew he was coming and were ready.

Noticing where the enforcement agents were headed, Gabriel decided to follow them. He listened as he heard explicit instructions to use deadly force on all except Gabriel. Gabriel was to be wounded in a non-critical way only, but the rest could be killed if able. Gabriel was to be given a plausible method of escape. It was critical that he not be detained. They were going to wait until contact was made with a particular student, then assault the room. No, the ministry knew he was there. He had given them away. A plan of this complexity is not built in mere moments. They had notice and to protect Gabriel's credibility in the resistance, they had decided to spare him, giving him a credible way to return to those he was betraying. This had Xavier written all over it.

The agents were in position and Gabriel watched as they began their assault on the classroom. The carnage was beyond anything that Gabriel had expected. Agent after agent fell as fire rained down on them, but still they came. He heard the status called out that Gabriel had been successfully injured, and to not target him further. Then he saw Tom raise his body to shield Gabriel to get him to safety. The agents were without mercy as they shot him multiple times before pulling back when cover fire began to come back from William. Gabriel marveled that there was no hesitancy in Tom's act to save him. If only he had been able to act with similar certainty when he could have made a difference.

He heard Tom's dying words and watched in horror as he saw Phillip disintegrate, taking Alaine with him, distributing mangled body parts in the concussive radius. William was knocked over, and Gabriel realized that William had also saved Gabriel great harm by taking much of the force of the blast. Gabriel watched as the agents fell back momentarily, then when the fire stopped from the window, began to edge forward. He watched as he fired a few shots and they briefly retreated. He had not hit anyone with his shots. And then the shooting stopped. The agents cautiously advanced and were given the all clear when learning that the drone indicated the area was now clear. A sweep of the area was ordered, and confusion had abounded where everyone had gone. Gabriel knew where they had gone. They had gone to their death, and all that he had done was ensure their bodies would not be further defiled, so their families could gain some level of closure in their grief.

Gabriel let full realization of what he had observed flow through him. There could be no doubt in his mind. His actions were responsible for the failure. Or at least his lack of action. To be silent was to be complicit, when speaking up would avert great harm. And for Isabella to have gone back and seen this, and still she offered forgiveness and ongoing fellowship? It completely exceeded Gabriel's comprehension but was not enough to erase the empty feeling deep within him. There had to be more. There had to be something he was missing. Something that would allow him to grow. For right now, all he felt was shame.

Gabriel reviewed the sequence many times and from many different perspectives. Each time, it was the same. He had failed. If only he had the courage to speak up – Courage to honor the tenants of the Order. Courage to display selflessness. To be willing to give of himself, even at the cost of his own life. If there was only a way to go back and undo the wrong, to make things whole. He would be willing to give up everything now, to do that if the choice were there.

Gabriel racked his brain. Maybe there was a way to undo it and make it right. His mind drifted back to the last book he had read by Aldous Kendell, *Dreaming with Purpose*. Kendell had said if you could find the seminal event that caused a chain reaction of outcomes, you could possibly change the course of events. Gabriel had studied this as an academic exercise and been explicitly told to not try to experiment with it, as it could cause great harm to himself and possibly others. But despite the danger of it, Gabriel saw hope at redemption. A way to make his wrongs right.

Gabriel redirected his timeline back to his time in the library. He reread Kendell's book. He checked the index for other books on the same topic, finding two and went to the time they were paged through and read them. He traveled back to view the author's discussions on the topics to learn more about it. One author had claimed to alter time a few seconds back. He spoke of the tremendous strength it took and how he had succeeded but had nearly killed him. His caution was that the further back you went, the more dangerous it was to the dreamer who tried to alter events. He had documented one dreamer who professed this gift, who had been found dead. He was believed to have died because he had gone back a few hours to try to save the life of his son. Unfortunately, his son was still dead and had added his own life to the tragedy.

He read how the ability to do this was extremely rare. But this did not deter Gabriel's resolve. If there was even a small chance to make things right, to restore Tom's life, to keep his team unharmed, and to prevent the unnecessary loss of life of that innocent little boy, he was going to do it – Even if it cost him his life. Gabriel had learned what he could and thought through his best option. He was ready to begin.

Gabriel paused before beginning to make sure he hadn't missed anything important. What if he failed? What if he met the fate of the father who died trying to rescue his son? Was he willing to leave

Isabella with the uncertainty of what had happened? Would he needlessly add to her grief? Gabriel realized that he was not willing to do that to her.

Finding a writing utensil on the table where Isabella had left the note, he began to write on an empty part of the page.

Dear Grandmother and other friends and family,

You cannot know how much I am sorry for the loss I have caused all of you. I go on a journey to try to make it right. Ask Teacher about Kendell's book and he will be able to tell you what I have tried to do. If I fail, I wanted you to know that I died in pursuit of the values I now hold dear. Know that I love you and my spirit will endeavor to be with you in whatever lies next on your journey.

Gabriel

Gabriel had given considerable thought to the seminal event that altered the course of events. Having read about the danger of going back too far in time, it needed to be as recent as possible. He had recounted the firefight over and over and saw a way to maybe get Tom to safety, but Alaine and Phillip would still die with William still on death's door. There had to be a second way that could save them all. He had reviewed the team's abort plans and fallbacks and it had come to him. If the first transport location appeared to be compromised, they would immediately move to the fallback one that was further away in the capital. If he had a way to scare them away from leaving the transport alcove, they would still have a dangerous mission, but he would not be the one compromising it. While the outcome would be uncertain, it appeared to be the closest thing to a seminal event he could identify.

Gabriel entered the dream state and transported himself to the underground hiding place below the storefront in the capital. He found where the secret door was and looked around this area for some way to warn his team. What would convince the team to abort for this location?

It would have to be some evidence of someone there, he thought, remembering them listening for sounds before opening the secret door. Gabriel looked in the area near the door for something that could make a suspicious sound. He found some light cells distributed around the area. They did not appear to be mounted. If he could find a way to drop them at the proper time, maybe that would be enough.

Gabriel tracked the team getting out of the transport pod as they came to the door, readying themselves to open it. Gabriel shifted himself to the other side of the door and focused his will on the light cell closest to the door. He was not sure how to press across this event as Kendell had described it but decided that he would try to translocate the light cell off of the ledge it was on to midair right beside the door. If he could do that, it would drop and hopefully make a noise loud enough to deter the team. He had never tried to do anything like this when timeline traveling. Visualizing the light cell, he then reimagined it in the target location. Gabriel felt a shockwave nearly knock him over followed by a clanging sound. He had moved it, but was it enough?

Gabriel shifted himself back to the other side of the door.

"Did you hear something?" Alaine asked to the rest of the team quietly. "I swear I heard a banging sound from the other side of the door."

Each team member shook their head indicating they did not.

"Let's hold up for a few in case someone is out there," Tom decided while whispering quietly. "If no one hears anything in the next five minutes, we will prop the door and see if we see anything."

The team nodded in agreement.

Gabriel watched with frustration. He had felt his strength wane considerably and he was having trouble staying focused in the dream state all of a sudden. He would have to do something again, if the team was going to not dismiss the clue he had given them. Seeing no other choice, Gabriel found a second light cell and repeated by dropping it right on top of the other one. Again, he felt a shockwave hit him and this time he was knocked over. Looking at his hands in front of him, he watched as they dimmed in intensity, began to lose substance, and then Gabriel's vision went completely dark.

CHAPTER 24

$\mathcal{J}$sabella, the High Seat, convened the governing council of Kayden. After the reading and normal introductions were concluded, she got down to business.

"What is our food situation?" Isabella asked.

"Better than those on the surface," the Keeper replied. "I estimate our current reserves will last for another four to six months, maybe longer if we can continue to supplement our food supplies undetected in the protected nature preserve areas. Also, as our dreamers have finished constructing living areas and been able to stay ahead of the ministry detection attempts, we have also been building underground grow areas. This takes quite a bit of energy to simulate sunlight. We have had to transport a lot of soil down, but it is secure, and will make our reserves last longer. I think it will be a very long time before we can produce enough using this method to supply the population down here, but every little bit helps."

"Good work on this," Isabella said with encouragement. "Also, good work with keeping the morale of the people up through this difficult time."

"Thank you," the Keeper said. "We have had a few victories lately that have raised everyone's spirits. I was getting really worried about our resolve a few weeks ago."

"Guardian," Isabella directed, "what is our latest intelligence assessment of the surface? Do we have a future point where we have leverage to win back our way of life?"

"The food situation is approaching dire proportions on the surface," the Guardian answered. "The ministry is trying to ramp up production of a synthetic equivalent, but you can see evidence of malnutrition starting to show in the general laborer class of the people. They are aware food is scarce and have begun to be less compliant to ministry edicts. Resentment is also building since the ministry officials do not seem to be suffering from the same shortages. There is great pressure on getting crop production increased, but the more supervision it is given, the more mistakes are made. It is a complete mess, which the government appears to be completely unprepared for. They have even had to increase policing of the nature reserve areas to keep people from trying to poach animals to eat. Animals haven't been a lawful food product for years!"

"Any rumblings of them softening their stance toward Xenon and the northern sectors?" Isabella asked.

"We have witnessed grumbling about letting things go back to how they were before clamping down, but we lack a direct line to the government. I have not yet been prepared to risk getting someone captured and killed to try to ascertain interest." He replied.

"I have an idea on that," Isabella said, "but I don't know how soon, if at all, it will be possible to do it. But everyone agrees if we get a way to approach the government to negotiate, we should pursue it?"

Seeing heads nodding around the table she moved on.

"Seeker," Isabella asked. "Any update on Gabriel?"

"No," the Seeker answered. "There has been no change for the past seven weeks. I will let you and the council know if anything changes."

Isabella nodded solemnly. Some things just needed time.

∞ ∞ ∞

Gabriel opened his eyes and found himself floating through a haze. It was like he could see a translucent image of the world around him, present but somewhat transparent. He had no idea how long he had been in this state. It could have been a moment or an eternity. He felt he should do something but lacked the focus or the strength. Then his world went dark again.

Again, he opened his eyes. Again, he felt that there was a lack of substance around him. He remembered opening his eyes before. He remembered he needed to do something, and again he blacked out.

This process repeated many times. Each time he remembered the prior, and each time his thoughts progressed just a little bit further along before again blacking out. He had decided he may be in the void. This was the place he had learned where something went if you started to translocate it and didn't succeed in getting it put back in the new place. It was an abyss of sorts. It was said that people had been lost to this place and had never come back. For sure, no one had ever returned on their own accord.

A sense of peaceful tranquility overcame Gabriel in his brief moments of awareness. He did not know if he had succeeded in what had brought him here, but he had truly done all he could. He had acted with faith and with true selflessness for the chance of saving the others. If it cost him his life and if he was to spend the remainder of his existence in this state of intermittent awareness, then it was a price well paid.

Gabriel wished he had made a bigger impact with his life. He wished he had showed more love. He wished he could go back and thank his parents for their sacrifice. He was grateful. Grateful for what he had learned and for the friendships he had experienced. For the love he was shown, even when he was not deserving. He wanted to go back and do more to help those he loved. To tell them what he now felt with surprising clarity. But on he continued to float, in and out in the void.

Recollection came over Gabriel as he floated through varying states of awareness. He had been lost before early on, when he had followed Isabella in his dream. What did Raelynn tell him then on how to get back? Memory came back as she had told him to focus on the time and place he had left. Would that work here? Before he had focused on the intermediate place with the field of lilies. Did he remember clear enough to return? He decided to find out.

Visualizing did not come easily, but he found himself back in this field of lilies. It was all he could do to keep clarity of his situation. He focused on the room from which he originally dreamed from in his hospital bed, and on seeing his body present there, willed himself into existence, while simultaneously exiting the dream state. He had awareness of his physical body but could not move. His body would not respond, and his eyes would not open. He was back, yet he was not.

Gabriel could hear voices come and go in his room. He recognized Raelynn's voice the most often, but also frequently heard his grandmother, his aunt and uncle and others that seemed familiar, but he did not recognize. There was concern in all their voices. They were somehow keeping him fed while he existed in this comatose state. Each day, he would hear someone say that there had been no change. He heard things like, "Did you hear what he did during the rescue mission?" He wondered what he had done. All he had remembered of the rescue mission was that he had lost nearly his whole team. Best he had been able to tell, he had been in this state for over seven weeks now. At least that is what it sounded like from the context of the comments he heard.

Slowly he felt strength returning to his body. It had been like his brain was out of phase from his sensory feeling and movement response. Slowly that connection seemed to synchronize. Gabriel was hopeful that he may have the ability to open his eyes soon and possibly speak. He had so many questions, but was stuck laying on a bed, in suspense, wondering if or what he had accomplished. Strangely, his time of existing in a self-loathing state had passed. While he was not proud of his earlier path, he realized that it had been necessary to give him the clarity he needed to choose the path he was now on. If his work to change the past did not work, he would still do all he could to redeem his prior actions, but he was now at peace with himself. He better understood the Path of the Lily and would dedicate his life to being true to its tenants.

Gabriel's thoughts were interrupted by a familiar voice. It could not be, could it?

"I know you are in there," a voice that sounded like Tom chided Gabriel. "What do I have to do to get you to come out of whatever state you have got yourself into? I always thought people from the capital were lazy, but I never thought they were this lazy!"

Gabriel jumped for joy inside himself. Tom was alive! He had somehow saved his friend. That jolt of realization triggered something within Gabriel, and suddenly he felt fully in sync with his body. Gabriel opened his eyes as a slight smile was now able to form on his face. Tom was safe! Tom was safe! Tom was safe!

"You are all alive," Gabriel said with a weak and excited voice.

"Of course, we are," Tom replied. "It is you who we have been worried about."

"I don't have any memory of what happened," Gabriel admitted with a slightly stronger voice, "I have bits and pieces but would really appreciate it if someone tell me how you all escaped and how I ended up in this bed."

"You don't even remember getting shot?" Phillip spoke up. "That was really exciting. I don't know how you could forget something like that.

"No, Phillip not even that," Gabriel replied.

"You got shot while we were pulling Phillip from his classroom," Tom interjected. "It has mostly healed up with as long as you were taking your nap, but it definitely needed some medical attention."

"Did we divert and take a different transport route?" Gabriel asked. "Was there a noise at the first one?"

"See, you are remembering somethings already," William said with a smile. "It may come back slowly but it is good it is coming back. Yeah, there was some sort of noise right outside the transport door. May have been someone down there. Didn't want to risk it so we redirected."

"That is good," Gabriel answered. "And how did I get shot?"

"I think they got an alarm when the necklace was taken off," Isabella answered walking in suddenly with a big smile on her face. "They sent their local security force but was only about six people who tried to attack. Tom and William were ready for them and got Phillip's secondary vest off before the school could get authorization to blow it."

"Thanks for explaining, Grandmother," Gabriel replied. "So how did I end up here?"

"We transported to the medical drop to get you taken care of and then you pushed us to get Phillip to his mother without you," Tom explained.

"Then we hear you just went unconscious. None of us thought the wound was that bad, but sometimes things happen."

"Since you were out of commission, we got assigned another dreamer to go rescue more kids," William said. "Sorry for just getting to visit you but we had to save as many as we could."

"I am disappointed I missed that," Gabriel said with genuine regret. "I am most glad you are all safe."

"I think we probably need to let Gabriel rest some more," Isabella interjected. "We can fill you in more later. Everyone should be nearby for a while unless something comes up."

It took a couple more weeks before Gabriel was strong enough to get up out of bed without help. Gabriel was being treated like a hero. Annabel and Isabella came by frequently while he was still in bed and seemed really happy he was alive and improving. There was very little speculation what had put him into the comatose state. Gabriel had realized that the confession he had made about being an agent was no longer known, and he owed it to those he loved to tell them the truth, regardless the cost. It should have been easier knowing how his grandmother had responded the first time with her note, but it was not. And then there was the sadness and seemingly emotional withdrawal he had seen when he had told Annabel. He was most afraid of seeing that again.

Today was the day he had decided to address this, and now that he was able to walk around again, had sought out his grandmother.

"Can we speak in private for a few minutes?" Gabriel asked her. There were always people entering and exiting her living space.

"Of course, Gabriel," Isabella answered. "Let me secure and mark what passes for a door, and I should not be interrupted."

Gabriel watched as she secured the space representing her door and then proceeded to tell her what had happened. He explained how he knew that she was the leader of Kayden and how he was an agent of the Ministry of Scientific Compliance still. He explained how he had gone back in time, to make up for his failures, and needed to tell the truth to those he cared most about.

Isabella had listened carefully without comment or judgement. He saw her show fear on her face when he explained how he had altered time, and he thought she showed pride when he shared how he had decided to come clean. When he finished the story, she gave him a big hug.

"Welcome truly home," his grandmother said warmly. "I am so proud of you."

Gabriel smiled as he partook in the love he was being freely offered.

"So, what now?" Gabriel asked. "For sure, I need to tell Annabel and the others, but it seems like I need to do more now that I have regained most of my strength."

Isabella paused for a moment in quiet contemplation.

"No," she said. "I agree that Annabel and Tom need to know but let me talk to them first. While coming clean will make you feel best, I think you can help the cause most if we keep this connection secret, save for a few trusted people."

Gabriel nodded, thinking he saw what may be coming.

"Ok," Gabriel said. "I can do it that way. What do you have in mind for me to help the cause?"

"Do you have a way to contact your old ministry still?" Isabella asked.

"Yes, I think so, but it is easiest if I have access to something on Oversite. I think I would have to go to the surface to get that. I have been off the grid with the ministry since we evacuated." Gabriel answered.

"Sources indicate that there may be interest in some sort of truce on the ministry side," Isabella explained. "If we could get some concessions, it may be in our best interests to return to the surface. I need a safe way to get them this message. Our people are not meant to live outside of the view of the sun. Plus, we don't want to be responsible for people starving or getting diseases due to malnutrition, even if they act against us. If we wanted that, we would be no better than they are."

"So, what do you want me to do?" Gabriel asked while indicating his interest in helping.

"I need you to get to the surface and give a report. I can monitor the Great Scientist Council to see if they are serious about agreeing to something meaningful. If they are, I am willing to take some steps to get some of our people back to the surface," Isabella answered.

"You do know if they agree to something, it will only last as long as they think it is in their advantage to keep the agreement?" Gabriel asked.

"Of course," Isabella answered. "But it will also give us time to get better prepared also. Frankly we can't last a year more without replenishing our food stocks. Time is working against us all."

"Ok," Gabriel replied, "I will do it."

Gabriel and Isabella spent some time discussing the terms that would be acceptable. They worked out a plan to successfully get Gabriel to the surface to make contact in a way that would preserve his credibility in the ministry and would get the outcome desired.

Gabriel made it to the surface and was able to log a very lengthy report on the state of the resistance and what he thought would be needed to get them to come back to operate the farms that were being dreadfully mismanaged. He indicated he was on a three-day surveillance mission and would check for any responses in two days before he was due to report back. He thought it may be months before he was sent on a similar mission again. He was still working to build up trust, and that this was the most autonomy they had given him, letting him travel unsupervised.

∞ ∞ ∞

Xavier reviewed Gabriel's comprehensive report. Amnesty was not a decision he could make on his own. While he had a lot of autonomy in this sector, the proposal that Gabriel had submitted would be like a bad tasting medicine. Sure, it may solve his problem, but that didn't make him excited to take it. Xavier made a request for an emergency meeting of the Great Scientist Council. After a few hours delay, he was told they would convene by remote first thing in the morning. The fact that they hadn't made him wait a week was evidence on how bad things had gotten.

People in all the sectors were not acting in a compliant manner. There was rioting. Ministry officials were not being treated with deference anymore and were even accosted in the street and in their homes with hope that they had food kits on them. There was a movement calling for consumption of meat acquired by hunting in the protected nature reserves and trapping fish in the waterways. This was all counter to the learning that had been accomplished in the name of science. Despite the Ministry of Information's best efforts, the southern sectors were not placing blame on the rebellious northern sectors. They were placing it on the government for provoking something that wasn't really a problem. Who cares if someone believed something stupid, if they did their job and got the food produced? At least then, they would have food to eat. So much progress was lost in just a short period of time.

Xavier was up early for his presentation to the emergency session he had asked for. He did not expect his presentation to be received well, but for the good of the nation it needed to be received. Xavier was surprisingly admitted right on time, and everyone was present with exception of his boss, the Minister of Scientific Compliance.

"You have the floor," the head of the council said without any other introduction.

Xavier nodded and began. "As some of you may know, I have a well-placed agent inside the Kayden organization who has been operating in a very high-risk position. He has been off the grid and out of communication since most of Xenon abandoned the surface. He has since been given a position of trust by the resistance and is currently on an assignment to spy on the state of the surface for three days. Yesterday, he was able to file a comprehensive report on the state of the resistance, who their leader is, and their prognosis for staying in an evacuated state. The bottom line is that they also are on a deadline where they will run out of food. Their deadline is much later than ours, but if the conditions were right, they could be convinced to return to the surface and resume their old jobs to restore the food supply. There would naturally be a few months delay of a growing season before we would see meaningful harvests, but it may be the best of many bad choices we have in front of us."

"Can you go over the conditions they require?" the Minister of Nutrition asked.

"First, they want all remaining children back who were taken," Xavier answered.

"Are there any left that they haven't taken back?" the Minister of Energy Conservation said sarcastically, eliciting a few uncomfortable chuckles from others.

"They also want the *Adherence to Myths Act* repealed," Xavier resumed. "Children staying with their own families, autonomy on their own farms like they had before, and an increase in the energy and water allotments for each farm plot. And no prosecution for any acts taken during the time of evacuation. A full scale amnesty."

"So, everything like before it started, except repealing the Adherence to Myths Act, and more energy and water quotas?" the Minister of Energy Conservation rejoined. "They farmed fine with original quotas when they left, I am certainly not on board with approving more than that."

"Do we really want full scale myth practice going unchecked?" the Minister of Transportation asked. "Didn't the problem come when we increased enforcement for more minor infractions? Do you think they would accept going back to that level?"

"My agent speculated on that," Xavier answered. "He thought that as long as they were permitted to pursue whatever beliefs they wanted in private, they would support it. I think if we modified the act to only arrest those who were actively and publicly trying to convince someone to follow a myth, they would go along with it. And we could make this allowance only in the northern sectors."

"You are from the Ministry of Scientific Compliance," the head of the council offered, "and yet you are advocating loosening laws governing scientific compliance. Why?"

Xavier paused to contemplate the enormity of the question. "Am I less resolute than I should be in enforcing the way of science? I don't think so. In nature I have seen an animal trapped and it chewed off its own appendage in order to save its life. We are fighting for the survival of our way of life, of our way of thinking. Seven of our ten sectors have been on the right path and three have introduced mayhem that has threatened our whole. If I must cut off the three to save the whole, I will do it. That doesn't mean I will lose hope for regaining the three that were cut loose. I will strive with all I am to undermine their rebellion, to infiltrate their ranks, and when the time is right, bring them back fully to the enlightened way of true scientific thought."

Xavier could tell his argument had won the day. Some details still needed to be worked out, but they would make a proposal. One he hoped would be accepted.

"You advised against the clamp-down that started this whole rebellion, didn't you?" the head of the council asked Xavier.

"I didn't think it was the right strategy at the time," Xavier replied. "But I have been fully aligned to the decision and am not about to question it now."

"The council appreciates those who speak their mind but still support the official decision with their full energy, even if it was not their preferred way," the council head stated. "Stay nearby Xavier, we will get you our answer, even if we have to stay all night."

∞ ∞ ∞

After the two days had passed, Gabriel checked back in, and was given instructions on how to intercept a government message on interest in amnesty, including the terms the government was willing to accept. There would be no more enforcement of the *Adherence to Myths Act* in the northern sectors, provided there was not active proselytizing going on and the forms of the meditations were observed. Children would be reunited with their families that remained separated, and government inspectors would be scaled back significantly to allow full control of farming to be back in the hands of native Xenon residents. They had not backed off on the energy and water quotas, but that would just mean that more dreamer interventions would be needed to bring in the harvests. They also asked for as much of Kayden's food reserves as could be spared. It wasn't everything that Isabella wanted, but Gabriel thought it would be enough and honestly more than he would have ever expected the Great Scientist Council to offer.

There was also a note from Quintin that he and Xavier were being recalled to the capital. Quintin did not seem optimistic about his future in the ministry. Gabriel was not so sure the blame would fall on them though. Both Xavier and Quintin both had valuable experience in Xenon. Only an idiot would throw that experience away, given the likely plans that would need hatched to undo the concessions that were about to be given. Either way, Gabriel had his answer, and after intercepting the message with the instructions he was given, he could now return to his grandmother with the good news.

EPILOGUE

*G*abriel looked out across his grandmother's farm. Well, it was now effectively his farm. He had identified his grandmother, at her request as the leader of Kayden. He needed some way to explain how he had come across the information on the resistance. No matter what the government said relative to the amnesty, she would no longer be safe. They may not arrest her, but they would gladly cause her to die in an accident or some other event. She now hid in an underground cavern that had not been used previously. This one even had an exit that would take her to sunshine if she needed it, hidden in the middle of one of the most remote nature preserves. Here, she camouflaged a small hidden garden to make her feel more at home.

As for Gabriel, he was enjoying the life of a farmer. He liked being in charge, and when he didn't know something, he just had to walk up the road and ask his cousin and good friend Tom. He was still using more general laborers than he wanted to since everyone had not come out of hiding yet. The distrust level was high, especially those with families who heard the horror stories how children not tested useful enough were being executed in the other sectors.

But slowly they came out. Living underground when you are a people born to the outdoors is one of the most unnatural things you can do. The Deerbarrow Inn even began to fill the common room again with socializing and some smiles. Gabriel felt like he was treated like royalty whenever he went there for a beer, which was beginning to become more tolerable to drink. They heard the stories how he had rescued

Phillip at great risk to his own life, and there were even more murmurs that he had done something even greater that could not be talked about.

Gabriel continued his learning. While he wanted to visit Teacher for an extended period and to comb the library, he instead spent his time reading the books that had been prepared for him through his dreams. He was finding that he had skills in areas of dreaming that he was not aware of previously. Most dreamers could only do one or two of them, but so far, he had some level of ability in every area he had tried. Raelynn and Isabella had told him how remarkable that was and kept encouraging him to continue to grow. Isabella was convinced the ability he was developing would fill a great need in the future. Gabriel was also happy the news of his prior role in the ministry had not soured his relationship with Raelynn. It only seemed to make it stronger.

He had been right about Xavier and Quintin. It wasn't Xavier who was punished for what had happened, it was the Minister of Scientific Compliance himself. Logs documented that Xavier had tried to talk him out of the path that had caused this disaster but had been overrode. With a new vacancy in the ministry, Xavier was promoted to take his spot. Quintin acted like he may be in line for a better position also but due to Gabriel's importance, remained his case officer. Gabriel was told he had been promoted also, but it didn't give him any happiness like it would have a few months earlier.

Gabriel kept getting peppered with questions about the resistance. What would be effective to undermine it, and how did he think Xenon could be persuaded to follow the path of science at a faster speed? And they really wanted to understand how people were relocated outside of the understanding of Oversite. Now that the food supply had been restored, there was beginning to be some impatience where the northern sectors were relative to scientific compliance.

The Ministry of Nutrition had begun to try to create some farms in the more loyal sectors using techniques that had been surveilled from watching Xenon farmers prepare. But they could never seem to get the energy and water quantities right. Plus, there was great reluctance to disrupt any protected nature areas. They still didn't know how Xenon was getting by with less. Gabriel smiled whenever he read that, and his advice was asked for. Gabriel claimed ignorance, and said he got help from others and it just got a better result before promising he would try to find out more.

Gabriel looked across the fields and reflected, considering all he had learned and how far his understanding had come. Until the government was willing to look beyond its predefined beliefs of how the world worked, they would never get complete answers to their questions. Reason corrupted without the benefit of faith was sure to fall short.

COMING SOON

Fresh off of a stunning rebuke in *Call of Kayden*, the government plots to seize back its control over the wayward sector of Xenon. To do this, the Ministry of Scientific Compliance recalls Gabriel back to the capital to fully debrief him.

While Gabriel is being debriefed, he learns about a diabolical new technology innovation– something that can detect people in the dream state. This new level of surveillance risks jeopardizing Kayden's many hard-fought gains.

Gabriel and others must work together to determine if Xenon will assimilate to the desires of the capital or find another way to thwart the totalitarian urges of those in power.

Planned release in 2020.